i

The Giant Killer

James Carmody

Pocol Press
Clifton, VA

POCOL PRESS
Published in the United States of America
by Pocol Press
6023 Pocol Drive
Clifton, VA 20124
www.pocolpress.com

Publisher's Cataloguing-in-Publication
Names: Carmody, James, 1961-, author.
Title: The Giant killer / James Carmody.
Description: Clifton, VA: Pocol Press, 2018.
Identifiers: ISBN 978-1-929763-82-5 | LCCN 2018943531
Subjects: LCSH New York (N.Y.). Police Department--History--Fiction.
| New York (N.Y.)--History--Fiction. | New York Giants (Baseball
team)--History--20th century--Fiction. | Terrorism--Fiction. | Murder--
Fiction. | Historical fiction. | Mystery and detective stories. | BISAC
FICTION / Mystery & Detective / Historical
Classification: LCC PS3603.A75545 G53 2018 | DDC 813.6--dc23

Library of Congress Control Number: 2018943531

ACKNOWLEDGEMENTS

A big THANKS goes to Sam Swope Founding Dean (2003-2016) of the Cullman Center Institute for Teachers at the New York Public Library. I was granted a fellowship in 2007 and this was where the research for this mystery story all began. I want to include the whole staff at the Cullman Center in my thanks, they continue to appreciate, enrich and support the practice of teachers. I also want to thank the team at the A. Bartlett Giamatti Research Library at the National Baseball Hall of Fame & Museum, especially Freddy Berowski who helped me with the stats on Christy Mathewson. A special thanks goes to Fred Huber and Jimmy Ross, two great book loving readers who read the manuscript and gave advice. Thanks should also go to Mr. Hetrick at Pocol Press for publishing my first book. Continuous thanks goes to my wife, Olga who supplied plenty of coffee, love and encouragement. I should thank my children Andrew, Mary and Peter for being good and not disturbing Daddy when he was writing. Finally, my father who gave me a love of words, my mother who enjoyed a good mystery, and my brother who got me first interested in baseball back in the days of the Big Red Machine. Also, thank you, dear reader for buying this book!

DEDICATION

I would like to dedicate this, my first book, to Olga, wife, soulmate, friend.

1

"If the time, money, energy, and brain-power which are wasted in the barber shops of America were applied in direct effort, the Panama canal would be dug in four hours." Gillette advertisement 1906.

Wednesday January 4, 1905 1143 First Avenue. 7:45PM.

Lieutenant Petrosino arrived at the scene of the crime forty minutes after the bomb went off. When he entered Fassett's barber shop on the upper east side of New York City, the cold of the frigid night followed him, pouring through the space that had been a window. Glass crunched under Petrosino's black oxfords as he slowly moved amidst the debris. Police officers took notice when their commanding officer appeared and straightened up, put their hands at their sides, and looked toward him. The five officers then snapped to attention, rigidly saluting, their breath temporarily suspended before them in a cloud of frost, until Petrosino said authoritatively, "Continue!" without glancing at them and they went back to their bending, searching, and examining.

Head down and serious, the small brown eyes of the lieutenant zigzagged across the crime scene and he noticed a smattering of white barber towels scattered throughout the shop and splashes of deep, red blood splattered over shattered glass and worn wooden floor. The explosion had also destroyed large glass canisters of hair treatments and gelling agents. An acrid mix of the lingering scent of dynamite and hair tonic added to the unreality of the scene. The haphazard blood patterns arrested his eyes and he imperceptibly squinted. His face was pockmarked, and he wore a black derby that looked a bit too large for his black-haired head. A blue suit was under his dark overcoat which covered his five-foot three inch strong, stocky frame. He seemed more like a well-dressed, unsuspecting customer looking for a late-night trim or a former prizefighter a bit past his prime rather than a detective of the NYPD come to investigate an explosion that killed a man.

Officer Muldoon, standing at six feet three inches with sandy hair and a handlebar moustache to match, was coatless despite the thirteen degree night, and he was the first and only officer to directly communicate with the senior man at the crime scene.

As Petrosino paused to look at the blood patterns on a face towel, Muldoon cautiously approached him. After years of working together, Muldoon had an almost sixth sense when it came to understanding Petrosino's moods, wants, or questions. Muldoon looked almost timid and apologetic when he approached Petrosino. This awkwardness gave no hint of the friendship the men shared.

"Good evening sir. Sorry to disturb you so late but I know you want to be involved in anything to do with the Black Hand, so I told the boys to roust you. The bomb went off at about 7 o'clock. Dynamite sticks as far as we can tell. We have one man dead, God rest his soul, a Mr. Ritchie Venuto, a regular customer here. The owner, a Mr. Fassett, was threatened by the Black Hand and he has all three notes used to threaten him. The boys found one eyewitness, a Mrs. Karobicek who didn't add too much. The owner himself was given the smelling salts and a bit o' the brandy and is sitting up, talking non-stop. As you know sir, not one Irishman on the force can speak Italian. His language has got us flummoxed."

Petrosino had turned to look up at the Irishman and Muldoon now moved aside to give the detective a proper view of the deceased. Glass was crushed like coarse Sicilian sea salt under Petrosino's foot as he approached the reclining corpse covered by the bloody barber towel. On the floor, near the body lay a personal shaving mug that was broken into three pieces. The foamy shaving cream seemed to try to hold the mug together. One of the pieces showed a drawing of a shovel. Petrosino briefly thought of his own shaving mug depicting an illustrated policeman's badge, which he kept in his bathroom. He tried to remember the last time he was relaxing in a barber chair. A slight grin came across the face of the detective despite the carnage around him. He imagined himself reclining in the chair, eyes closed, face fully lathered. He would be an easy target for his enemies in that situation.

From the shovel on the shaving mug of the deceased, the detective surmised that Mr. Venuto dug subway tunnels. He moved one of the pieces with his shoe to see it better and some of the shaving cream attached itself to the tip of his black oxford. Petrosino wore Italian shoes of the best kind but he didn't try to shake the small glob off. He was thinking about the shaving mug and what it might reveal about the deceased. New York desperately needed immigrants to dig the underground tunnels that were being planned all around the metropolis. Petrosino looked at the hand that protruded from the towel. Rough thick hands and dirt under the fingernails added to the digger of subways theory. Even this blizzard, the worst since 1888, did not prevent the urgent underground work. For the first time since he had entered the barbershop, Petrosino took his hands out of his coat pockets and he bent as if peeking under a table and lifted the white, red stained towel. There were shards of glass everywhere, the sheet bits of glass tinkled to the floor sounding like the ice crystals outside being blown by the wind. The glass that had penetrated Venuto's neck killed him and looked like a bizarre icicle. Despite years of witnessing death in many gruesome ways, Petrosino shuddered. So subtle that not even Muldoon, about three feet behind him noticed this slight release of emotion.

The patrons silently fidgeted in their chairs. They wanted to go home. Their unshaven faces with upturned eyebrows and lips pressed together silently considered this short, new policeman. Unlike the Irish cops, this one looked like an uncle, neighbor or brother. They were all thinking the same thing, "Who was this man who was saluted by Irish cops rather than ignored?"

Muldoon approached his superior with authority, determined yet deferential, "The owner has some injuries, scratches mostly, he was lucky. He is in the back with some of the boys and a Mr. Kundera. Kundera owns the shoe store that shares the hallway with the barber. He was working at the time of the explosion but saw nothing. The customers here would like to go home to their wives and wee ones. None of them were hurt seriously, just cuts and scratches. Those that fared a little worse are in the back being taken care of, nobody needs the hospital and nobody seems to have anything to add," said Muldoon anticipating Petrosino's questions.

"Dismiss them. I want to speak to the eyewitness and then Fassett himself."

"Yes sir. My man will show you the way to Mrs. Karobicek. Tunney!"

A young, pale, freckled, red haired, youth appeared shivering from either the cold or the chance to meet Petrosino.

"Show the lieutenant to the home of the eyewitness," commanded Muldoon.

Tunney, a stick-like figure in police blue with a blue coat that hung on him as it would a flimsy hanger, led Petrosino outside. The detective paused, crouched and looked to where the bomb had gone off.

"Muldoon, collect what you can here. You know what I am looking for," ordered Petrosino, shouting through the cold space where the window had been.

"Done sir!" boomed the big fellow.

Petrosino then followed the spindly, shivering and shaking Tunney over ice and around piles of snow to the home of Mrs. Karobicek. Tunney looked like a giant, moving stick drawing and Petrosino wondered how such a man could get a job on the force. No doubt a father or uncle knew somebody that knew somebody or some money went under the table. Petrosino knew that President Roosevelt had tried to clean up favoritism and bribery during his brief stint as Police Commissioner eight years ago, but he had not been entirely successful. Petrosino sighed to himself.

Tunney mounted the steps that had been neatly shoveled of the almost two feet of snow that had collected there. Through a first floor window Petrosino noticed a dim candlelight move in the shadows as they approached. Petrosino turned to look at the barber shop across the street. Tunney paused at the top step to look up at the dark brown brick residence in search of a knocker. The door was opened before he could use it.

"Come in, come in," Petrosino heard the impatient voice from where he stood on the sidewalk, hands in his pockets. He turned to see a short, compact woman with thin arms and legs, carrying the candle the detective had seen a moment ago in the window. She was beaming, perhaps thought Petrosino from a genuine hospitality or perhaps from the perceived adventure this calamity had brought. Petrosino quickly mounted the steps and the door slammed behind them. Petrosino removed his hat in the hall. The woman quickly spoke again, "I'll show you where I sat as I saw the whole thing."

She led them to a room on the immediate left of the front door. Petrosino examined the room by the light of the low-lit gas lamps on the wall. Recent issues of *The Sun* and *The New Yorker Staatszeitung* were stacked neatly on the table near a blue water jar and basin. A comfortable looking, well-used chair flopped near the window next to a table filled with brown pharmacy bottles and teaspoons. There was the faint smell of residual smoke from the dying embers in the fireplace. The fast tick tock of the German cuckoo clock, its dark animal figures immobile and staring, was the only sound. Petrosino deduced that this was the room where Mrs. Karobicek spent most of her time. There was no sign of maleness, although the detective had noticed a man's boots in the hall as he entered. There was this single chair in the room, yet Karobicek wore a wedding ring. Was she a widow? Who did the boots belong to?

"I was sitting here as I usually do," she began when she was interrupted by a whistle that started low, increased and remained at a high pitch. "How about some tea... ah.."

"Lieutenant Petrosino."

"Yes, how about some tea? It'll take the chill off. I need it, this night has added years to my life."

She turned and went to get the tea.

"Thank you," Petrosino said. Tunney allowed a smile to cross his face as he saluted and took his position in the hall, near the front door. Petrosino understood from experience that the drinking of tea in familiar surroundings with eyewitnesses seemed more like gossip than a police inquiry and it usually produced better results.

Tunney rubbed his hands in the cold, dark hallway.

"Young man, come here and bring this chair into the parlor," shouted the eyewitness from the kitchen.

"Now," she began, "I suppose you will want to know what he looked like," she said as she brought in a silver tray laden with fine china cups and a pot of tea. She placed the tray on a small side table.

"That is a good place to begin, Mrs. Karobicek," stated Petrosino as he sat down in the chair provided by Tunney.

"I saw a lone figure outside of the shop just before the explosion. I admit it was not easy to look through a window with opera glasses but my windows, like the rest of my home, is immaculate. I became suspicious when he stopped and stooped, as if to tie his shoe."

"Mrs. Karobicek," interrupted Petrosino, "What is suspicious about tying a shoe?"

"Well, Lieutenant ahh?"

"Petrosino."

"Well Lieutenant Petrosino, you figure it out. On a night that is so cold and all that ice and wind and snow, who would even notice that their shoe is untied? And if they did wouldn't they want to get home as soon as possible?" She poured the tea into one cup.

"How do you know it was a man?" questioned the detective.

"I'm sure you know that this is a respectable neighborhood. Good women do not go out at night unattended. Especially on nights such as this with all this snow and ice underfoot."

She poured the tea into the other cup and the splash gurgle of tea against fine china gave the impression of a tea party rather than a police investigation.

"How do you like your tea? Sugar, milk?"

"Both."

With a nod of her head, she completed her task, handed the cup and saucer to the seated detective, and sat down with her own cup in her chair.

With an impish grin that showed her teeth she scrunched her eyes and asked, "Can that bag of bones standing out there please put some wood on that fire?"

"Yes, of course. Tunney!"

The redhead appeared standing straight and stiff-backed, his hat under his left arm and saluting his superior with his right.

"Yes sir!"

"Tunney, please light the fire for Mrs. Karobicek."

As the spindly policeman was kneeling at the hearth, the hostess continued, "I looked more closely because I thought that on such a cold night everyone would want to get home as soon as possible. Just sitting here looking out the window I could feel the cold. More tea?"

"No thank you."

"The man then stood up and started to run. I saw a small glow and focused my glasses on what I knew had been dynamite. Without thinking, I lifted the window and closed the wooden shutters, protecting my windows from breakage. That cold chilled me to the bone! My husband made those shutters. He did a fine job on them too. They prevented dynamite from blowing my windows to bits like it did to every other window on the block."

"How did you know it was dynamite, Mrs. Karobicek?"

"Who else would be out on such a night except the Black Hand? And they always use dynamite, don't they?"

"How is it that you know about the Black Hand?"

"Who doesn't? The Black Hand is mentioned in the German papers as well. Ah! We've got neighbors that are the well-to-do Italians and they are afraid of the Black Hand too. If they can go after Caruso, they can go after anybody."

"Why Mrs. Karobicek, were you looking out your window in the first place?" The fire was now crackling and Tunney left the room as stiff and awkward as he entered it.

"I was looking for the man that made those shutters. He should have been home hours ago."

"Should the police look into this?" the detective questioned noticing how calmly everything was related.

"There is no mystery here sir; he is at the Hofbrau drinking growler after growler with his friends. I am just glad I closed my shutters in time. I might not be talking to you now if I didn't have those shutters."

"Tell me more about the figure himself. Describe him again. Are you sure he was alone?" The description given by Mrs. Annie Karobicek did not help much, no limp, no distinctive clothing, no view of the face. He had been dressed in warm winter clothing and a scarf was pulled up over his nose. Here, the detective finished his tea and gently laid the cup in the saucer. The ping of saucer and empty cup was the signal that ended the interview. They looked at each other in silence for a moment.

"I'll have one of my men contact you if we need further information. Thank you for the tea."

"Well, I won't be able to go to the station. I am a sick woman. All my energy is used to clean the house. I have been doctoring for a while and in my condition, I shouldn't be going out of the house. You and your men are welcome here anytime, she smiled.

"Thank you. I'll remember that. Thanks again for the tea."

"You could have another. I made enough. The weather outside is frightful."

"I must go! Thank you, Mrs. Karobicek," said Petrosino. He passed the young Tunney, saying, "Don't forget to put the chair back and have some tea with her if she offers it to you. Goodnight Tunney!"

Petrosino exited the building. The young policeman slightly touched his forehead with a silent salute, maintaining it after the detective closed the door. Stories were already beginning to form inside of his head about how he had assisted the great Petrosino after only two years on the job. How envious all the rookies and some veterans would be! Tunney grinned.

"Young man! Won't you have some tea? I made plenty!" called the voice from the other room.

In the small back room behind the barbershop, the small square card table that in happier times hosted glasses of Chianti, chunks of Asiago, and loaves of fresh baked bread as well as the regular game of scopa, was now laden with a black doctor's bag, bandages and assorted bottles and vials. A doctor was attending to the cuts, bruises and abrasions that some of Fassett's customers had received as a result of the blast. The room was filled with cigarette smoke and the unshaven faces of the arguing men flashed disheveled teeth and impatiently sent smoke through their noses. Kundera, the shoe salesman, was sitting next to Fassett attempting to calm him. Muldoon had handed three threatening letters that Fassett had received from the Black Hand to Petrosino.

Fassett, when introduced to the detective pleaded, his brown eyes wide in exaggeration and fear, "Mr. Petrosino, you must help me. My wife was right. I should have paid!" He grabbed the coat lapels of the detective.

Petrosino grabbed Fassett's wrists and gently removed the barber's hands from his coat, "Try to calm down and tell me what happened," Petrosino said with something akin to brotherly affection.

"Well after the first two notes. I still didn't pay attention. This is not downtown where we have another Italy. Here, I live among Americans! Anyway, late last night, while I was shaving my last customer, a man walks in and wants to speak to me. I told him to sit and wait. He sat. I finished. I said what do you want? A shave? He had a moustache; I figured he wanted to get rid of the moustache. He said, did you get the note? I said, what note? He said, from the Black Hand! Mr. Petrosino, I grabbed my heart. I was ready to die. I pleaded, leave me alone! He told me I am in the soup! He warned me that if I didn't have three hundred dollars my shop would be blown up! I told him I don't have that kind of money! He then said there is going to be a twin killing! He said he didn't want to apply the whitewash. I asked why me? Why me? I ask him why do you do this to me? He told me it's not about me. I asked what is it about? He told me it's all because he didn't play! I said what do you mean? He didn't answer. The man said again he should have played."

7

Here Fassett became louder and faster in speech, "I became scared because the man talked crazy! I said please leave me alone. I'm an honest man. He walked away! Tonight the bomb! They will kill me! You must help me!"

Petrosino tried to sound reassuring, "What did he look like? Describe him again."

"Tall, thin, moustache, nice blue pinstriped suit, white shoes, Italiano!" Fassett clapped his hands, rubbing his palms as he did so, his two hands ended in a self-embrace, clasping and shaking.

"Did you speak in Italian or English with the man?"

"He spoke English, so I spoke English!"

"Are you accurate in what you said to me? Did he use those phrases, twin kill and apply the whitewash?"

"Yes he's a crazy man. I couldn't forget those words! And now Ritchie Venuto is dead!"

"Who is this Ritchie Venuto?"

"One of my best customers," Fassett gingerly touched the bandages that had been wrapped around his head. "He was a good man, a family man!"

"Did he dig in the subways?"

"Yes! He did! How do you know?"

"Mr Fassett, it is my job to know."

"What do you think he meant by, 'he didn't play?'" asked the lieutenant.

"I don't know. I don't know! The man, he talks in riddles!"

Petrosino felt that this is all the information he would get, "If you see this man again, you must contact us immediately. I've ordered Muldoon to assign an officer to protect you. Is there anything else Mr. Fassett?"

"No, well... yes! How could I forget? The crazy one left something behind."

Fassett shuffled over to a drawer, talking to Petrosino as he walked, "the crazy one noticed his shoes, he had white shoes, he noticed his shoes were untied and he bent over to tie them. When he did that the Pisano left this on my shelf," the barber pulled out a yellow tin, and handed it to Petrosino.

It was a Tuxedo tobacco pocket tin with the face of Christy Mathewson, pitcher for the National League Champion New York Giants baseball team on it. Above the ballplayer's head printed in red, script letters was TUXEDO and then, alongside that was printed, *"THE PERFECT TOBACCO"*. The slogan, which appeared underneath the bust of the pitcher read, *"Tuxedo gets to me in a natural, pleasant way. It's what I call good, honest, companionable tobacco-the kind to stick to.*" When opened there was some tobacco inside.

"I will need this," Petrosino said, as he pocketed the tin.

"Take it, I don't use the stuff!" waved Mr. Fassett.

"Good night Mr. Fassett," he then turned to the big man, "We'll talk in the morning Muldoon, it looks like the Black Hand is behind this murder. I'll see you at Lanza's at eight tomorrow morning. Did you find the key I gave you to his back door?"

"It was acting like a bookmark! That is what I get for reading so late into the night!"

"What is it that keeps you up all night?"

"Well, I finally found a copy of *Play Ball*, King Kelly's autobiography. Now that was a ballplayer, did you know…"

Petrosino raised his hand palm outward "Tell me tomorrow morning over coffee." He turned to leave.

"Sir?"

"Yes?"

"This time we'll get The Wolf," said Muldoon.

"El Lupo? He outsmarted me once. If it is him that has done this I will not let him get away again." He upturned his collar, pushed his hands into his coat pockets. There he felt the three Black Hand letters within. He then stepped out into the bitter night and began the long walk to his home downtown. If it was El Lupo why had he not stayed in the Italian neighborhood downtown? Why did he come so far uptown? Was he enlarging his territory? What did the man with the white shoes mean when he said "he didn't play."?

In his other pocket he clutched the tobacco tin with the face of the greatest pitcher in baseball and tried to understand how it might lead him to the killer of Richie Venuto.

2

"You miserable cur." The Black Hand in an extortion note to Sam
Fasset.

*"As far as they can be traced, threatening letters are generally a
hoax; some of them are attempts at blackmail by inexperienced
criminals, who have had the idea suggested to them by reading about the
Black Hand in the sensational papers; but the number of threatening
letters sent with the deliberate intention of using violence as a last resort
to extort money is ridiculously small."*
-Lieutenant Petrosino

He pushed the saucer and small, thick, white ceramic cup of
espresso slowly to the edge of the checkered red and white tablecloth.
Once again he laid the Black Hand messages written to Fassett side-by-
side to compare them. All three were written in Italian on the same
cheap, nondescript, common stock paper with no identifying
characteristics. Petrosino would not get much from the paper, so he
decided to focus on the handwriting and the language.
The first letter received on December 6, 1904 read as follows:

Dear Friend:
Meet us at the end of the Third Avenue route at One Hundred and
Twenty-ninth Street. And please bring $300 in a basket. Failure to come
means injury.
(Signed) THE BLACK HAND
Written in Italian and postmarked Station H, Forty-Fourth Street
and Lexington Avenue.

Dec 10, 1904
Dear Friend: We notified you to come with $300. You did not
show up. But we will give you one more chance. If you do not show up
we will kill you. We will kill you and we don't care for the police. So it
will do you no good to tell them. We will meet you at the same place.
(Signed) THE BLACK HAND
Illegible postmark.

January 4, 1905
Station Y, Sixty-Eighth Street and Third Ave.

You miserable cur. You did not show up. Now we will have to blow up your shop and kill you.

The usual signature with the addition of a red skull and crudely drawn cross bones was on the note.

That night the bomb exploded.

Petrosino wondered who the "we" referred to and if this was El Lupo and his gang or was it a Black Hand imposter? The description given by Mrs. Karobicek was not much help. Was it the same man with the white shoes who left his tobacco tin behind? The eyewitness did say the bomber was alone. So who is the other part of "we"? But of course, El Lupo would never set dynamite himself. He would always get an underling to do it.

Petrosino looked at postmarks and drop off location. Forty fourth and Lexington, Third and Sixty eighth. The addresses may be important. They were both on the east side, twenty four blocks apart but adjoining avenues. The bombing itself occurred at 1143 First Avenue was between 62nd and 63rd Street. The bomber may live nearby. The postmarks are close enough. It would make sense, if someone saw him on the night of January fourth. He could explain his being in the neighborhood, and he could get home quick enough. He could pass by Fassett's every day and never be noticed. People do not notice the familiar.

The ink was slightly smudged, this could mean that the letter writer was left handed, causing his hand to drag behind his writing and blurring the ink before it dried properly. Petrosino sipped his espresso and looked around the room. The detective had enjoyed this restaurant that had opened the year before by a friend named Michael Lanza. Michael was another past victim of the Black Hand that had been helped by Petrosino. The wainscoting, the tiled floor, the tin ceiling, the soft electric lights, the impressionist paintings of the Italian countryside dominated by yellow splashes of wheat with white swirls of clouds above, all came together to form a sense of comfort. Mostly though it was his respect for the proprietor and the light marinara sauce served over the homemade spaghetti and fresh bread with farm butter from Queens that kept the detective coming back.

Then he saw her. Adelina. His Italian *princessa*. He was surprised to see her so early in the morning. She came straight through the front door with a big, wide Italian smile that showed off her perfect teeth. He stood as she approached.

"Adelina, what are you doing here?" asked Petrosino trying not to show his agitation as he kissed her hand.

"Aren't you happy to see me?" she replied, sensing his reserve.

"Yes of course, but I didn't expect you."

"Don't you like surprises?"

"In my line of work, surprises could mean death."

The short Adelina, with brown hair and rich brown eyes the color of dark coffee beans, looked at the detective with a smile of joy on her face, "Joseph, I am a good surprise," she said.

Her appearance was noticed by the watchful owner, Michael Lanza, who now came to the table with his clean white apron wrapped around his waist.

"Hello, Michael," said Adelina.

"Adelina, as beautiful as ever! How is work in the trade union coming along?"

"The work can be difficult. So many men are against us but we will get the vote."

"Mr. Lanza, isn't she beautiful?" said Petrosino hoping to change the subject.

"Oh, Mr. Lanza, my husband to be does not want me to tell you that once again we were harassed by police for standing on a sidewalk with signs!"

"The police are doing their job. It is against the law to loiter and you know that," said the detective while looking down at the table.

"But!" Adelina pounded the table which rattled the small spoon resting on the white saucer, "How can the powerless change a law without breaking a law? Politicians don't want to hear us. Most newspapers will not print our letters. Standing on the street talking to women and men as they pass is the best way to get people to believe in our cause."

"You may have a friend in President Roosevelt. I've heard he is sympathetic to your cause," said Petrosino.

"What does that mean, sympathetic to the cause? Those are just words! We need action! The women in this country should be able to vote and I if I get arrested while I am marching or picketing. Then, at least, everyone will know that Adelina does more than talk!"

Mr. Lanza, sensing the rising action asked, "When are you going to be Mr. and Mrs. Petrosino?"

The couple looked on uneasily. "For our breakfast we'll have two *crostata frutti di bosco* and a large loaf of bread with butter, and two espressos," said Petrosino.

Lanza, thin with a well-trimmed beard and moustache, simply said, "Very good sir."

Adelina spoke up to the back of the restaurateur, "When we do get married, you must be there Mr. Lanza!"

"I would be honored," said the owner pausing, turning while

holding his hand to his breast and bowing his head slightly to the left.

When he had left, Petrosino said, "Adelina, dear Adelina I am surrounded by people that would kill me if they had a chance. If we were married, I would constantly be worried about you."

"I want to have a family and I can think of no better man than you Giuseppe. If you will not be a part of my life, I could never love another man. You would always be in my heart."

"What about your safety?"

"I'd rather have you for a day as a husband than to never have you. If we are married or not married the ones who want to kill you will kill you anyway."

Michael brought the espresso. "I've been reading about the Black Hand bombings in the papers. Are you making any progress in eliminating them?"

"Mr. Lanza, you always know what to say. It is difficult. The Black Hand is ruthless. In time, I think I will be able to... eliminate them," replied Petrosino, as he stirred the hot coffee.

"I'll bring the *crostata*," said Lanza as he disappeared behind the green curtain which led into the kitchen area in the back of the restaurant.

Petrosino then took Adelina's hand into his own and held it there gently, "Adelina, maybe we can get married after I defeat the Black Hand."

"I may be an old lady by then."

"Well then, let's focus on the present for now and wait on marriage," countered Petrosino.

"I cannot wait forever," said Adelina.

The bread, butter, and some jam came with the *crostata*.

"Don't let her get away Giuseppe, she is a beauty!" said Michael Lanza.

"Oh, I know she is a beauty," said Petrosino and smiled keeping his eyes on Adelina.

The bell tinkled above the doorway. A customer walked in and looked directly at Petrosino. It was the man who had followed him from police headquarters. The man was rather short and round. He wore a dark black coat with a heavy fur collar that surrounded his small head. Petrosino, who always sat in the back of the restaurant with his back to the wall, noticed him immediately upon his entrance. The man paused and slowly moved toward Petrosino. The detective kept a small gun strapped around his lower leg. He rolled up his pants leg. The detective bent down as if to scratch his leg and removed the gun from the holster. The short balding, man, still looking at Petrosino, came closer still. The man put his hands into his pocket. The detective held his gun under the table trying to aim it at the man.

Adelina had noticed the change in her love and asked, "What is wrong?"

"Oh nothing. I just realized how hungry I am. I hope this is enough."

"Have some bread," said Adelina, ripping the bread and offering him a chunk.

Just as the strange man with vulture-like features was very close to the table, Michael Lanza came out with plate of thinly sliced *mortadella* and came between the man and the couple.

"Enjoy!" said Michael, "It is on the house."

"Thank you." said Petrosino as he stared at the man which Mr. Lanza noticed immediately.

Michael whirled around and approached the bald customer. The man still standing, ordered a glass of red wine and nothing more. He sat in a chair at a table very close to where Petrosino and Adelina sat. The vulture-like man with his large round, sunken eyes that blinked too often, and his overextended big nose looked intently and said, "You are Petrosino, aren't you? The great detective?"

With Adelina between him and the new customer, Petrosino looked right at the man and said, "No, you are mistaken."

Lanza came with the wine just in time to hear the man say, "You look like Lieutenant Petrosino!"

Lanza said, "This man is a friend of mine and I assure you he is not Lieutenant Petrosino, although now that you mention it, there is a resemblance."

Lanza served the wine to the man and turned to Petrosino and said loud enough, because there was nobody else in the restaurant, "Frank, I promise not to tell your wife about this but if she comes in here and catches you two together, I don't want to know about it!"

"My wife will never know," Petrosino said going along with the ruse.

Adelina kept quiet. Feeling this was enough and not wanting to arouse suspicion, Lanza retreated to the kitchen.

The man kept staring at the couple. They were seated very closely to him and they felt that they could not continue their conversation, so they continued the ruse.

"If your wife comes in here, I will tell her to go out!" said Adelina playing along with the deception."

"OK, I am tired of her. She cannot cook anyway. That is why I am always here with you!"

The man fidgeted in his seat and blinked once, twice, and brought his left hand up to rub his bald head. Without touching the wine that had been served the short man blinked three times, got up from the table. Staring at Petrosino, he approached the couple with both hands in the pockets of his coat. From underneath his table, Petrosino pointed the small derringer at the legs of the man, although at this angle, Adelina was dangerously close to the line of fire.

3

"Suffrage is the pivotal right." -Susan B. Anthony

"You look like the detective," said the vulture.

"Why are you so interested in this man Petrosino?" asked the detective.

"I have never met the man, but I have seen plenty of photographs. I wanted to shake the hand of such a great man."

"Well maybe someday you will get the chance to do so," said the detective.

"Yes, maybe I will," answered the man. The vulture man shifted his weight from one foot to another. He stretched his mouth across his face showing large, yellowed teeth. He looked at Adelina and back to the Lieutenant. His jaw tightened. Petrosino shifted his small gun saying a quick prayer that his love would not get hit. Then the vulture man blinked, turned and walked out of the restaurant leaving his wine untouched.

Lanza came out from behind a curtain which hung over the entrance to the kitchen. "Lieutenant, I had that man in my sights all the time. The first sign of trouble would have given him a bullet from my revolver."

"Thanks Michael. I had him covered under the table but Adelina was blocking the shot."

"Well excuse me for being in the way!"

"Your espresso must be cold. Can I get you a hot one?" asked Michael.

"This will be fine, thank you," said the detective.

When Lanza was back in the kitchen, Petrosino asked his love, "Why did you say that?"

"Well, I was in the way. If I weren't here, you would have had him. Do you think that man wanted to kill you?"

"Yes, of course. He was probably a man who killed for money, … a professional killer. If you weren't here he might have tried to kill me and if he did that I would have him as my captive now. I would beat it out of him and he would tell me who hired him but I could not do that because I didn't want to put you in any danger. When he saw you here and the story that Michael told well, that confused him. He didn't want to shoot the wrong man. Professional killers never want to kill the wrong person. It would look bad for them. Still, he will be back for me. He will not get paid until I am dead."

"How did he know you were here?"

"He followed me here from police headquarters. I thought I had gotten rid of him but he appeared again a few blocks south. He is very good at what he does. This is why I was … slightly alarmed when you walked in, I knew that the man had bad intentions. If you were not here guns would have been fired. My enemies do not know about you yet and they do not know that I enjoy this restaurant. Now, they will know and the next time, I will have to fire my gun."

"Couldn't you just arrest him?"

"For what? Following me? There is no crime in that. I could have tried to catch him and beat him but as soon as I got up he may have pulled his gun and I couldn't let anything happen to you."

Adelina tore her pastry and said, "I accept all of this."

"But I do not. I could have been killed today. If we get married and have children the Black Hand will know that and they will go after you. You will be in constant danger. For me, that is an unacceptable risk. I have a picture of this man in my mind. I will remember him should I see him again. But he also has a picture of you in his mind. We must be careful. If I knew you were coming here today I would have taken extra precautions. I underestimated this man."

"Who was that man? Where is he from?"

"If he is not part of the Black Hand then he was probably hired by them. I'm sure I will see him again."

"I thought we would have some fun. I thought you would be happy with the surprise of seeing me."

"I am always happy to be with you. Your life is more important to me than my own."

"Then let me live my life as I want and marry me!"

"Adelina, this is not easy for me to say but…"

"Then don't say it. You know where to find me if you want to see me Giuseppe. I have work to do for our right to vote movement! There is a march planned for next week."

"Just make sure you don't get arrested. I would not want…"

The detective did not have time to finish his sentence. Adelina rose from the table, her large brown eyes filling with tears. But before they could run down her cheek, she turned to leave. Her beautiful brown hair was trailing behind her. Petrosino watched her as her right hand was raised to her face to wipe her tears.

Just then Muldoon appeared from behind the curtain.

"Isn't that Adelina?"

"Yes it is," said Petrosino watching her go. "Sit down and have some *mortadella* with me.

The big man sat down and instantly grabbed two slices of the meat. He tore off some bread and as he was slathering it with butter, he asked, "Did I miss anything?"

In other baseball news: "Shumza Sugimoto is 23 years old, an outfielder, and played last year with the Cuban Giants. While McGraw does not expect the Japanese to make the team, he has consented to take him South and see what there is in him. Sugimoto is a jiu jitsu expert and while exhibiting his prowess in a clubroom here successfully tackled Mike Donlin the outfielder of the New York team. Sugimoto weighs only 118 pounds but it is said that he can handle a man who tops the scales at 170." February 10, 1905 New York Times

4

"Savannah, GA: Detectives were scouring the city tonight for thieves who broke into the ballpark clubhouse and stole gloves, masks, protectors, shoes, bats and other property of the New York National League baseball team worth between $2,000 and $3,000. Manager McGraw hopes to recover the stolen items through the aid of the local police department."
March 10, 1905 New York Times.

"That man is the best American who has in him the American spirit, the American soul. Such a man fears not the strong and harms not the weak. He scorns what is base or cruel or dishonest."
-President Theodore Roosevelt to the Friendly Sons of St. Patrick on the occasion of their 126th anniversary dinner. Friday March 17, 1905, Delmonico's New York

"A little monograph on the ashes of one hundred and forty different varieties of pipe, cigar, and cigarette tobacco."
-Sir Arthur Conan Doyle 1859-1930

St. Patrick's Day, 1905.

"The fate of the twentieth century will in no small degree depend upon the quality of citizenship developed on this continent. Surely such a thought must thrill us with the resolute purpose so to bear ourselves that the name American shall stand as the symbol of just, generous and fearless treatment of all men and all nations. Let us be true to ourselves for we cannot then be false to any man." BANG! Teddy Roosevelt pounded the podium behind which he stood, chin thrust out into the crowd, right arm raised for drama.

This concluded T.R.'s speech to the *Friendly Sons of St. Patrick*. The crowd was hollering and clapping, smoking and whistling, drinking and laughing. It was a tumultuous night at Delmonico's. President Roosevelt, who had Irish on his mother's side and was one of the founders of the American Irish Society in Manhattan, was a good friend to the Irish and they were a good friend to him. Roosevelt clearly enjoyed the enthusiasm. He made his way to a table prepared for him in the smoke-filled room and a pint of the black gold appeared before him. He stood, and with a wide grin, waved the stout like a patriot waving a flag. He drank down the dark, velvety brew to the continued cheers of

19

the crowd. A second Guinness arrived and he sat down for this one. Next to him was Petrosino.

"I never expected to see you here! You are an Italian surrounded by Irishmen!" bellowed the president.

"Just like the police force. How was the wedding?" asked the detective changing the subject.

"Franklin is a bit of a dandy you know, but Eleanor will please his mother. My niece's bridal trousseau was lovely."

"I didn't know you were a judge of such things!" said Petrosino, attempting to be lighthearted.

"I'm not, but the dandy said it four times! By the way there were plenty of orange blossoms in the Bridal Bouquet, and you know what that means!"

"No, I don't know."

"It means plenty of children. That's what orange blossoms signify! Plenty of children!"

"That bit of information had… escaped me."

Roosevelt considered the quiet detective, "Well, it's not your field!"

The president lifted the beer to his mouth and gulped. It left a ring of foam around his upper lip which he wiped by extending his lower lip, "The wedding itself was boring. This...," he gestured to the Delmonico's crowd, again using the beer glass like a conductor would wave a baton to abruptly silence the orchestra "...is really why the President of the United States is in New York on St. Patrick's Day."

The man stood up, larger than life, always dramatic, always increasing the intensity of the moment. Roosevelt shouted, "Men!" The friendly crowd immediately began to quiet down.

"Men of Ireland, now men of America, I was born not far from here, a native son of this great metropolis, I raise my glass to the future of this great country that so many of you, born across the sea now call home. We are united in our purpose to fulfill the destiny of our land." Cheers and more cheers. An Irish ballad began and steadily rose so that it filled the room. Roosevelt, clearly enjoying himself, sat down again.

"What brings you here?" Roosevelt asked, staring through his thick glasses knowing that the ballad would keep things private between himself and the great detective.

"I know that you are an expert in tobacco," began Petrosino.

"I am an expert in many things. Tobacco is just one," half joked the President.

"What can you tell me about this?" said Petrosino, as he produced the tobacco that had been left behind by the terrorist as well as a tin of usual Tuxedo tobacco he had purchased.

"Well Joseph, the first thing I notice is that the Tuxedo tobacco is twist tobacco, see how it is tied into little knots? It can be chewed or smoked in a pipe. This other, lighter color tobacco is chew tobacco. Mind if I try it?"

"Please do."

Roosevelt took a large wad between his thumb and middle finger and inserted it deep into his mouth. After a while he said, "Good quality. Very good quality. It is smooth and mellow. Where did you get it?"

"A killer left it in a barber shop."

"I can't be sure but I think it is Redman. I chewed Redman out West. If it is, Redman is very rare in these parts. It hasn't come to New York as far as I know. It is mostly sold west of the Mississippi."

"So the man I am looking for either comes from the Midwest or purchased it in a store that would sell Redman. How can you be sure it is Redman?"

"Well I can't, but if you give that to me I will take it to Washington with me and have the boys in the bureau of investigation look at it and get back to you."

"That would be appreciated."

Teddy placed his strong hand on the shoulder of Petrosino. "You made me look good when I was police commissioner and if anyone had listened to us, President McKinley would not have been assassinated. I feel that I owe you a lot. This is the least I can do for a fine citizen and a friend."

Petrosino paused to sip his coffee.

Roosevelt continued, "It is situations like this McKinley incident that show a need for a special branch in government to act as intelligence for state and local matters. Men like yourself with a passion for this type of thing and a goodness that cannot be shaken. I am thinking about calling it The Federal Bureau of Investigation, or FBI. What do you think?"

"I totally agree Mr. President."

"When the time comes to begin this endeavor I will call you. For now, let's drink a bit more eh? Where is your stout?" bellowed the big fellow.

"I'm not drinking, Mr. President. I'm on duty."

"You're always on duty! But I guess that is why you are so good."

"Thank you, sir, and my congratulations on the marriage of your niece today."

"The dandy! It's time for some song!" roared the president, his face coming forward, his neck extending, his eyes bulging through his thick glasses.

"I must go then. I will wait to hear from your men," said Petrosino.

"Very well then, I don't think you'll know any of these ballads anyway! HA! Carry on soldier!" With that, Roosevelt gave Petrosino a terrific side slap on the shoulder that reminded the lieutenant of the days when Roosevelt was Police Commissioner of New York. The big man stood up. Through the cloud of thick tobacco smoke quieted the general chatter with:

"Men! A song," The president then began to sing and continued until the whole room was singing in one all male chorus:

The minstrel boy to the war is gone,
In the ranks of death you'll find him; ....

On the twentieth of April, an official telegram from Washington came to Petrosino. The telegram identified the tobacco and the sole New York proprietor. The President's hunch had been correct, it was Redman Chew. What is more, he had also been correct in saying that it was rare in New York. It was so rare that only one tobacconist in the city sold Redman: Rossi's Fine Tobacco at 174 Pearl Street. Petrosino would have to visit Rossi's incognito. Why was such exclusive tobacco found in such an ordinary tin? Was the man in the white shoes that carried a tin with Mathewson's face on it connected to baseball in any way?

5

*"I learned early to drink beer, wine and whiskey,
and I think I was about five when I first chewed tobacco."*
-Babe Ruth

Early April, 1905.

The bells tinkled above the doorway as Petrosino shuffled into Rossi's Fine Tobacco Shop at 174 Pearl Street, the center of the tobacco district in Manhattan. It was still early and the store was empty. The master detective was disguised as a Spanish aristocrat. Petrosino looked around and saw a usual tobacco shop with well-stocked shelves of various colored tins. A glass case holding pipes and other special items ran alongside the right of the shop, almost to the end, where there was a break to allow access to the back room. In the back of the shop was an all-wooden counter with a solitary register on it. A dark green velvet curtain extended down the length of the opening in the back wall and from this, a well-dressed man carrying a walking stick appeared. Ignoring him, Petrosino looked for Redman tobacco among the products. The shop, although it did not smell like smoke, did have the sweet smell of raw tobacco. Petrosino felt that the well-dressed man was studying him. The detective enacted a much-practiced stutter step. He was slightly bent which made him look even shorter. The detective had dressed well for the occasion. The crisp, dark brown suit, the expensive cuff links peeking from the sleeves, and the highly-polished shoes gave the impression of affluence. The derby, a more expensive one than he usually wore, remained on his head, the only outward sign that this was Petrosino. An expert wig of stringy gray hair extended from the derby. His face was thoroughly rubbed with beet juice to give him a darker complexion.

"Can I help you?" asked the well-dressed man behind the counter, laying the walking stick on the clean, wooden top.

Petrosino, who knew many Italian dialects, detected a northern Italian accent in this man.

"I am looking for something very special, but I do not see it," said the detective, masking his voice in a perfect Spanish accent.

"What can I do for you today?" replied the man, oblivious to the last remark.

"I am looking for Redman chewing tobacco."

Without hesitation the well-dressed man said, "Yes, of course. This is usually not sold by me. May I ask who told you that I sell it?"

23

The detective hid his enthusiasm, "You have it or you don't. A friend told me that you would have it."

"I do have it in limited quantities and I give it only to special customers. Your friend has good taste. May I ask who your friend is so I can thank him for sending me a new customer?"

"What! What are all of these questions? I want to speak to Mr. Rossi!" Petrosino barely raised his voice but he spoke slower and accentuated the Castilian.

The man squared his shoulders, "I am Mr. Rossi. I did not mean to upset you. I can sell you a limited amount. If you want more, I will have to order it. What I have is reserved for certain clientele, your friend no doubt among them. How much do you want?"

Petrosino detected an accent in Rossi that would put his hometown close to the border of Switzerland.

"Fill this please," said Petrosino as he produced a fine pocket tin from his suit jacket and handed it to Rossi.

Rossi, with his fine gray suit and yellow handkerchief artfully displayed from his breast pocket, disappeared behind the green velvet curtain. Petrosino approached the walking stick left on the counter. It was of dark wood, noticeably thick, topped by a beautiful greyhound dog's head, done in silver. It looked heavy. Petrosino wanted to pick it up but the tinkling of the bell above the entrance door caused him to turn around. A tall thin man, with a slight moustache entered the shop. He was dressed in a dark blue pinstriped suit and wore white shoes. He was hatless. When the man saw Petrosino he paused and remained in front of the shop.

The detective turned back to the cane. Mr. Rossi appeared and looked directly at the man who just entered.

"Take this as my compliment. If you would like more please let me know and I will order it for you," said Rossi.

"Gracias," replied Petrosino.

"Good day, and I apologize for upsetting you," said Mr. Rossi, picking up the cane and disappearing into the back of the shop once more.

Petrosino pocketed the tobacco and made his way slowly to the door. He pretended to be interested in the pipes displayed in the old wooden showcase. The long gray hair fell to the side of his face. Petrosino bent over, causing the stringy wig to cover his face. He was concealed from those to his left and right, but could look at them with a side glance without being detected. The wig was the perfect cover for close observation. The new customer, a thin man of medium height, had his back to the hunched detective. Petrosino struggled within himself. Should he reveal himself to question the man with the white shoes? This disguise was a valuable one and Petrosino knew that he would have to abandon it if he revealed himself. The newcomer matched the description given to him by the barber Fassett. Yet sometimes it was better to remain incognito and learn more. Also, he didn't want his enemies to know that he was a master of disguises. If he revealed himself now, he would be losing a lot in the future.

With all of this in mind, Petrosino decided to leave the shop rather than arouse suspicion. As he passed, the man in white shoes looked away and seemed to study something in the case. As soon as Petrosino closed the door behind him, he quickened his pace somewhat to cross to the other side of Pearl Street. He entered Flaherty's at 171 Pearl Street almost directly across from Rossi's and looked through both shop windows. He saw Rossi approach the newcomer, cane in hand and meet him over the counter. The detective could see them talking although he lost some detail in the glare caused by the rising sun. The newcomer was very animated and apparently irritated. Rossi looked calm, holding his walking stick and shaking his head slightly from left to right and back again. The man in the blue pinstriped suit was now visibly angry and suddenly grabbed his nose with his right hand. The hand then flew out toward Rossi and looked like a claw as it did so. Rossi stood like a statue and the man with the white shoes abruptly turned and quickly left the shop. Rossi then looked out the window and saw Petrosino staring back at him.

April 23, 1905

In other baseball news, Brooklyn played against Boston on a Sunday, which was against the law. Police officers watched the game in Washington Park without making an arrest because no admission was charged. However, scorecards cost anywhere from 25 cents to one dollar, depending on seat location.

6

1905: REGULATION: "Tobacco" does not appear in the US Pharmacopoeia, an official government listing of drugs. "The removal of tobacco from the Pharmacopoeia was the price that had to be paid to get the support of tobacco state legislators for the Food and Drug Act of 1906. The elimination of the word tobacco automatically removed the leaf from FDA supervision."

Smoking and Politics: Policymaking and the Federal Bureaucracy Fritschler, A. Lee. 1969, p. 37.

The disguised Petrosino busied himself with the window display, choosing a brown tobacco pouch and holding it aloft for a few seconds to allow Rossi to see.

Petrosino had to make another quick decision. He decided to keep Rossi ignorant rather than following the thin man with the white shoes.

"Ya want that one do ya?" asked the brogue behind him.

"How much?" counter-questioned the detective, turning his back on Rossi's Fine Tobacco and its well-dressed proprietor.

In his disguise the detective walked to St. Patrick's Cathedral on the corner of Prince and Mulberry Street. Since 1884 church authorities had given Petrosino the use of a small room as thanks for solving the mystery of *The Graveyard at Old St. Patrick's*. He entered the church through a side door with a special key. Once inside the church he went down to the crypt, making sure he was not noticed. The basement was damp and seemed like a natural cave in places with a dirt floor and exposed rock wall. Petrosino went to a locked door and opened it with another key. Inside this room were all his disguises. Only Archbishop Farley, and the pastor of the parish knew of this secret location. Someday, some intelligent or persistent individual could discover where Petrosino lived and may get past the precautions arranged to prevent anyone from entering his apartment when he was not home. If this unlikely event did occur, the intruder would not see any of the disguises that took so long to cultivate. This small church room, hidden in the catacombs underneath the church, is also where the great detective hid during part of the Tong Wars. The Four Brothers had feuded in Chinatown just a few years earlier. This hidden room was filled with clothing of all sorts. Mirrors, various headpieces, and jewelry used in his disguises were stocked around the room. The hidden room was also a good hiding place when Petrosino didn't want the underworld to know of his whereabouts. Sometimes, he wanted the criminals to think he was out of the city. Thus, he hid here. After Petrosino removed his disguise and cleaned his face, he left the room and entered the main body of the church. He paused to say a prayer and light a candle for all policemen killed in the line of duty. He then exited the church through the main doors and headed for police headquarters on Mulberry Street. Once there, Petrosino summoned the police artist to draw a sketch of the man he had seen in Rossi's shop.

The artist, a small man who spoke with a German accent steadied himself at his desk. "You may begin. I am ready."

Petrosino described the face of the man he had seen. "His face is thin, so much so that his cheeks seem hollow. His chin is almost like a bony point. His nose is rather large but thin and comes away from his face at a sharp angle. His nostrils are large. His nose seems to take up more space than his eyes and mouth together. He has a thin, brown moustache that matches the color of his thinning hair which is cut short well above the ear. His eyes may be a muted green or hazel. They are the shape of almonds and not far apart. His eyebrows are very thin they are not very pronounced, almost invisible. There are no marks of distinction on his face. His mouth is small with thin, pale lips. His hair is well kept, short around the ears, parted on the left. His ears are close to his head but distinctive in their shape which is similar to looking at the opening of a tuba. The ear lobe is very small and the top part of the ear is a bit elongated. His forehead is large. His complexion is pale. He is shaved and has on overall neat appearance even if he seems very thin to the point of being ill."

In silence, the artist quickly worked. "How iz thiz?"

"The nose needs to be a little longer and the bone of the nose should have less skin around it, be more pronounced."

"Fine. That iz fine," said the artist as he busily made adjustment and then held it up again.

"This is very good. Can you make one more like it?"

Once finished, the artist handed one to Petrosino and the other was to be displayed in the Rogue's Gallery where all of the police force would have a glimpse of this man in the blue striped suit and white shoes. Petrosino placed this new drawing between another Italian man who had stabbed a policeman on Carmine Street and the vulture man that had followed him to Lanza's. Underneath the drawing of the man with the white shoes who may have been the same one that had visited Fassett, Petrosino had printed: Do not arrest! Follow to learn whereabouts and notify Lieutenant Petrosino.

Early April 1905.

Joe Petrosino returned to Rossi's Fine Tobacco Shop and walked through the now familiar store. At the sound of the overhead bell, Rossi again appeared. This time his suit was a dark green with a burgundy handkerchief flowering out of the breast pocket. Petrosino strode confidently to the back of the shop. He wore his dark gray suit and derby.

"Good day sir, how can I help you?" He held the familiar cane down at his side; it seemed to be a part of him.

Petrosino came right down to the crux of the matter.

"I am with the New York City Police Department," he said as he flashed his badge, which was pinned on the inside of his suit lapel and he revealed it by flipping the lapel. It was an odd place to keep a badge, but the great detective did not want anyone to see the inside of his suit jackets with their many pockets and hidden belongings. The contents of his inner jacket pockets consisted of the following: a small flask of Sambuca used for reviving himself or others, a burglar's tools for lock picking, a pocket watch on a chain, a police whistle, opera glasses, a switchblade, and five twenty-dollar bills.

"And I need, ... your assistance," said Petrosino.

Rossi arched his eyebrows a bit and brought his cane to his waist in a non-threatening way, "How can I be of service, Inspector ahh…?"

"Lieutenant Petrosino."

"Yes. Lieutenant Petrosino. How can I be of service?" Rossi stared at the detective, expressing no real emotion except perhaps that of annoyance.

"I need a list from you of certain customers."

"May I ask what this is for?"

"No."

"Well I see no harm in assisting the police."

"Good. Then I will need a list of all of your customers who buy Redman Chew tobacco."

Rossi allowed a grin, "There was a gentleman in here just the other day looking for Redman. I wonder if he has anything to do with this." He let the tip of his cane kiss the floor.

"Can you describe this man?" asked Petrosino, continuing yesterday's deception.

"Oh yes. He left quite an impression. He was well dressed. His hair was gray and quite long. I didn't get a good look at his face but he had a ruddy complexion and he was certainly of Spanish origin."

"Very good. Anything else?"

"Well he was about your height, perhaps a little shorter and as I say, he was very well dressed and he appeared to be some sort of an aristocrat. He wanted Redman Tobacco. I had never seen him before. I usually buy enough just for certain customers but I sold him some."

"This is very good but I will still need the list of customers who buy Redman," said Petrosino pleased that his disguise had fooled the proprietor.

"Yes. It is a very short list."

"Why is it such a short list?" asked he detective, feeling he was getting somewhere with his inquiry.

"By making a good tobacco exclusive, I can make more money from it. I believe I am the only tobacconist in Manhattan that sells Redman."

"The list please," the detective ordered.

"Yes. That would be James Hazen Hyde, John McGraw, and Elmer Dundy."

"Only three! How can this be profitable?"

"Yes. Well. These three gentlemen are quite accomplished and are willing to pay a bit more for exclusivity."

"Are there any other customers?"

"No, this is all, excepting the Spanish gentleman the other day."

Petrosino, armed with this information, tipped his derby, "There is one more question."

"What would this be?" asked Rossi, seeming slightly amused.

"Have you ever been threatened by the Black Hand?"

Petrosino noticed a slight change in the face of Rossi. His blue eyes became slightly narrowed and his lips came together. Subtle but perceptible. Petrosino studied faces and reactions and after many years he was very good at it.

"Why do you ask?"

"I feel you may be in danger."

Rossi seemed to consider what the detective had told him.

"Yes," the older man began. "I have been threatened by the Black Hand, but I do not want to turn this into a police matter."

"Have you kept the threatening notes?"

"No, I have not. Please, I do prefer to handle this in my own way."

"I do…, advise against it."

"If I need your assistance Lieutenant, I will contact the police. But for now, I believe I can manage my own affairs."

Here Petrosino produced the drawing of the man in the white shoes, "Have you seen this man?"

Rossi paused. "Why, who is he?"

"He has been identified in connection with a bomb that killed a man. Have you seen him?"

Rossi paused again. "Lieutenant, I would like to deal with things in my own way."

"These men can be dangerous and should not be trifled with, once again, I urge you to relate to me everything that has happened regarding the Black Hand," Petrosino said, slightly raising his voice. He had seen and heard about so many victims that refused to come to the police out of fear of retaliation by the Black Hand and, he hated to admit, a mistrust of the police.

"Lieutenant, I must ask you to respect my privacy. I feel that I can handle this. I was warned that if the police were to get involved, I would be hurt." Rossi again let the cane's tip touch the floor.

"Very well. But if you need the police, call the station and ask for me."

"I will. Now is there anything you would like? I can give you anything in the shop as a sign of my thanks for your generous offer of assistance." Rossi offered a slight bow of his head and the closing of his eyes as he brought a close to the conversation.

"Nothing today," said Petrosino shaking his head. He turned around to leave the store.

"Lieutenant, how shall I contact you if I need you?"

"Call police headquarters and ask for Petrosino."

"Thank you. Good day."

McGraw of baseball, Dundy of the Hippodrome, and Hyde of the Equitable Life Assurance Society were in his mind as he walked among the downtown peddlers hawking their wares. As he moved he heard "Soap! Soap! Knives sharpened here! Fresh asparagus here! Fresh asparagus! Matches! Matches! Maaatchesssss!" He also heard many Italian dialects, Yiddish and German, Irish brogues and Russian. The cacophony outside of his head could not drown out the noise inside of his head. The question almost screamed at him, demanding an answer. "How could Redman Chew, if only given to these illustrious individuals end up at the scene of a murder in a tin that had Christy Mathewson's face on it?"

7

"Life without baseball had very little meaning to him. It was his meat, drink, dream, his blood and breath, his very reason for existence."
-Blanche McGraw on her husband, John McGraw manager of the New York Giants.

"It was a contest in name only." The New York World, April 15, 1905.

As the Giants were warming up for their opening day contest, Muldoon stepped onto the playing field at the Polo Grounds from the outfield. When Muldoon made it to the infield McGraw yelled, "No cranks!"

Muldoon kept coming. McGraw, who had been hitting fly balls, stopped and let the tip of the bat touch the ground and repeated, "No cranks."

Muldoon, towering over the short Giants manager, said, "I am a fan, but I am here on business."

"What business is that?" asked McGraw, who was never intimidated by bigger men.

"Police business," said Muldoon, dressed in his usual, off duty clothing, a white vest with faint dark stripes over a white long sleeve shirt. The vest had four pockets and pearl buttons. The pants were a light fabric, grayish in color.

"Oh a copper!"

"And a former baseball player. I played with King Kelly!"

"You don't say," said McGraw, slightly intrigued.

"Back in the late 1870's we played for the Cincinnati team. I played first base and outfield."

"How did your career end?"

"Well, I didn't like being sent to the Syracuse Stars so I quit."

"Could you hit?"

"I batted .376 for most of the season back in '78."

"Why would they send you to the Stars with that average?"

"They needed money and the manager had a brother that hit .260 but he wanted to play. That was baseball back then!"

"Well, I don't talk to coppers," McGraw turned his back and picked up a ball to continue the batting practice.

Muldoon, knowing McGraw was a gambling man and feeling confident in himself said, "If I can get a hit off Red Ames in three pitches, we talk. If I don't, I'll walk."

McGraw smiled and keeping his eyes fixed on the field said, "Deal."

McGraw signaled for all of the team to gather together. "It's time for a little fun boys. This copper thinks he can hit a big league pitch!" McGraw beckoned to Red Ames, "Hey Red, throw three pitches to this gent. Put all three of them over the plate. Bresnahan, get behind the plate."

Players stepped back to allow Muldoon room at the plate. Muldoon picked up the largest bat he could find, swung it a few times and took his place at the plate.

"Oh! A lefty!" shouted the manager and everyone laughed.

Red threw the first pitch and Muldoon swung and missed. Muldoon purposefully looked awkward to deceive Red. Everyone laughed. Someone yelled, "He can't hit the side of a barn with that swing!" It was the same for the second pitch. The big man made himself look totally uncoordinated. Arms flew in all directions; he lost his balance and dropped the bat in an over exaggerated attempt at deception. The entire Giants team was now laughing, watching this clown try to get a hit off a major leaguer. "He can't handle the ash!" said one. Another yelled, "He's carving the air!" The players were having fun. Some walked away.

The third and final pitch was different. Red didn't bear down too hard, he threw an easy pitch, taunting Muldoon to get a hit. It was what the policeman wanted. An easy one over the plate. All he had to do was hit it. It looked like a grapefruit as it came in. The big man gripped the bat and went into a stance that the Giants had not seen during the first two pitches. His big bat sliced the air effortlessly. The big man grunted as he connected with a loud crack and sent the ball zooming deep into the outfield. There were no fielders out there so it sailed, landed and rolled. The Giants were dumbfounded at first, but when Muldoon started to trot towards first, the Giants responded by clapping, as he stepped on second, they were cheering and as he made his way home, the team, including Red gathered around the plate to greet him. McGraw however, stood apart arms folded and looking grim. Muldoon shook hands and accepted good natured slaps on the back and yells of, "Sign him up!" and "Nice cloud scraper!" He left the players behind and walked toward the manager.

"You bastard! Can you catch?" asked McGraw.

Muldoon, still smiling and feeling exhilarated said, "Sure! But I'm not here for that boyo!"

"I feel I've been tricked but I always pay my debts," said McGraw, who now respected the policeman, but kept his arms akimbo. "What is it you want to know?"

"I'm interested in yer tobacco."

"What about my tobacco?"

"What is it that you chew?"

"What's this all about anyway?"

Muldoon grinned, "That's not the deal laddie!" His face turned dead serious, "Now answer the question."

"I use Redman Chew."

"Fine. Fine. And where do you buy your Redman Chew."

"I also have a job to do and I can't be wasting my time in talk like this," said McGraw annoyed.

"Would ye rather travel to Mulberry Street with me?"

"I buy from a place called Rossi's Fine Tobacco."

"How much do you buy?"

"As much as I need," said McGraw growing increasingly impatient.

"Do you share it with anybody?"

"I give it to some of the players."

"How much do you give them?"

"When I get some new stuff, I pass it around and they each take a small amount. Taylor, Bresnahan, Donlin, maybe a few others, take it regularly in small amounts."

"Do you have any extra?"

"I always have extra."

"Where do you keep it?"

"With my gear."

"Does anybody have access to it?"

"Nobody touches my things."

"OK. Thanks. Don't let Honus Wagner beat you."

"Aren't you going to tell me what this is all about?"

"Not while the case is going on! If you win the World Series then maybe I'll tell ye!" Muldoon grinned and turned to leave.

McGraw smiled and said, "If you get tired of police work, you can try out for this team."

Muldoon went the way he came, exchanging a few good natured slaps with the players lingering around second base. He then sauntered into the outfield remembering the glorious baseball days of his early adult life. He started to trot, then run. He wanted to turn around and see the ball coming towards him. He wanted to measure the speed and arc of the ball, he wanted to stretch and throw his body to the ground just at the point where the ball was landing. He wanted to smell the grass up close,

33

feel its coolness on his face. He wanted to hold the glove aloft with the ball in it. He wanted to hear the roar of the hometown crowd. Instead, he kept running and ran past the outfield and into the waiting city.

On Friday April 14, 1905, over 24,000 cranks traveled to the Polo Grounds to watch the New York Giants open the season against the Boston Beaneaters. Hundreds more fought for a spot on Coogan's Bluff to get a partial look at what most fans thought was the best team in baseball. The following day, the *New York Times* would report on the tremendous turnout by describing the Polo Grounds thus, "They filled every nick and crevice that a human body could squeeze into."

In the Autumn of 1904, John McGraw's National League champions sat out the second World Series, refusing to play the upstart American League champions. Most fans on this April day now felt that the fall contest was certain and that the whole season was a warm up to prepare the New York club for the new World Series.

The Polo Grounds never looked better. Flags and bunting were everywhere and the fifty-six piece Seventh Regiment Band played to keep the fans amused while they waited for their team.

George McClellan, New York City's mayor and Police Commissioner McAdoo were in places of honor for this long awaited event. Sitting to the left of McAdoo, was Joseph Petrosino. The detective had asked to come along because he had been following a trail in a Black Hand bomber case that began with a death and a tobacco tin left in a barber shop which had led him to the New York Giants. There was one person in particular whom Petrosino would be studying. This is what the Italian policeman did; he studied, contemplated, and acted. Petrosino tried to find out everything he could about the suspects in his cases. Many people would scoff at Petrosino for suspecting *this* particular man. Petrosino was never influenced by public opinion or the press and thus he would not flinch in bringing to justice a man that thousands of people in New York admired. The man under suspicion was for now a secret between Petrosino, Muldoon and one of the Giant groundskeepers. A groundskeeper in debt to Petrosino for keeping his brother out of jail years ago was now only too happy to help the great detective in any way he could. The suspect in this case was none other than Little Napoleon, otherwise known as Mr. John McGraw. Petrosino studied him. He was the Manager of the National League Champions. His players called him Mr. McGraw. If you wanted to be cursed at or have a fight with him, then you would call him Muggsy.

McGraw was the first baseball player to make $10,000 a year. He was feisty, a gambler on horses, a loud mouthed Irishman, a disrespecting son of a gun, and a winner. He made a name for himself playing "inside baseball" or "Irish baseball" for the Baltimore club. Now he was in New York playing the same brand of ball and New York loved him.

Petrosino, on the other hand, was quiet, reserved, and tough when he had to be, physically strong and like John McGraw, highly intelligent. New York loved him, too. Petrosino caught many criminals that had eluded lesser detectives using his powers of logic and deduction. The detective was also known to use his fists when the occasion called for it. Petrosino respected intelligence. When his opponent was clever it increased the thrill of the chase although the overriding principle that motivated Petrosino was one of justice.

This sense of justice in the detective was tinged with a frustration that the world of men would never really improve, no matter how many criminals were captured.

Both the lieutenant and the manager had enemies that despised them. Petrosino and McGraw were like two sides of the same coin. Although their personalities were very different, something was the same in their essence, their nature.

Now that Petrosino had strong suspicions about Muggsy, he wanted to see where it would lead. From experience he knew that even the smallest, most unlikely hint may reveal the central aspect of the mystery he was concerned with. He would pursue this unexpected turn the tobacco tin had produced. He would soon see where it would take him. Perhaps it would be a dead end. Perhaps not.

A parade of players started downtown a little late for the scheduled 3PM appearance at the Polo Grounds. People were cheering their heroes and admiring the cars they rode in as the parade made its way up Eighth Avenue to Harlem. Prominent citizens had loaned their automobiles for this unprecedented and unplanned event. The Giants players came first, followed by the Boston men. Fans who couldn't make it to the ballpark cheered and waved to McGraw the "Little Napolean" and manager; Christy "the Christian Gentleman" Mathewson; Mike "Iron Man" McGinnity; "Turkey" Mike Donlin; "Moonlight" Graham; "Boileryard" Clark; "Red" Ames; "Cap" Dan McGann; Sam "Sandow" Mertes; "Bad Bill" Dahlen; Roger Bresnahan, "the Duke of Tralee"; Sammy Strang, the "Dixie Thrush"; Hooks Wiltse; Billy Gilbert; Art Devlin; George Brown; and the clubhouse clown, "Dummy" Taylor. Some onlookers were more impressed with the other names in the parade; those of Studebaker, Buick, Ranier, Raulang, Oldsmobile, Locomobile, Stanley, and Pierce Arrow. Sixteen automobiles in all honked and chugged up the Avenue. Last came a maroon Columbia Electric Brougham. For four thousand dollars one could have the "fastest (18 miles an hour), most efficient, and luxuriously appointed electric carriage ever built."

When this select group entered the Polo Grounds the cheers and applause rose like a great ocean swell. It drowned out the band that played on as the players arrived. Petrosino couldn't hear the music above the roar but the swift, chaotic movements of the conductor was evidence that the music continued as the ballplayers passed into the Polo Grounds. The grounds crew started to roll up the tarp that had been covering the home plate area. The one Italian member of the grounds crew, an informer for Petrosino, knew secrecy was paramount and never looked up. Revealed, the large blue banner with gilt letters read, "GIANTS. CHAMPION BASEBALL CLUB OF NATIONAL LEAGUE 1904."

After a brief warm up that delighted the fans, the home team took the field in earnest.

"Do you know anything about the game or are you here strictly for business?" asked Police Commissioner McAdoo. McAdoo, on the job for less than one year, knew of Petrosino's reputation. Month after month the Italian detective proved himself to be one of the major assets of the department. When Petrosino asked to come along for the Giants' opening day, McAdoo did not ask any questions. He let men like Petrosino do their work unencumbered. Besides, shortly after he was appointed as Commissioner, McAdoo got a call from President Theodore Roosevelt, a personal friend of Petrosino. "Let him do what he wants!" urged the big fellow. When he was Police Commissioner for New York, Roosevelt's enthusiasm and support of Petrosino had helped advance the Italian policeman's career. The present commissioner knew this man beside him and the President were still close and he believed they contacted each other semi-regularly. Being "good" to Petrosino could be helpful to his own career. For a moment, McAdoo fancied himself with a direct line to the White House.

"I have a mild interest in the game," said the detective, breaking the reverie of his superior. Petrosino never took his eyes off of the field.

McAdoo studied him. On this windy Friday, Petrosino was dressed in an undistinguished three-piece gray suit and a derby. Petrosino's stature was well below the department height regulation of five feet seven. The derby and the thick soled shoes offset the height difference somewhat; still Petrosino was noticeably shorter than the men he worked with. His face, always serious, was pockmarked due to small pox at a young age. Petrosino was a solitary man. He didn't speak much. He was all business. To many, this solver of mysteries was a mystery himself. His only friend seemed to be Muldoon, a man he would have to get to know.

McAdoo understood the strengths of his most valuable detective. Recognizing clues, and where they led, however absurd, was a strength of Petrosino. In his preliminary research, which was always a combination of tapping into a huge network of informers, reading newspapers, teaching himself about any new subject which may apply to the present puzzle, and discreetly observing suspects, Petrosino informed his mind to further his deductions.

What do you know about McGraw, Joe?"

Without altering his gaze but leaning a little closer to McAdoo he said, "I discovered that McGraw would do anything to win. While he was with the Baltimore club he had the groundskeeper make the dirt extra hard a certain distance from the plate. His players knew where the hard spot was and aimed for it. When a player hit it just right the ball would bounce very high and by the time the fielder caught the ball, the home team would have a man on first. Today, any hit of a high bouncer in front of home plate is called the "Baltimore Chop". Another trick McGraw used was to mix fine soap chips in with the dirt around the pitcher's mound. When the opposing thrower picked up some dirt to better grip the ball, the opposite would happen and the ball would slip. The groundskeeper, Murphy was so good at what he did that McGraw brought him to New York to work at the Polo Grounds."

"That certainly doesn't make the papers," quipped McAdoo.

The detective remained silent. Getting this information was not difficult for a man like Petrosino. His reputation and experience opened many doors for him in all strata of society. In this instance he had saved the brother of the only Italian groundskeeper at the Polo Grounds from prison by capturing the real killer. Joseph Petrosino had an incredible memory and he was not afraid to call in chips that were owed to him.

McGinnity, the Iron Man, gave up three weak infield hits to the Beaneaters and they went down easily in their first time at bat. Donlin, the center fielder, yelled something at the pitcher and then led off the bottom of the first for the Giants with a double to left.

"Do you chew tobacco?" asked Petrosino.

"I can't say that I do. I like a pipe now and then with the evening edition of the *Post*."

The commissioner knew that his Lieutenant was absorbed and focused in his work. This question was not an attempt at conversation but a question that looked for information concerning some aspect of a case that his subordinate was trying to solve. When Petrosino asked no further questions the commissioner kept silent and tried to enjoy the game.

Strang bunted back towards the mound. The ball died on the grass between catcher and pitcher. The pitcher was slow in retrieving the ball and the speedy Donlin was on third with Strang safe at first. This was a perfect example of what some would call "Irish baseball," getting on base by bunting and then advancing runners, always being unpredictable and aggressive.

Petrosino could see McGraw, hands on his hips, barking something or other to his players on the bench. McGraw clapped as Donlin went to third standing up.

McGann, the first baseman, was next and after yelling at the umpire about the second pitch he hit the third pitch to right field. Donlin crossed the plate for the first run of the game and the noise level increased tenfold. The right fielder made an errant throw to third base and Strang scored from first. McGann took second then third as the catcher Needham made a high throw to try to catch McGann at second. McGann gave the second baseman an elbow to the mouth which was missed by the sole umpire, but seen by most of the home crowd. The ballpark became louder. The Beaneaters looked nervous and unprepared for the efficiency of the New York club. The visiting team was also intimidated by the noise. The New York fans were many and they were obnoxious.

"Go eat yer beans in Boston!" shouted one.

"All this bean eatin' is creating wind!" teased another.

Everyone around the detective was shouting, clapping, laughing and smiling. Joe Petrosino looked like a Beaneater fan, standing stock still, amid the crazy tumult all around him. He was watching the players interact with each other and with their manager. He was remembering what Muldoon had told him of his encounter with the team during practice. The home team and its skipper were aggressive, confident and they executed well.

Dahlen, the fifth batter of the inning, looped the first pitch over the head of the first baseman. McGann tried to reach home from second on the hit but was thrown out. Dahlen charged for third but got caught between second and third on a fine throw by Needham. He was tagged easily for the final out and collectively everyone went, "Ohhhh!" The quick double play silenced the crowd momentarily.

Petrosino knew that being overly aggressive and too cocky turned strengths into weaknesses. There was a certain point when the criminal mind became too confident in past successes and this over confidence caused them to be sloppy. For Petrosino this overconfidence was a matter of waiting because this inflated belief in immunity from detection seemed to be a part of human nature. The Giants as a team and as individuals were not immune to this law. That last double play made them look bad. Petrosino, despite being a newcomer to baseball, understood that had McGann and Dahlen held up the Giants would have first and third with one out and a chance to break the opening day game wide open.

"Two to nothing in the first is not a bad way to start the season," said McAdoo.

"That base running that ended the inning didn't look good." said Petrosino, looking at McAdoo for the first time since the players marched onto the field.

"I suppose this crowd and the early mistakes by the Beaneaters made our Giants think they could do anything," replied the Commissioner, shrugging his shoulders, not knowing what else to say.

"Does McGraw call the play or do the players run on their own?" questioned Petrosino.

"Oh! I see the game interests you after all," said McAdoo, ready to talk a little baseball. "Well, from the way I understand it; all the players are taught to be aggressive by Muggsy. He lets them run when they want. He was very aggressive with Baltimore."

Petrosino turned to the field and resumed his vigil. McAdoo frowned, stuffed his hands into his coat pockets, and looked at the players. McAdoo, a growing fan, eager to talk about nuances and statistics, kept quiet as his subordinate soaked in the surroundings. McAdoo never questioned the detective about what he was looking for or why he wanted to attend the game. It was better to do as the President advised and keep out of his way. McAdoo thought that if he handled Petrosino correctly, he may advance his own career.

In the bottom of the fourth when Donlin hit an inside the park home run, the crowd really blew up.

Someone yelled, "That was a Chinese home run!" Those around him ignored his taunt and clapped, whistled and shouted. Boston's poor defense and the strength of the Iron Man were a combination that doomed the Beaneaters.

Burkeville, that section of distant bleachers was filled as usual with loud Irishmen who paid two bits to get in and they would, especially on this day, get their two bits worth. The Irish came out to the ball park in droves. After all, 80% of all the players in baseball were of Irish descent. McGraw was one of theirs as was Donlin, McGann, and Bresnahan.

Petrosino turned towards McAdoo, "Can you get Muldoon into the Giants' dugout?"

McAdoo attempted humor, "Why, do you want an autographed ball from the boys?"

Petrosino failed to appreciate it, "Can you or can't you? This is important."

McAdoo felt embarrassed at his readiness to become friendly with the taciturn detective, "Yes, of course, I can arrange that," not knowing if he truly could.

Petrosino was excited for the first time since he entered the stadium, "Good. The sooner the better" and he turned to leave.

"Won't you stay for the rest of the game?"

"I have someone else I must meet."

McAdoo watched Petrosino go, the derby getting lost in the crowd of cranks. Petrosino was absorbed, focused, determined and highly skilled. McAdoo would define his lieutenant as a man of tenacity and an unwavering sense of justice. He knew the Italian would never let go until he solved a case. Maybe he would accompany Muldoon when he visited the Giants. It would probably be very instructive and he might be able to get some of the boys to sign a baseball. He then sent a policeman to inform the photographers that the police commissioner and mayor were ready to be photographed. The photographers, eager to get a picture, were held off at the behest of the great detective who did not like to be photographed, especially in public.

Meanwhile, Petrosino walked around to the edge of the Polo Grounds to meet someone that was waiting for him. The fans were focused on the big game. Many circled around the outfield grass watching the game from the edge of the field. About ten yards beyond this outfield perimeter of fans was another semicircle of cranks sitting in carriages and open automobiles, also focused on the players. It was next to them that the detective walked. The Lieutenant kept his head down as he passed the fans, mostly men, clad in dark suits and wearing top hats. In fact, very few men were hatless and even fewer wore light colored clothing. Petrosino fit in perfectly. He looked beyond the well-dressed fans standing along the perimeter of the outfield to the field itself. The Giants were crouched waiting for the ball, their backs to him, and far in the distance one of Boston's boys was hoping to get a hit. Finally, moving closer to the edge of the elevated stands that extended beyond first base and into right field, the detective saw the small door in the back end of the stands slightly ajar. He entered.

The April sun peeked through the boards. The ceiling in the half-lit interior was a confusion of wood crisscrossing the space to add support to the bleachers. The interior sloped dramatically towards the field to a height barely exceeding that of a man. It was at this lowest point among shadows and wood, in which a solitary figure motionlessly stood. The thin rays of light on the dirt floor striped the detective as he moved and the continuous creaking and cracking of the support beams as fans jostled about on the stands and the smell of dry wood gave the impression of an expressionist barn as it would appear in a bizarre nightmare.

Petrosino approached the figure and they spoke in Italian.

"Good day," said the detective extending his hand.

40

The man took the hand and kissed it with the same intensity and sincerity as a devout Catholic would kiss the papal ring.

"So good to see you, Mr. Petrosino."

"How is your brother?"

The man smiled, "Since the baptism of his third child he has never been happier!"

"How is my godchild?"

"Little Giuseppe is wonderful! He grows big and strong. His older brother is now an altar boy at Our Lady of Pompeii. All of our happiness is due to you!"

"Do you have any news?"

"Well, I know that McGraw is generous with his tobacco. He shares it with a few of the players."

"Do you know who?"

"I see them take from him during practice, when I am working on the grass. I've seen Taylor, Donlin, Bresnahan and McGann take from the manager."

"Is there anything else?"

"McGann, the first baseman is always in trouble with McGraw. It seems that McGann is sometimes out very late and he is very tired during work outs. One day before a game started, I was raking the infield and McGann showed up late for practice. When McGann went to first base to take some throws McGraw let him have it."

"What did he say?"

"You're out too late! Stop the drinking! McGann then told him that is not about the drink. McGraw wanted to know what it was all about. McGann told him it was none of his business."

"How did McGraw react to that?" questioned Petrosino.

"He fined him ten dollars for being late to practice."

"It would be nice to know what McGann does all night. I'll have Muldoon follow him. Thanks for the information. If you find out anything else, you know how to contact me."

"Yes. I promise."

"Go now before anyone gets suspicious."

"No one is thinking about the groundskeeper while the game is going on."

"Where is your boss, Mr. Murphy?"

"He is probably at the racetrack."

"Still, you do have an obligation to your work. Do you remember how to contact me if you have news?" asked the detective.

"Yes. I will light the green candle that I always carry with me and place it at the foot of the St. Anthony statue after the 9AM mass, then I will wait for you to find me. If there is no news, I will not light anything. But I will still say a prayer!"

"Good. Remember if you see me at mass don't come to me. We can meet after this case is over."

"God bless you," said the groundskeeper as if he would never see the detective again.

Petrosino exited from the small door in which he had entered. He closed it and moved away from the action on the field. Head down and walking swiftly, the mind of the great detective was exploring possibilities when he heard the following: "Peanuts! Cracker Jacks! Get your red hots! Red hots here!" The detective approached the stand owned by Harry Mozley Stevens.

"Hi Harry."

"Holy smokes! It's Joe Petrosino! I didn't know you were a fan of the game."

"I am now."

"How can you not like the Giants? What can I get for you?"

"I'll have a red hot."

"The works?"

"Sure."

"Coming right up."

Petrosino was handed a hot sausage with mustard and sauerkraut wrapped in Vienna bread.

Petrosino started to look for the five cents in his pockets but as soon as he began Harry bellowed, "Forget about it! I owe you one. This one's on me. Enjoy the hot dog."

"Thanks Harry," Petrosino sauntered off enjoying his "hot dog." The crowd was cheering for the home team. Petrosino turned to look at the players. He could see the Giants were on the field and either somebody made a great defensive play or one of the A's was striking wind because the fans were out of their seats, clapping and cheering. It was loud. The Giants eventually crushed Boston 10-1. The Iron Man threw a three hitter, allowed one walk, hit one batter and faced only thirty two men. Donlin with a single, a double and a homer provided all of the firepower needed to subdue the Boston nine. It was the Giants' first win on the first day of the 1905 championship season. Petrosino began to focus on some of the Giant players.

8

Tuesday May 6, 1905.

*The Beaneaters get revenge from their opening day humiliation by
defeating Christy Mathewson 2-1. It is Mathewson's first loss against his
three wins. New York is 13-4.*

*"You can learn little from a victory, you can learn everything
from defeat."*
-Christy Mathewson

*The saloon and the brothel are "the two great obstacles in the
way of success of the majority of professional ballplayers."*
-Spalding Guide to Baseball 1889

Early May 1905.

The bomb that went off in front of Iannacone's Meats sent
baloney flying into the streets. A woman passing by was killed in the
blast. Dan McGann, who was standing in the shadows, discreetly
watching and waiting, saw what happened. His first reaction was to run
to the aid of the woman. Then, he was shocked into being immobile.
Finally, he realized that she was dead because of him. He didn't want to
do what he was doing, but to cause a death was a sin. He never wanted
to be responsible for the death of someone. People gathered. Voices
were nervous and excited. Still, McGann remained hidden. There was
nothing to do. To reveal himself might invite suspicion. As everyone
raced towards the scene of the explosion, the first baseman, with head
down, moved in the opposite direction.

Mr. Iannacone, the owner of the Italian meat store, had been
visited by an individual three days prior. This individual, a thin Italian
with a moustache, had pleaded with Iannacone to pay up. After the
unwanted visitor left, Iannacone closed up shop and went to Police
Headquarters, asking for Lieutenant Petrosino. The word on the street
was that Petrosino was a good cop and a son of Italy who would protect
his countrymen when they needed him.

Iannacone nervously waved the Black Hand note in the face of the
desk sergeant who looked annoyed. All Iannacone could say in English
was "Please."

"Please, Petrosino."

The sergeant on duty, who had barely poured his tea, was in no mood for this.

"OK! OK! I'll make sure he gets it. He is not in at the moment."

"Please Petrosino, please," he answered.

"Give it to me! He'll get it."

"Petrosino please." He started and continued in Italian.

"The Lieutenant is not in." At this point the sergeant leaned over the desk and snatched the paper. He looked at it and saw that it was a Black Hand note. Then, with a wave of his hand, he dismissed the butcher as one would shoo a fly.

"Go on now, Jesus Mary and Joseph! Go sell your olive oil or whatever yer sellin!"

Slightly confused, but half understanding, Iannacone left the station house.

The sergeant put the Black Hand note under yesterday's edition of *The Irish Examiner*. Eventually that note got lost in the mess of the front desk and Petrosino never saw it until early August when a new recruit, decided to straighten the desk. Iannacone had written Petrosino's name on it. The Lieutenant was furious at the lapse in attention and demanded to know who was responsible. No one would confess.

Officer Muldoon, blond hair colored black, teeth blackened and a birthmark added to the right cheek, wore a wool cap with a dirty white shirt, and old, dark trousers from which a longshoreman's hook hung at the waist. His dark, scuffed shoes finished a disguise put together by Petrosino himself. Muldoon discreetly followed Dan McGann into the three story, squat brick house at 326 Spring Street. The sign over the door said *Thomas Cloke Liquor*. The room was filled with longshoreman, assorted riff-raff, and other hang abouts. The air was a stale mixture of tobacco smoke and dry beer. Patrons, speaking Gaelic, a language that he himself knew, 'crowded the bar as others sat at rickety tables in dilapidated chairs. There was a boy at the back wall near a large blackboard. He was reading the days' early scores from the Western Union ticker tape and writing those numbers on the board. The only score put up on Cloke's board read Highlanders 1 Detroit 0.

When some patrons saw that the other New York team was winning they said, "The Yankees are winning their game but they will never win a championship!"

McGann took a place at the bar and no one seemed to notice the more polished, less physically imposing customer who played first base for the New York Giants. Muldoon didn't break stride, spotting McGann almost immediately, despite the crowd. The big Irishman confidently made his way through the saloon, gently pushing, slightly nudging his way to get close to the first baseman. Muldoon, at three inches over six feet was big among big men. His shoes slipped and sometimes softly stuck on the beer and spit combination that stained the slightly uneven floor.

Standing behind McGann, Muldoon forced his way to the bar. McGann moved to his left.

"Give me a plain!" yelled Muldoon as he slapped down a quarter on the bar. After a few minutes the bartender approached with the Guinness, Muldoon produced a yellow Tuxedo tin with Mathewson's face on it.

"Can you put one penny's worth in that tin?"

The bartender, laying down the pint, picked up the tin took it to the center of the bar and dug into a barrel, scooped, shook and filled the tin with chewing tobacco. He returned it to the bar.

Muldoon left it untouched where the bartender had placed it. The Christy Mathewson face looked up and away towards the dark pint.

McGann did not seem to notice any of this. Muldoon gulped down the pint. Halfway through, he slammed the glass on the bar and waited. McGann continued to look ahead, nursing his own Guinness.

"Not a bad pint," yelled Muldoon to McGann, hoping to start a conversation.

McGann twisted his head and slightly looked up. "I don't come here to talk."

"Suit yerself!" yelled Muldoon as he took another gulp.

Suddenly, Muldoon felt a slap on his back.

"I don't recognize you," said the stranger.

Muldoon turned to his right to face a longshoreman wearing a dirty t-shirt from which extended thick pink arms and a heavy neck supporting a head of pure white hair.

"That's because this is my first time in here," answered Muldoon.

"And where are you from?"

"Cork."

"Is that Cork city or County?"

"Well, are you meaning me mother or father?"

"Your father man. Your father, if you still know who he is!"

"Me father is from the county."

"I thought so. I know the look. The name's Farrell." He extended his hand. Muldoon took it.

"O'Rourke."

"Well now, O'Rourke, ye haven't been working long with that hook that's hanging from yer waist."

"For a longshoreman you're pretty smart!"

"Well for an Irishman, I'm a jackass!" Farrell laughed and slapped Muldoon on the back for the second time.

"How do you know what you know Farrell?"

"Jesus Mary and Joseph, yer hands man! They're too damn soft to be working long with the hook."

At this juncture, Muldoon noticed that McGann left his drink on the bar to look for something in his pockets. The big Irishman knocked the drink over with his elbow to get a conversation started with the suspect.

"What a sin! Let me buy this one palie!" said Muldoon.

"Why is every other Irishman an idiot?" snarled a combative McGann.

Farrell, who heard everything, came around to face McGann.

"Stop acting the goat," said Farrell seeming to relish the thought of a fight.

"Chase yourself," said McGann gently brushing Farrell's chest with the back of his hand. That was all he had to do.

"You need your arse wiped!" quipped Farrell.

Muldoon had seen enough but it was too late. McGann, like lightning, punched Farrell full in the face. Blood spurted immediately. McGann jabbed to the face again, this time with a left.

"That's enough!" Muldoon stepped forward but another patron, perhaps a friend of Farrell, perhaps an inebriated loner with no life, wrapped his arm around the neck of McGann and jerked him backwards. The first baseman had an answer.

McGann rammed his elbow into the soft gut of his assailant. This caused the man to loosen his grip somewhat. McGann then grabbed the arm around Farrell's neck with both of his hands and twisted the arm while turning his body around. To complete the dance, the knee of the Giant came up to the face of the off-balance tough guy.

Muldoon grabbed McGann, actually lifted him off the ground, spun him around and yelled, "Enough laddie!" McGann was slammed to the floor.

The first baseman, getting up from the floor, reached for the overturned glass on the bar that had started the ruckus, grabbed it, smashed it, and swung it at Muldoon. Farrell intercepted his arm and twisted it back. McGann dropped the glass in his right hand and with his left hand and off balance, as if he were catching a low scorcher down the line and bringing it up out of the dirt, miraculously grabbed the hook from Muldoon's waist and swung at Farrell before Muldoon could react. Surprised, Farrell let go and stepped back and fell to the floor.

"Look out!" yelled Farrell from where he lay. Everyone went off balance but the hook still managed to scrape Farrell. A gash opened up on Farrell's arm and blood was still coming from his nose. Muldoon picked up the first baseman from behind and tossed him backwards.

"You're gone man!" yelled the police officer who had still not revealed himself as such. No one approached the first baseman while he held the hook.

McGann waved the hook menacingly. "You look familiar!" said the first baseman, perhaps remembering Muldoon from the day he hit the home run off Red Ames.

People moved aside. An old timer at the far end of the bar was trying to order a whiskey. Others, looked, and moved aside. Some placed bets on who would bleed next. The hook cleared a path to the door. Staring at Muldoon, McGann said, "I'll remember you and if I see you again, I will kill you." McGann turned to leave the bar. Muldoon did not pursue.

Muldoon, hands on knees, bent to look at Farrell. "Are you ready for another?"

"Is it a fight or a drink yer talking about?"

"A drink man! A drink!"

As he lay on the ground, Farrell looked up at Muldoon.

"I saw that hook coming toward me and…"

"He was a fast bastard!"

"I saw the hook coming toward me and thought of me brother Kevin and how he left this earth."

Muldoon, grinning, said, "How did it happen?"

"He drowned in Dublin"

"Drowned in the River Liffey?"

"Jesus no! He drowned in a vat of Guinness!"

"At least he didn't suffer," smiled Muldoon.

"I should say not. He got out three times to take a piss!"

"Let me help you to yer feet," said the smiling Muldoon, "And get a towel for your nose."

Holding his head back, Farrell said, "Me nose is me soft spot."

"Two more pints!" yelled Muldoon to the bartender who was nearby and attentive.

As the drinks were being poured, Muldoon dressed the arm wound of Farrell with a clean bar towel. The injuries were not that bad after all.

The hero who grabbed McGann from behind, walked out of the bar with a bloody nose and without saying a word. Cloke's resumed its state of normalcy. These men who frequented Thomas Cloke's saw fighting all the time, in alleys, in bars, on ships and especially in their bedrooms. They didn't want to get involved. It was none of their business. Better to drink the Guinness and sleep rather than fight. Fights give you black eyes. Black eyes mean trouble. Troublemakers don't get picked to work on ships. No work no pay.

Muldoon looked at Farrell.

"I like you Farrell! You're smart, and not afraid to fight. We could use men like you. Do you want to work with me?"

Farrell smiled. "Me father was from Tipperary and he hated the Corkmen. They always had the best hurlers. But then he married my Ma, a lass from Cork in St. Anne's Church! What might ye line of work be?"

"Well, you have to talk to my boss first and I can't tell you right now, but don't fret it is nothin' illegal."

The towel around Farrell's arm was a deep red.

"Well if I don't bleed to death first, I'd like to hear what ye hav' to say."

Thursday May 11, 1905

Matty pitches his first complete game shutout of the season against St. Louis allowing only five hits in the Giant win that improves their record to 16-5.

9

"It couldn't have happened anywhere but in little old New York."
-O. Henry

Muldoon stopped for a drink at Pete's Tavern before he went up to his rooms. Living above this fine pub at 129 East 18th Street had its benefits. He was given free beer and snacks, and in return whenever there was trouble the bartender could summon him. Rarely was there any trouble. The crowd here was convivial. One of the bunch, Sydney Porter, approached the big man.

"Hello! Hello! We haven't seen you around here for a while!"

"Sydney, how are you! Are you still writing?"

"If I don't how will I have money for the beer? Say, why don't you join me at my table I want to ask you a few questions about police work. I am going to write a short story and there is a policeman involved who meets his old chum after many years, maybe you can help me with the details."

"Sure Sydney, but don't tell me how the story ends!"

The men laughed and made their way to a middle table one off from the window. As they moved through the bar, various customers acknowledged the pair.

"Muldoon!"

"Hey Sid!"

"Hey Jimmy!"

One of the men stepped out in front of Muldoon, "Is it really you? Have you come back from the dead?"

"No. No," laughed Muldoon, "It is not my time. I've just been away."

"Well, where have you been then?"

"Catching robbers!"

Everyone within earshot laughed.

At the table the two talked for hours and drank more than a few pints. Finally, better sense came to him and Muldoon decided to call it a night. He still had business to attend to and a visitor to speak with.

"Time for me to go. If I want to grow big and strong I need me rest," said Muldoon.

"My friend, you are so big and strong that you look like you have been sleeping more than Rip Van Winkle!"

They finished their pints. Sydney scribbled on his paper. Muldoon reached over the table and slapped Sydney on the back.

"I look forward to the next story, Sid!"

Porter took this as a compliment; he knew how well-read Muldoon was.

"Good night Sid!"

"Good night to you Jimmy!"

Muldoon called to the bartender, "Jack, I'm through!" He handed the bartender a nickel, "Knock if you need me! Oh, and by the way, Petrosino is coming and when he comes can you bring up a pot of tea and something sweet?"

"Of course Jimmy!"

Muldoon went upstairs to his rooms. He had two. Some of his meals were taken downstairs but mostly he ate out, so he had no need of a kitchen or dining room. One room was a sparsely furnished and very plain, akin to the cell of a monk. There was a large unmade bed, a small table with a well-worn bible on it and a crucifix above the bed. There was another table with a washstand on it, a large pitcher for wash water and a few crumpled face towels piled haphazardly around the blue pitcher. A big bathtub filled what was left of the room. The other room was his study. The study was where Muldoon lived. A desk, chairs, a horse-hair stuffed sofa and plenty of books. Books so varied in topic that he seemed like a collection of three individuals rather than one. Many of his books were purchased on Book Row. Back in 1896 when he teamed up with Petrosino to solve a murder involving rare books, the owners of various shops showed their appreciation by selling him books at big discounts. Some books were even foisted upon him and he never refused. Muldoon lived a solitary life, and had little time for women. He loved hurling, boxing, books, baseball, chess, Ireland, New York City, and the Church. Muldoon had coached Petrosino in English during their early years. They had been on many adventures together. In his time off he followed baseball and he traveled to the hurling matches once in a while, but mostly he read books and studied chess. He boxed, rowed and swam in the East River and looked for birds in Central Park. He missed female companionship, but it was to be expected with his police work.

There was a knock at the door.

"Come in Lieutenant."

Joseph Petrosino walked in, removing his hat and extending his arm.

"James, good to see you."

"Sir there is tea on the way."

Muldoon carefully lifted the chess board from a chair and put it on a large table on which rested many books. The board showed a Paul Morphy position.

"Wait a minute. Let me look at that," said Petrosino who was also interested in chess.

Another knock came at the door this one a repetitive, softer sound.

"Your tea," said a voice through the door.

"Come in! Come in," boomed Muldoon.

A boy came in and awaited orders.

"Set it there lad," said Muldoon pointing to the table he had just cleared.

The boy did as he was told and laid the tea things on the table.

Muldoon went to the fireplace and from a teapot he took a penny and handed it to the youngster.

"Thank you sir," said the boy.

"Thanks Tommy."

Muldoon sat on the sofa and poured the tea.

"Which game is this James?"

"It is Anderssen-Morphy 1858 in Paris."

"Which opening did Anderssen play?"

"Ruy Lopez."

"I thought so. Morphy is aggressive," noted Petrosino as he moved away from the chessboard and towards the tea things. He sat on the Victorian chair with the lavender velvet.

"I hope you'll have time for a game later on, after we discussed what we have to discuss."

"Yes," replied Petrosino with a smile, "I was hoping we would have the time. I want to work on the Sicilian Defense."

"I'll be happy to oblige," said Muldoon and continued, "I remember Marshall helping us solve that chess murder years ago, a wee lad he was, but I knew one day that he would be a champion."

"Let's save Frank Marshall for later. Tell me again how it went with the Giants, and McGann," said Petrosino as he had a cannoli from DeRobertis Pastry Shop. Muldoon knew that Petrosino liked to hear a story at least twice, and when possible, from different angles.

"I forgot to thank the boy," said Petrosino. The lad at Pete's Tavern known as Tommy always ran to DeRobertis to get pastries when Petrosino visited. He would say, "They are for Petrosino!" and he would be given a few free pastries.

"I didn't get too much from the Giants. A bit disappointing it all was. McGraw gets Redman from Rossi's and gives the players a small amount. He has extra on him that he claims no one would touch. It seems there are four or five players who take the stuff from him regularly but in small amounts. Probably enough for one or two chews, McGraw doesn't have that much to begin with. I followed McGann to

Cloke's down on Spring Street and we got into a fight with McGann. I got careless and McGann grabbed my longshoreman hook."

"Who is we?"

"I met a feller there named Farrell, pretty sharp and he doesn't back down from a fight. I asked him to come and meet you. Perhaps we can find a place for him on the force."

"Bring him in. We could use good men. Well, James, we don't have much to go on but it is something. Do you think McGraw is capable of ordering a storefront to be bombed? What could his motive be? He certainly has enough money."

"Difficult to say sir. I am not sure what kind of a motive a man like McGraw would have to do a thing like this. It seems to me that if he focused on winning ballgames, he wouldn't have time for this."

"This is what I thought, Muldoon. The ballplayers themselves are more likely to do something like this. We have to get to know them," said Petrosino.

"Baseball men sir, are a bit aggressive a bit uncivilized but for the most part they are a good bunch. It is difficult for me to think that a baseball player is doing this, although you never can tell, all kinds of men play ball." Muldoon then related the incident at Cloke's in more detail.

"I'll visit McGraw myself. I need to get a feel for the man. There are other suspects and other possibilities of course," said Petrosino.

Petrosino was going to explain what they were when there was a sudden, urgent knock at the door.

"Who could this be?" questioned Muldoon as he went to answer the door. Petrosino pulled the revolver from under his pants leg and faced the door.

Muldoon yelled, "Who is it?" as he grabbed a Billy club that he always kept hanging on a nail near the front door.

"Just me sir," said Tommy who had delivered the pastries.

The door swung open. "Yes lad, what is it?" asked Muldoon exhaling as if he were blowing out candles on a birthday cake.

"There is something you should know sir," said the lad.

Muldoon's face looked serious, "Well then, come in and tell us all about it." He ushered the boy in and closed the door.

"What is it you want to say?" asked Petrosino.

"Well sir, when I went to DeRobertis to get the pastries, I told Mr. DeRobertis that they were for you, like I normally do it, sir. There was a man in the shop behind me who heard me say it and I noticed that he left his bread on the counter and followed me out. I tried to lose him in the park but he is downstairs now at the bar. He's having Pete's Ale but he's not drinking it."

"You'll be a fine policeman someday," said Muldoon.

"I want to be just like Mr. Petrosino!"

"What does the man look like?"

"Well, he is scary looking. He is bald with big eyes that looked pushed into his face. He is not very tall. I'm almost as tall as him."

Petrosino looked at Muldoon, and thought of the man at Lanza's, "I know this man. He is dangerous. I am sure he has a gun and his intention is to kill me."

"What do we do sir?" asked Muldoon.

"Did the ugly man see you go up here?" asked Petrosino

"No, I don't think so, he is sitting at the end of the bar and he can't see into the hallway."

"Good, you must stay here, until this is finished," said Petrosino.

"Can't I come? I want to watch you catch the bad guy."

"No, your place is here, where it will be safe, there may be violence."

"Oh boy! Is this fun!"

Petrosino's demeanor changed, "It is not fun! This is never fun. It is work, I do it because I have to!" The great detective turned towards Muldoon, "You go out the back way and come in using the front door, this man doesn't know you. Stand close to him. Stay behind him. I will follow shortly and come from the back room. I don't think he will try anything in the bar, he doesn't want to get caught. He is a professional. I will walk past him, he will see me and follow me out. I will walk towards Gramercy Park. You follow him. Before we get to Gramercy, you will catch up with him and beat him. Together we will give him the beating of his life. We will retrieve his weapon, fingerprint him and keep him in jail for a while."

"What if he goes for the gun downstairs?"

"You'll pounce on him as soon as he draws it but I don't think he will. He doesn't want to kill me in a place with so many witnesses."

"Good work lad," said Muldoon.

"Take a pistol with you. Pause in the pub before you follow him out, he may have some friends waiting outside. Look to see if there is any unusual movement when I exit."

There was a thick, hollow book called *Irish Ballads* under the collection of Sherlock Holmes stories where Muldoon kept his pistol. Nearby were other hollow books where he kept his ammunition. Thieves never bothered with books. Muldoon also slept with his gun under his pillow. He opened *Irish Ballads*, took out his pistol and loaded it. He clicked it into place and said, "Ready."

"After this we'll play chess, and I will try the Sicilian Defense." said Petrosino.

Muldoon exited through the back way, walked around the block and came in through the front door. He stood there and then he realized that they had both made a mistake. He identified the short balding man at the bar in the thinning crowd, one of the only people he didn't know. Would Petrosino recognize the mistake before it was too late? He tried to back out onto the street but he was not quick enough.

A slightly inebriated Sydney Porter was the first to acknowledge Muldoon, "Hey! Where did you come from? I thought you were through for the night."

"Sydney can you keep it down? I'm on police work," whispered Muldoon.

Petrosino appeared at the other end of the bar. The strange man shifted his position and slipped his hand into his pocket.

"Police work! That is exactly what I want to know more about," blurted Sydney. At this, the man with the large eyes turned around quickly and saw Muldoon staring at him. Petrosino observed and his mind instantly saw his mistake in trying to keep Muldoon undercover in a pub where everyone knew him. A child's mistake! The professional criminal knew he had been identified and felt trapped. The vulture man blinked his eyes three times in quick succession. In an instant, never having been in this situation before and never really knowing how he would react, the criminal decided to draw his weapon.

10

"Turn of the century New York: So naive, so ostentatious, so proud and so captivated with itself that it produced the Hippodrome Theater."
-Norman Clarke in The Mighty Hippodrome

May 18, 1905
The Pittsburgh Pirates, the major obstacle between the New York Giants and an appearance in the World Series, visit the Polo Grounds for the first time in the season. Led by Honus Wagner, the Flying Dutchman, one of the greatest players of all time, the Pirates tag Mathewson 7-2.

The man who looked like a vulture awkwardly jumped up from his stool. He knocked it over in the process and there was a loud bang when the chair hit the floor. Some customers stopped talking. The patrons looked at the man, thinking at first that he might be drunk. The man blinked and moved like someone reeling from a punch or waking from a nightmare. Being lefthanded, the vulture had to step out, away from the bar to get a clear shot at the master detective. But this also exposed him. It took a few more seconds for some to understand what was happening. Excited voices began to fill the room as customers saw the gun.

"Look out!" someone yelled. "Jesus Mary and Joseph." said another.

Petrosino pulled his gun, thanked God that there weren't many people left in the pub and fired, hitting his assailant in the upper body. Muldoon grabbed the ugly-faced man from behind, but the man was already dead.

People screamed. Chairs fell over. Wooden stools bounced off the wooden floor. Glasses broke.

Muldoon, still holding the lifeless body yelled, "It's over everybody. It's over! You are safe now. Drinks are on me! Line up for drinks!"

Panic and fright gave way to a sense of relief and amusement. Muldoon and Petrosino dragged the body to the back room as the crowd, excited at having witnessed gunfire at such close range, moved toward the bar. As the bartender started pouring Pete's, he yelled to the boy who had brought pastries to Petrosino, "Tommy! There's glass on the floor. Let's clean it up! Tommy!" Tommy did not hear because he had stayed in Muldoon's rooms as he was told and was now exploring the Irishman's living quarters. The pourer of drinks made a note to himself to speak to Tommy about his invisibility and yelled, "One at a time folks, there is plenty of beer in the barrel, one at a time!"

Some people left, but most stayed for the free pint. Porter wrote feverishly on a napkin, having run out of paper hours ago.

"Check his pockets, Muldoon. Maybe we can figure out who he is," started the detective.

There was no identification but there was a key, and a ticket stub from a New York Giants game dated Saturday May 6 against the Boston Beaneaters, and a Giants schedule.

After the police came and the body was taken away, Muldoon paid the eight dollars to pay the house for the drinks. The two detectives found themselves over the chessboard in Muldoon's library.

"What an amateur mistake!" bemoaned Petrosino.

"We all make mistakes," reassured Muldoon.

"Yes, but someone could have been killed!"

As Petrosino took the white rook off the board Muldoon said, "I see tonight's events haven't hurt your game. I resign."

"Tonight's events were disturbing but I must put them out of my mind. Otherwise, I could not function. I made a mistake tonight and it cost a life. I regret it."

"It is interesting that he had a New York Giants schedule and ticket stubs in his pocket. I wonder if he is connected to your case or is he just a Giants fan?"

"Time will tell. Shall we have one more game?"

Tuesday, May 9, 1905.

Petrosino made his way up Sixth Avenue to 43rd Street. He could see the oversized, ornate arabesque roofs of the Hippodrome while still a few blocks off. He had read about the great theater built by Thompson and Dundy, the same men who had built Luna Park in Coney Island, but he had not been there for the much anticipated and hugely successful opening night last month. He preferred the opera. What on earth could compare to Enrico Caruso?

The great detective approached the Hippodrome and showed his badge at the door.

"Just a minute. How do I know that badge is the real thing?" said a thin old man, pointing a bony finger at the badge.

"Mr. Thompson and Mr. Dundy are expecting me," replied the detective, unfazed.

"Wait here. Hey Jerry! Go tell Thompson that, whatz your name?" wheezed the old timer.

"Petrosino."

"Jerry, tell him Petraseeeno is here!"

The man called Jerry disappeared.

The detective looked at the old man and estimated that he was about 90 years old, so he asked, "Were your parents born in the colonies or the States?

"My father was born in the colonies. My mother was born in the State of Connecticut. I was born in Richmond town. I will be ninety-three on February 4."

"And you're doing a good job as watchman," said Petrosino earnestly.

"You could be police, but I have my orders and if I want to get paid, I follow them."

"Understood," chimed Petrosino nodding his head and barely touching the brim of his derby.

Jerry came back followed by a tall thin man in a coffee color suit, Thompson himself.

"Petrosino!" he yelled, running towards him, hand outstretched, "It's always good to have the coppers around! Keeps things honest!"

Petrosino took the offered hand and was led inside.

"We don't have too much time. How important is this?"

"This is very important. It is related to a case I am working on. I won't be long."

"Sounds exciting, maybe there is a script in this. How about a drink in my office?"

"I never drink during work."

Thompson abruptly stopped walking and stared at Petrosino who had taken two additional steps. He said, "Never drink during work? That's too bad, I always do."

"May I move about freely?" asked the detective as they continued their walk.

"Of course. Of course. Have you seen the show yet?"

"No."

"Well, it is fantastic, and all the papers agree with me! Here are two tickets for you," he reached into his breast pocket, "and two tickets for the commissioner."

Petrosino took them, realizing this was not a bribe, and he was not working for the owners of the Hippodrome, "Thank you."

Thompson led Petrosino down the side isles, marble elephants with gold tusks protruded from red velvet walls. The elephant motif was everywhere, elephant heads, supporting the boxes, elephants standing guard outside the Men's room and the ladies powder room.

"Let's sit here for a moment, you sure you don't want a drink?" Thompson didn't wait for an answer. He led the detective to the center of 5,200 seats. The repetition of the seat forms called to mind the House of Mirrors at Luna Park. Instead of his reflection, Petrosino saw seats and the marble elephants in the distance, illuminated by light bulbs at the end of their golden tusks.   Hundreds of players were on the stage moving about. Cranes were lifting scenery.

"You came at a good time; they are practicing for *Andersonville, a Story of Wilson's Raiders.* Who will you be questioning?"

"I need to speak to Mike Donlin, the outfielder for the New York Giants."

"Well, what do you want to know? He seems like a good kid. Good looking. I think he's sweet on one of my chorus girls."

"What can you tell me about Mr. Donlin other than that?"

"Look, he is one of 480 soldiers in *Andersonville,* how am I supposed to know him? Sure, he plays baseball for the Giants, but he has a part that will not be missed. He gets shot in the water in the big battle scene. If he has to play ball out of town, we get somebody else. We have so many players here that we need a small army of stand-ins ready to do anything should someone not show up. I hired Donlin because he is good publicity. If the Giants win the World Series, and Dundy has more than one bet that they will, we can give Donlin a more important role during the winter. He'll bring in some fans. He's good for business. Watch the show. Donlin will be appearing soon."

Petrosino looked at the gigantic stage. According to the program, rebels were chasing down Captain John Barnes of the Union Army. The sets looked surprisingly realistic. Aided by his Southern sweetheart, the captain was given a fresh horse and was able to distance himself from the Confederates, but they were in hot pursuit. Suddenly, the cranes were in motion, a bridge was placed on stage. The scene changed.

"You'll love this." exclaimed Thompson proudly.

The stage lowered, gushing water could be heard.

"One hundred and fifty thousand gallons of water every minute!" yelled Thompson, clearly enjoying the spectacle.

A lake formed onstage. Soldiers, horses, and cannons appeared. Captain Barnes had led the confederate army into a trap. Rifle shots zipped this way and that. There was orchestrated chaos.

"There's Donlin!" whispered Thompson pointing to the tumult by the lake.

Petrosino tried to find Donlin in the frenzy but it was impossible.

"There! Donlin just took a shot in the back and fell into the water. It is the exact same way every night! In the exact same place!" Thompson was clearly proud. "The audience loves that lake."

As the Appomattox Court House came into view, Thompson got up and said, "Your man is done for now. This is a good time to talk to him. Please use those tickets they are two dollar box seats! The best in the house!" Briefly, Petrosino imagined his princessa and himself enjoying a show from the two-dollar seats, an extravagance he could not normally afford.

"Who would know Mr. Donlin the best?" questioned Petrosino.

"I would say Mountjoy Walker, costumes, he knows everybody. Last call for drinks!"

"No thank you," said Petrosino as he moved toward the aisle to approach the stage in search of Mountjoy and Turkey Mike Donlin, "I will need to talk to Mr. Dundy personally after that, I hope he is available."

"We got that message. At the moment he is busy with one of our chorus girls. Just come up to the office when you are finished."

The detective knew that Dundy was a ladies man and he surmised that the "business" with the chorus girl was a cover for something more sordid.

"I'll come up!" promised the detective as he made his way to the giant stage.

At the sides of the huge stage which measured 110 feet across by 200 feet deep, there were two clear glass lion cages. In these, the lions were being fed. The rest of the animals were kept in a zoo under the stage. The place was a buzz of activity. Costumed women moving this way, scenery being hoisted and lowered, shouting, cursing, laughing, panic and delight were all present at once on the great stage. Once on stage, Petrosino approached a group of five Union soldiers standing off to the side in different states of dishevelment.

"Gentlemen," began the detective, "can anyone tell me where Mr. Donlin might be?"

"Who wants to know?" questioned a wet soldier with a towel around his shoulders, half turning.

"This is a private matter."

"Is it an autograph you want?" asked another soldier who was straightening his cap.

"No, nothing like that."

"He's back there," said the one with the towel, motioning to the side wall.

Petrosino walked over and saw Mike Donlin. At five feet nine inches, a sturdy build, a long scar down the left side of his face and his cheek always filled with chewing tobacco, the outfielder was easy to identify. He was standing behind heavy ropes that descended from the high scaffolding.

He was talking to a group of individuals who looked like circus people. Their appearances differed from one another.

"Mr. Donlin?"

"That's me."

"I would like to talk to you."

"I'm sorry," said the ballplayer in the Union uniform, "I am not giving out autographs today."

"This is a police matter."

"I'm clean. You've got nothin on me."

"We need some privacy, Mr. Donlin."

"Whatever you got to say, say it quick. You can speak in front of these men. They are my friends. Let me introduce you to them. This is Colonel Gaston Bordeverry, Marksman, Alexander, the Hindu Magician, Chinko the Juggler, Marceline, the Clown, and Brad with Coco the Monkey. They are some of the best vaudeville actors alive.

Petrosino considered his options. He looked at the performers. Sad faced Marceline stared at the detective, his makeup made him look droll. The Hindu magician was wrapped in white robes and a large white turban, in contrast to Brad who was dressed all in black and feeding Coco, perched on his shoulder, the monkey's tail wrapped in the armpit of his trainer. Chinko, dressed brightly and smiling, had large rings over his shoulders. The colonel wore two six shooters that had to be loaded with blanks. Donlin was still wet from the battle scene.

"Very well, Donlin," began the detective, "In March of 1902 you were caught urinating in public and were sentenced to six months in jail for how shall I say it, *accosting* two chorus girls. You served five months with the Baltimore club before they let you go. You were picked up by the Cincinnati team and despite having a good year you went on another bender while in St. Louis and Manager Kelly suspended you for thirty games. You were then traded to the New York Giants. Shall I go on?"

Marceline looked even sadder as Petrosino revealed these facts. Alexander the magician disappeared. Chinko kept smiling.

"OK, alright, let's walk," said Donlin. "We can walk to the end of the stage and then back. Nobody will pay attention to us here. On this stage, everyone is focused on themselves and their job."

As they moved toward that part of the stage where the scenery was kept, Donlin began, "Talk about me pissin in public but what about talking about the boy from Peoria who was orphaned at a young age and is tryin' to make somethin' of his life? I was a great pitcher before I could hit and if it wasn't for Wagner, my .351 in 1903 would have been a batting title! Same thing with my .329 last year, only Wagner was better! That Kraut bastard!"

They stood among the forest scenery. Donlin leaned against a tree. Petrosino studied him. He contemplated. Was this man a criminal?

"I must ask you. What tobacco is that you have in your mouth?"

The question was like a cue to spit and Donlin did so into a nearby spittoon. "We can chew only during rehearsals and we're fined if we miss the spittoon and get caught. Why do you want to know? Am I breaking the law?"

Petrosino, putting his left arm out to lean on a tree and the right arm held akimbo said, "This is police business and I will ask the questions."

"This is Redman Chew."

"Where do you get it?"

"This is crazy! Just tell me what you want!"

"I want you to tell me where you get it."

"From Mr. McGraw."

"Where else?"

"What do you mean where else?"

"Who else gives you Redman Chew?"

"Nobody else. Mr. McGraw is the only one giving me any tobacco. Everything else I buy."

"Where do you buy the Redman?"

"I don't buy Redman. I buy Tuxedo!"

"Why don't you buy Redman?"

"I don't know where to buy it."

"Why do you buy Tuxedo?"

"I can afford it. Matty's face is on it and that's what ballplayers chew, I guess. What is this all about? I don't have to answer your stupid questions."

"Let me see your tobacco tin."

Donlin produced the tin from the inside of his Union soldier costume. It was a personal tin. Blue with gold trim, slightly worn. Petrosino took the lid off of the tin and inspected the contents. It was all Redman.

"How often does McGraw give you the Redman?"

"I don't pay attention to that. What's this all about anyway?"

Donlin shifted by coming off the tree and staring at the women of the next number *Dance of the Hours*, who were dressed like colorful daisies.

Petrosino shifted his line of questioning.

"Who were those men I saw you with?"

61

"Those vaudevillians are my friends."

"An interesting group."

"Marcelino, Chinko and even the Colonel are going to help me into vaudeville. I'd like to change out of these wet clothes."

Petrosino persisted, "Why vaudeville, when you play for the New York Giants?"

"I can make more money in show business. Baseball doesn't pay that much."

"How much do you make?"

"What kind of a question is that?"

"This is police business."

"I still don't know what this is all about. If you must know McGinnity is the highest paid player in baseball and he makes five thousand a year. I'm an everyday player and I don't make that much. Nowhere near it."

"So all of this is to make more money," questioned the detective.

"I know I can make it. I just need a break. I met a girl named Mabel Hite and I want to marry her and live a life in show business. I am writing a play called *Stealing Home*. I am through with pissin in public!"

"Is money a problem for you?"

"No! Well, yeah sometimes."

"How do you make extra money?"

"I work here! Isn't it obvious?"

"Tell me what you know about John McGraw."

"A great man! A true leader. None like him!"

A few stage hands came by and wanted to move the trees and the bridge that were part of the battle scene. Things were always moving backstage.

"Clear the stage everybody. All clear!"

Another man came towards them, "Move aside gents, we are opening the lake."

Donlin paused and asked, "Do you want to see things from the scaffold? It's a grand view. You'll see how amazing that lake is from up there."

Petrosino thought this may be a trap, but he always gave the suspects a chance to reveal themselves. Instead of being afraid to accompany the muscular Donlin onto the wooden planks hanging high above their heads, he welcomed it. The detective understood that Donlin would be a sturdy opponent in a fight, but he felt he could take care of himself. They ascended some steps against the side wall which led to a series of scaffolds. They passed the first two scaffolds as everyone on the stage below them was moving about in all directions. They arrived at the third scaffold. Petrosino observed that a fall from this height could kill a man. Did Donlin know that Petrosino was working on the Black Hand Bomber case? The nimble Donlin mounted the planks, holding the ropes as he did so. Was Donlin lighting dynamite for the Black Hand to make some extra money? He admitted to having money problems. Donlin walked toward the end of another higher scaffold that extended further out over the stage.

"Off the stage, everybody," bellowed a voice below from a bullhorn, "Clear the stage!"

"I love it up here! Come on and join me," said Donlin.

As the detective stepped onto the scaffold to join Donlin, it swayed slightly under his weight. He held onto the ropes to his left and right. He then looked up and noticed a third man on the planks. The man looked at Petrosino and their eyes locked. Petrosino thought, "Italian, laborer, nervous, tense."

The man's face twitched and he turned away and left the protection of the ropes. He walked to the end of the plank and his weight caused the scaffold to slant dangerously. He then undid a rope just over his head and the scaffold slanted even more.

Donlin yelled, "You're crazy!"

Petrosino remembered the picture from the Rogue's gallery down at police headquarters. The one next to the man with the white shoes. *Knife, Killed Policeman.*

"Let me through Donlin!" cried Petrosino.

"Everyone off the stage! Last call!" came the distant voice.

The cop killer holding the rope with one hand, extended his leg across the air like a trapeze artist and threw his weight to the adjoining scaffold. It swung wildly when he landed but he held on.

Now Petrosino was at the far end of the first scaffold.

"Jesus Mary and Joseph! Can you tell me what is going on?" screamed Donlin as he hung tightly to the guide ropes, trying to maintain his balance.

The killer steadied himself, turned, pulled a switchblade from his pocket, flipped it open, and threw it at the detective. It was an excellent throw that showed speed and accuracy. Petrosino didn't have much room for lateral movement so he went down. As he went down, the scaffold pitched forward due to the untied rope and his weight caused the detective to tumble forward and off the front end of the scaffold. He managed to hold onto the lower rope and remained dangling high above the stage below. The scaffold now supported only one rope at this end. Petrosino's legs moved awkwardly in the air, automatically looking for a foothold where there was none. The knife missed its mark fell about fifty feet and clattered on the wooden floor. Costumed people looked up. They gasped and began pointing and talking excitedly. Then there was another noise. The machine that lowered the floor and pumped 150,000 gallons of water a minute to form the lake was being tested. It rumbled and the water churned. The killer saw the detective hanging on for life. Mike Donlin also saw the detective and approached him to try to help him up. The killer saw an opportunity and tried to hop back again so that he could rid himself of the detective. As Donlin approached Petrosino, his added weight made the scaffold act like a see saw. Both men on the same side caused the scaffold to appear more vertical than horizontal. Donlin started to slide. He grabbed the ropes and tried to get back to where he began. He looked as if he were running up a slide. The rope dug into Petrosino's hands. The killer took a mid-air step and threw his weight forward just at the time that Donlin upset the balance on the scaffold. As the killer reached for the scaffold that held Petrosino, the scaffold moved away from him and he was in a free fall. He plummeted into the water. People screamed. The water gushed and frothed below. The killer disappeared into the lake, his body engulfed by the white torrent. He never screamed or flailed about. Dressed all in brown, he floated to the top when the storm on the lake was over. Face down, his jacket floated around him. His brown cap was in the water thirty feet away.

With the help of the brave Donlin, Petrosino regained his position on the scaffold. When the detective and the baseball player had made their way down to the stage, Union and Confederate soldiers alike were pulling the dead man from the lake. On the stage, surrounding the dead body, an odd circle of onlookers were murmuring to themselves and pointing to the deceased, the detective, and to Donlin. One woman became more distraught than Petrosino thought necessary and had to be comforted. Through the ring of onlookers, Thompson appeared pushing his way forward, followed by Elmer Dundy.

"Gentleman, there has been, an unfortunate circumstance unrelated to my purpose here," began the detective.

Dundy, a tall, good looking man, who wore a headpiece because of premature balding, spoke first.

"Everybody, back to work! Let's go!" CLAP! CLAP! "It's just a dead body! Lieutenant, please come to our office immediately. The police have been called. Our in-house dick will take care of things until they arrive."

Petrosino turned to Donlin, "You and I are through for today. If I want to speak with you again, and I may, I know how to find you. Thank you for helping me off the scaffold."

In the office of Dundy and Thompson, architects of Luna Park and now the Hippodrome, Thompson was ready to make a martini.

"I use only Plymouth Gin, Lieutenant so you can be assured of a good drink. Do you prefer your martini shaken or stirred?" asked Thompson.

"No, thank you."

"Does that mean you want it straight? Do you want it on the rocks?"

"I've already told you, I do not drink while I am working," said a somewhat impatient detective.

Dundy spoke next, "What is this all about Lieutenant? Why do you want to speak to me? I know nothing of this dead man nor do I know Donlin. Thompson hired him. It was his idea to hire a ballplayer."

Ignoring this, Petrosino questioned both, "Does Donlin ever ask for money or does he have money problems?"

Dundy spoke up as Thompson drank, "I want to cooperate with you fully, and before Donlin tells you, I will."

At this point Dundy pulled off his headpiece, pocketed it, and then very quickly said, "Donlin gambles. I take his bets. I sometimes give him money to clear his debts."

Petrosino remained silent about the gambling because his most important questions were yet to come.

"Is Donlin violent?"

Thompson piped up, "He had a big fight with Bozo the clown last week. I don't know what it was about but the whole company heard the ranting and raving. He was like a madman!"

Dundy turned to his partner, "His name is Marceline. Bozo is the name of the cat. Marceline the Clown. Marceline is a favorite of the fans. His name is not Bozo. It is Marceline. You have had too much to drink. Put that gin away will you? You can see, Lieutenant what I have to put up with."

Just then came a knock at the door.

"Come in!" barked Dundy.

One of the Daisies waltzed in.

"Elmer, we have an appointment."

"I'm busy at the moment. Can you wait outside?"

The daisy pouted, seemed to wilt and then left the room, closing the door behind her.

"Petrosino, let's finish this up, I have business with this lady that cannot wait!"

Petrosino contemplated and said, "Before the press arrives, I ...."

"Wait!" said Dundy showing the palm of his hand. The press is not coming in to see any of this. They only come in here if I want them in here. I am a showman lieutenant but first I am a business man. This "tragedy" could be bad for business. Unless we give backstage tours and

65

include the death scene. Did anyone turn in the knife he tried to kill you with?"

Petrosino, in a surprise move, came to the point, "Do you chew Redman tobacco?"

It seemed to work. Dundy fidgeted in his seat. His shoulders moved awkwardly as if he had an itch he couldn't scratch.

"Yes I do, how do you know that?" He produced the headpiece and haphazardly put it on.

"Where do you get Redman Chew?"

Petrosino could see Dundy shifting his eyes, not looking at Petrosino. Finally, he said, "I buy it at a shop downtown."

"What is the name of the shop?"

There was a perceptible pause, as if deciding what to say, "Rossi's, Rossi's Fine Tobacco."

"Why go so far for tobacco?"

"I don't go, I send somebody for it! Look, what does this have to do with anything?"

Petrosino was now making connections, forming theories, weighing possibilities.

"How did you begin chewing Redman?"

"Do I have to answer these ridiculous questions? Someone is waiting for me. I will have my own performance soon if you know what I mean!" Here a fake smile came across Dundy's face. Thompson was dozing in his chair.

"You can answer my questions here or downtown. That is up to you." Petrosino stared at Dundy.

"Well, James Hyde first gave me the Redman. I liked it and asked him where he got it. He told me and that is it."

"How did you meet James Hazen Hyde?"

"Really, Lieutenant, what does a dead man in my lake, and Mike Donlin of the Giants, have to do with how I met Mr. Hyde?"

"Just answer the questions please."

"Well, I bet on his coaching years back and I won. I won big. I personally thanked him for allowing me to make such good money without breaking a sweat. He asked me if I chewed, I said once in a while and he let me try Redman. I like it and he told me where he got it. What is wrong with that?"

"Well, aside from the gambling, nothing. Do you share this Redman with anyone?"

"No, I don't."

"What about the person who picks it up for you? Could he take any?"

"If you must know, Lieutenant, I usually send one of my lady friends to Rossi's."

"Are you still in contact with James Hazen Hyde?"

"No."

"Do you gamble regularly?"

"Yes."

"Explain."

"Every new show here is a gamble. The stage holds over 600 people, I needed 15,000 tons of steel for the roof and balcony of this place, there are 9,000 lights on this stage, I need to fill 5,200 seats and I am not sure whether the next show, *The Romance of a Hindoo Princess* will be a success! Every day I open the doors I gamble. So please, stop wasting my time, I have nothing further to say."

"If I have any further questions, I will contact you."

"I'll get Jerry to see you out."

"No need. I shall find my own way out. Good day."

"Good day Lieutenant."

After Petrosino left, a daisy waltzed in, "I'm ready when you are Mr. Dundy!"

"I'll have to see you later. Something has come up that I must attend to. I'll look for you downstairs."

"I've waited so long!"

"I do have a business to run. I'll see you downstairs. Close the door behind you."

As the door clicked shut, Dundy picked up his phone and dialed a number. On the second ring it was picked up.

"Hello?"

"Hello this is Dundy."

"Yes?"

"Lieutenant Petrosino was just here asking questions."

"What kind of questions?"

"He wanted to know where I got my tobacco. He also wanted to speak to Donlin. I don't like it. I think he may know about what we are doing. I can't afford any unwanted publicity. It is bad for business."

"What do you want me to do?" asked the voice.

"I want out. I don't need coppers around here asking me questions."

"Don't worry about Petrosino. I'll take care of him. Don't call me anymore and don't say anything to him. He is dangerous."

"Fine, fine but what... hello? Hello? Hello?"

Dundy stared at his voiceless phone, surprised by the abrupt ending.

May 19, 1905

Mr. Martini had a sawdust route. Every week he delivered bales of sawdust to saloons, meat markets and barber shops from his horse-drawn cart. He cleaned out the old and laid the new. It kept people from slipping and kept the dust and dirt down. The sawdust man kept bales of the stuff in a shed, near the stables downtown. In the early morning of the nineteenth of May a bomb blew everything to nothing. After he got over the initial shock, Mr. Martini walked into police headquarters and sat across from Petrosino.

"How do you know it was the same man who visited Fassett, your barber?" questioned Petrosino from his desk, at headquarters.

"Please. He was well dressed. Italian, moustache and most of all white shoes. Who wears white shoes? Also, he uses hands a lot when he talks."

"Fassett never mentioned this."

"What? His hands? Maybe Sammy thinks it don't matter but I'm telling you he uses his hands. We laughed about it. Sammy would imitate the man while he was a shaving me. Hands all over the place."

"When did this man visit you?"

"Two, maybe three days ago."

"Show me how he used his hands."

Mr. Martini's hands were a whirlwind of movement that made no sense.

"Show me the note."

Martini stood up and pulled papers from his black trouser pocket with a flourish, as if bringing forth a white bird from his pocket at the end of a magic trick.

The note was consistent in every way with those that Fassett had received regarding paper, penmanship, and prose. It read: "We give you a chance. Pay us $300 and leave it in a barrel tomorrow night that will be marked with an X in front of 38 Peck Slip.

"I will need to keep this. You can go."

"The bastard killed my horse! What about my horse?"

Ignoring this, Petrosino asked, "Why do you think the man with the white shoes warned you to pay?"

Mr. Martini thought for a moment, I guess he'd rather have the money than blow up my shop."

May 28. In other baseball news, the issue of Sunday baseball is in the courts and until it is resolved, New York City Police Commissioner McAdoo decided to prevent the grand old game from being played for money on the day of rest. The Giants-Brooklyn game in Washington Park is stopped so McGinnity went down to pitch in a semipro game taking place at 46 Street and 2nd Ave. As the players don their uniforms, the pitcher got into an argument about pay. He refused to put on a uniform until the issue is resolved. During the argument, the police came and arrested the players, except for the star Giants pitcher who is not in uniform.

11

June 9, 1905.

The Giants are embarrassed by their main rivals, the Pirates at Exposition Park. The New Yorkers commit six errors and Matty gets hammered for his third loss of the season. Pittsburgh defeats New York 12-6.

"The house stands right on top of the hill, separated by fields and belts of woodland from all other houses, and looks out over the bay and the Sound. We see the sun go down beyond long reaches of land and water."

-Theodore Roosevelt on his home, Sagamore Hill in Oyster Bay, New York.

June 10, 1905.

Abruzzi sold pastries and cappuccino to wealthier Italians and Germans and Irish and even some Jews. Abruzzi was happy with his life. Coming to America had been a good decision. Everything was fine until the Black Hand messages started to appear threatening him with violence if he did not pay. At first, Mr. Abruzzi did not want to pay but when a thin man appeared in his café urging him to pay or face the consequences, he decided to pay the man. He took the three hundred dollars from a drawer and handed it to the man with the moustache. Politely, the man ordered a cappuccino.

"You are wise to pay up," said the man standing at the marble bar.

Abruzzi steamed the milk and the shhhhhh shhhhh sound broke the attempt at conversation. Abruzzi served his blackmailing patron.

"The Black Hand shows no mercy."

"How's the cappuccino?" asked Abruzzi, barely breathing.

"Excellent! Just like in Roma!" At this point the man looked sad. "If I were not in this business, I would be a regular customer here. You have a fine café."

Abruzzi did not know what to say. A patron walked in and sat at one of the pink, round tables with thin, black iron legs that dotted the cafe.

"Excuse me. I have a customer."

"I don't have time anyway," said the Black Hand member with the white shoes.

After the new customer had placed his order, Abruzzi looked up but the man with the thin moustache was gone. That was three days ago.

Gino Abruzzi was surprised and angered when the bomb went off on June 10. He thought it had been settled. Abruzzi marched down to police headquarters the following day and demanded to see Petrosino. He had heard from friends that Petrosino would help. As he made his way down Broadway, he thought that this is what he should have done after the first note from the Black Hand. He should never have given the money to that man. He arrived at the Police Headquarters.

Still angry, he yelled, "I want to see Petrosino!"

A short, stocky man dressed in a brown suit and bowler pivoted quickly on his heels.

"I am Lieutenant Petrosino!" He extended his hand. Abruzzi took it saying, "The most terrible thing has just happened!"

"Yes?"

"The Black Hand has bombed my café!"

"Give me the details."

"I received a few notes, threatening me…"

"Did you keep them?"

"No."

"Go on."

"I threw the notes out, ignoring them until I was visited a few days ago by one of the Black Hand gang. I gave him three hundred dollars!"

"This man who visited you, what did he look like?"

"Tall, rather thin. A moustache."

"What about his clothing?"

"He wore a blue suit with…"

"With white shoes!" said the detective.

"Yes, how do you know that?"

"It is my business to know. I will be asking the questions. What did he say exactly, can you remember?"

"Well, he ordered a cappuccino and he liked it. He told me if he weren't in this business he would come to my café regularly. He told me it was a good idea that I paid up because the Black Hand is ruthless. Then a customer came in."

"And he left?"

"Yes."

"Did he finish the cappuccino? Did he say goodbye?"

"Well he did finish the cappuccino. He didn't say goodbye. Why is that important?"

"Please Mr. Ahh?"

"Abruzzi."

"Mr. Abruzzi, allow me to ask questions. You paid him the money he wanted?"

"Yes."

"The full amount?"

"Yes of course, I counted it twice."

"This is interesting. How can I contact you?"

"I live at 23 West Fourth Street. I don't have a phone if that is what you mean."

"That is not what I mean. Most people do not have a phone. Your address is sufficient."

"What about my shop?"

"There is nothing I can do. You must call me before they set the bomb."

Petrosino left the man standing there and weighed everything in his mind as he walked out into the busy metropolis.

In a small windowless room on the second floor of Police Headquarters on Mulberry Street Muldoon was talking to Farrell in a place used exclusively by Muldoon and Petrosino.

"I never thought you'd be asking me to do police work!" said the surprised Farrell.

"Of course, you must take a test, everything has to be on the up and up."

"Why me?"

"When ye commented on me hands bein' soft for a longshoreman I knew you was a thinking man and then when you went after that bully like ya did, well, I knew you were fearless as well. My boss has asked us to be on the lookout for men like yerself. Are ye honest?"

"I am honest as the day is long!"

"I'll need some references and if they check out, you can take the exam. I'll help you study for it."

"Grand."

"One more question. How are ye with the drink?"

"We get along fine!"

"I mean can ya go eight or ten hours without it?"

"Now, wait a minute. I have seen with my own eyes, plenty of policemen drinking at Cloke's."

"I know I know. But this is what we are trying to battle. We need men that will stay out of the pub and on the streets, doing their jobs," said Muldoon.

"This is Mr. Roosevelt's idea isn't it? I remember reading about him walking around at night looking for men drinking on the job," said Farrell.

"That's right, Farrell. Mr. Roosevelt started it and we are not going to let his hard work go to waste! Now what do you say? Can you be without the drink for ten hours?"

"I can."

"Good, give me your references."

Traveling to Oyster Bay, Long Island in 1905 to visit the summer White House of President Roosevelt, was a day in the country. A coach was waiting for Petrosino as he disembarked the Long Island Railroad car.

The secret service stopped Petrosino as his cab approached the house known as Sagamore Hill. With an official air, the guard called the President on the house phone. Petrosino could hear the President bellow through the phone, "Let him through!" Petrosino walked the short path and climbed the wooden steps that led to a large front porch. Petrosino admired the sun glistening off Long Island Sound. Quickly the door was opened to reveal a smiling President Roosevelt.

"Good to see you! Come on in!" yelled the big man. The President was, as usual, wearing dark trousers, and despite the heat, a dark vest buttoned over a white shirt. He led Petrosino into the interior of the big house.

It took a minute or so for the detective to get used to the darkness of the rooms within. The dark wood and lack of outside light in the main hall hid the animal heads on the walls. They silently came to view as if there were a sunrise in some distant jungle slowly revealing and defining shapes hidden in darkness. Petrosino saw everything as he remembered it. Beyond the mounted antelope and bison heads was a new room. At seeing the detective stare into the new room, Roosevelt offered Petrosino a tour.

"Come to the North Room, it is just finished. I am quite proud of it."

The men walked to the rear of the great hall.

Huge elephant tusks framed the doorway of the new room.

"These are gifts from the King of Abyssinia," said the President, rubbing the magnificent tusks with his hands. "They are beautiful things, wouldn't you agree?"

"Very much so," replied Petrosino, looking but not touching.

They stood on a raised platform looking into the new addition called the North Room. The room was two stories and measured close to 30X40 feet. Rich mahogany and other woods set the tone for a room that looked, with abundant animal trophies and books lining the room, somewhat like an exhibit at the American Museum of Natural History. Roosevelt's saber and hat from the Spanish American War were on display not far from the huge elk head protruding from the north wall. Roosevelt picked up a sepia-toned, framed photograph off a nearby table.

"That was in Newport, 1892." said Petrosino immediately. The picture showed a slimmer Roosevelt in a full body bathing suit and Petrosino's fully clothed pant legs rolled up almost to the knee, at a beach. Roosevelt has his trademark, exaggerated grin with arms akimbo, while Petrosino remained stoic with hands at his side. Behind them, down the shoreline, is a hulking summer "cottage," grainy and indistinct in detail.

"Incredible, how you solved that! You should write all of this down, it would make thrilling reading!"

"Someone is writing everything down for me!"

"Be careful who you tell!"

"This man can be trusted. I have known him for a long time."

The President replaced the photograph and offered some refreshment.

"Come sit down outside and have some iced tea!"

On the porch they sat down at a table covered with a white tablecloth. The President addressed a personal and favorite servant, James Amos standing nearby.

"James can you please bring us some iced tea?"

"Sir," Petrosino began, "I want to ask you about James Hazen Hyde."

"Never a better coachman!" boomed the President.

"What else can you say about him?" inquired the detective.

"Well, lets' see... back in 1901 he set the round-trip coach record from New York to Philadelphia in just over nineteen hours and thirty five minutes! That's 224 miles! That takes a lot of skill! He's a fine sportsman although a bit of a dandy! A bit of a dandy!"

Petrosino tried to be discreet, "What if anything do you think would be his vices?"

Although Roosevelt and Hyde were sometimes traveling in the same circles, Petrosino knew that Roosevelt's sense of justice would supersede any sense of friendship to Hyde. Roosevelt knew that Petrosino would not ask if it were not connected to a case.

"He'll gamble on anything!"

The President and the detective were served iced tea in tall glasses. A sprig of mint floated in the center.

"What does he gamble on?" asked the detective as James placed the iced tea on the table.

"Anything that may strike his fancy! Thank you, James. Horses, coaching, yacht racing!" Roosevelt emptied the glass without coming up for air, "Ah that was good to the last drop!"

"Do you think Hyde is capable of violence?" inquired the lieutenant.

74

"Hyde? No, I don't think so. What are you getting at Petrosino?"

"I am… directing a line of inquiry concerning the Redman Chew that your boys in Washington helped me identify. James Hazen Hyde is one of the few people in New York that is chewing this tobacco."

"Who are the others?" questioned the president as he contemplated the natural beauty around him from his position on the porch in a chair which was almost too small for him.

"John McGraw and Elmer Dundy," answered Petrosino.

The President raised his eyebrows, "Finding Redman Chew in a Tuxedo tin left at the premises of an establishment that was blown up by the Black Hand has led you to these men eh? Remarkable! I don't think Hyde is capable of that sort of mischief. You have an interesting life! But I still wouldn't trade it with my own. I'm enjoying every minute of my presidency!"

"One never knows, Mr. President. Perhaps Hyde shared the tobacco with a servant or acquaintance." Petrosino was looking to the President for ideas and suggestions.

James Amos returned with more iced tea, this time lemon slices artfully hanging over the glass rim.

"Thank you, James," said the president.

They both sipped their drinks in silence. Roosevelt was considering something. Finally, he spoke, "Would you like to meet the man?"

"Can you arrange it?"

"We can meet here at my home. We'll have dinner!"

"That would be excellent!" said Petrosino, pleased that his trip to the northern shore of Long Island had produced some substantial gain.

The conversation turned to Newport, and the case that Petrosino solved there that his chronicler would later write as *Death Comes to Newport*. They also shared remembrances of police work in New York City, Italian gardens, and of course, one of the President's favorite topics, botany. The President, a mere forty-six years old, the lieutenant two years his junior, strolled in the garden as the late spring afternoon slowly waned.

Roosevelt consulted his pocket watch and announced, "By Jove! It is nearly 4PM! I have a very important appointment to keep at four. I must not be late! I can send you back to New York in a coach."

Petrosino accepted. They said goodbye and Petrosino unceremoniously boarded the coach. As the coach pulled away from the summer White House, the detective could see the President down on all fours on the front lawn roughhousing with his children, his daily four o'clock appointment.

Traveling on the deserted roads of Long Island, Petrosino looked forward to dinner at the summer White House with James Hazen Hyde, not only because he would progress in his line of inquiry, but also because dinner at Oyster Bay was always engaging and interesting due to its enigmatic host.

12

Tuesday July 4, 1905

The Giants split the holiday doubleheader at the Baker Bowl in Philadelphia. Matty loses the first one, his fourth loss 2-0. Iron Man McGinnity wins the second 6-3 and the Giants lead against Pittsburgh is 7 games.

"Murder has been a common crime, and the dynamiting of houses and shops, the kidnaping of children, with every species of blackmail and extortion, was of so frequent occurrence that the mind became dulled to the enormity of these offenses."

-Gaetano D'Amato former president of the United Italian Societies on the crimes of the Black Hand in New York City.

July 5, 1905

Joey Ruggerio walked down East 12th Street to his shoe store. He noticed a large crowd gathered outside. Then he saw the debris and knew he should have listened to the thin man. Why hadn't he understood it when the stylish man had told him to pay up because the Black Hand showed no mercy? As a seller of men's fine footwear, Ruggerio could afford the three hundred dollars. Now this.

"Make way! Move aside. Watch out!" He yelled in broken English. He pushed and forced his way through the crowd. Police had already arrived to hold back looters.

Ruggerio approached a large, mustachioed policeman and said, "I'm the owner here."

"Very good, man," replied Muldoon, "Petrosino is on his way."

"Who is that?"

"Here he is, let him answer that for you."

"What do we have here, Muldoon?" asked Petrosino.

"It's dynamite sir, looks like our man. This here is the owner."

Petrosino turned to look at the victim, "I'm Lieutenant Petrosino with the New York City Police Department."

"My name is Ruggerio, I own the shop. I'm sure this is the work of the Black Hand, Lieutenant."

"How do you know?"

"There was blackmail. There was even a visit. I should have come to the police straight away."

"Describe this man, who visited you."

77

"Taller than me, thin, moustache I think, yes definitely a moustache, nicely dressed."

"Did you remember his shoes?"

"How could I not as a seller of shoes myself? He wore white shoes. I have them here but I don't sell many. They are hard to keep clean in this city. His were pretty clean."

"You are the latest victim in a line of bombings that are …unique. The bomber warns his victims in person before he commits his crime. Why do you think this is?"

"He probably wants the money. I should have given him the money."

"Even this is no guarantee that you will be spared."

"What do you mean?"

"Despite paying, a victim was bombed by the Black Hand. Why do you think this is?"

"Lieutenant, I don't know."

"What will you do now? You do not seem so upset."

"I'll go back to San Giovanni, my hometown. At least in Italy women still cook and stand by their men. Here, women want rights. Besides in Italy, I will live well with all of the dollars I have saved."

"Were there any notes?"

"I didn't keep them."

"Was there anything else? Anything unusual?"

"Yes, but I don't think it has anything to do with the crime."

"I will determine that. What did he say?"

"Well, he asked me if I thought Christy Mathewson would win his July 4 game against Philadelphia."

"And you said?" asked Petrosino seemingly interested.

"I said, I don't know. I don't follow this American game. Then he left."

"Contact me downtown if you have anything further to say. Thank you." The detective lightly touched his hat.

"Did Mathewson win that July 4 game?" asked Ruggerio.

Petrosino turned and said, "Mathewson lost 2 to 0."

"So many Italians I know follow this American game! What makes it so interesting, Lieutenant?"

Petrosino paused and looked at the scattered shoes in the street. "The more I apply baseball to real life the more everything makes sense."

"Will you catch him Lieutenant?"

"Well, it helps when people talk to me before the bombings, but people are afraid and others do not take it seriously, but yes, I think I will catch him. He has made a few mistakes this, I have no name for him but …Mad bomber!"

Petrosino put his hands behind his back and surveyed the scene. Bits of glass lay among scattered shoes. This blast was noticeably smaller than previous attacks. Less dynamite was used. "Why is this?" he thought to himself.

Later that day, three men sat in police headquarters. Muldoon, Mattarrazzo a baker, who had been threatened by the Black Hand, and had, at the promptings of his wife come to the police, and Petrosino. They went over it again.

"I will follow you in disguise, Muldoon will also be nearby. The Black Hand wants your money. They do not want to harm you if you think that you will pay," said Petrosino.

"What if something should go wrong?"

"We will have trained men from my Italian squad posted along the route. They will be in various disguises. You should be safe if you stick to our plan in the most… exact way."

"I'm worried."

"Muldoon, hand me the note," commanded the detective.

Muldoon handed his superior the Black Hand note, noticing the usual smudge and cheap paper that was now identified with the man in the white shoes. Also, Mattarrazzo had been visited by *Angelo*, Petrosino's new nickname for the man who warned and sometimes pleaded with his "victims" to pay or face the consequences. This verbal warning is what set the case apart along with the pattern that was developing in the bombings.

Petrosino read the note: "You worthless dog. We want $300 to be dropped in a bag. Go to Jeannette Park. Friday night July 7 at midnight you will go to the park and drop the money. There will be an oyster stand outside of the park. Lay the bag with the money on the ground near the stand. Cover the bag with horse dung. There will be a dry pile nearby. Leave. If you do not do this we will kill you. Then we will cover you with the horse dung. If you tell police we will know and we will deal with you.

Signed The Black Hand."

Mattarrazzo broke out into a sweat, "Maybe I should just pay them."

"No," said Petrosino "We are close to getting them. If you pay them, they will strike again."

"Think for a minute Mattarrazzo," said Muldoon "If they kill you, someone may see them, they could leave behind clues! No! Their idea is to collect the money long after you're gone. That is where we come in. The Lieutenant will be in disguise, waiting. I will also be in disguise not far off. Our men will be in various positions in relation to the park. We will communicate with whistles. There will be a human net around the park. I'll be in the horse cart and I will park myself outside the pub across from the park. You just cover the bag with the dung and go home."

"I have a bad feeling about all of this. Can't you disguise yourself as me?" asked Mattarrazzo, playing with his tie.

"You must deliver the money. It could be someone you know intimately and even in the dark they would recognize an imposter," said Petrosino.

"I trust you Mr. Petrosino, but I am worried."

"I understand. Do you have the money ready?"

"Yes."

"Good. Get home then and rest. Tomorrow is a big night. If everything goes well, I am confident in catching a member of the Black Hand Gang!"

13

"Tis the old secret of the Gods that they come in low disguises."
-Ralph Waldo Emerson.

July 12, 1905
Chicago's Three Finger Brown pitches masterfully at the Polo
Grounds allowing only two hits as Chicago easily defeats New York 8-1.
The Giants commit five errors and Matty gives up 12 hits.

July 7, 1905
Petrosino unrolled his dirty clothes that smelled like oil and
grease. He donned the black ensemble and put on the fake beard and
battered, black hat. He spread some dark grease on his face and then
attempted to wipe it off. He pushed his fingers into the black grease and
allowed it to seep under his fingernails. He then tied the shoelaces of the
decrepit black shoes. He lifted his sack of dirty rags and put others over
his free shoulder. He blew out the candle. In complete darkness, he
effortlessly made his way to the heavy wooden door that led to the
underground passageway under Old St. Patrick's Cathedral. The old
metal key in the black padlock made a slight click as it turned that
echoed through the underground chambers. Petrosino then walked into
the crypt below. Leaving the dead that lay beneath the church, he went
up a small stairway which led to the exit on Mulberry Street. Soon, he
would be waiting for the bomber. Or the man controlling the bomber.
Petrosino walked towards the Brooklyn Bridge and from there to
Coenties Slip, where Jeanette Park was located. It was almost midnight
and very dark, the full moon being obscured by the clouds. Petrosino
walked past Muldoon, also in disguise. Muldoon, in his empty horse car,
saw the rag picker pause and shift his bundle. Muldoon was the only
person who knew of Petrosino's disguises. Five minutes later, Muldoon
slowly pulled away from his spot near the Brooklyn Bridge.
Mattarrazzo, who had been watching Muldoon, started to walk down
South Street when Muldoon moved. Mattarrazzo clutched his bags and
nervously looked about; his legs were stiff with fright. Mattarrazzo knew
that Petrosino would follow him to the drop-off destination but he did
not know what Petrosino would look like. He saw a drunken sailor in a
white uniform bobbing and zig-zagging like a ghost. Could that be
Petrosino or one of the Italian Squad?
Petrosino, the rag picker, moved further into the shadows and
waited. The detective put his rags down and took a sip from the cheap

flask that contained Sambuca. As he did so, Mattarrazzo passed the detective. Mattarrazzo became more anxious the closer he got to the drop-off site. He did not know where the detective was; he had only the promise that he would be safe. Mattarrazzo coughed as he was instructed to do so that Petrosino could monitor his safety in the darkness of the night. Mattarrazzo felt that the cough sounded fake and forced and thought that the criminals would see through the detective's plan and shoot him in the back. How could even Petrosino say he would be safe when the Black Hand could be lurking anywhere? As they approached the drop-off point not far from the Coenties Slip docks, someone up ahead lit a cigarette. Mattarrazzo paused. Petrosino, about twenty yards behind, had anticipated that Mattarrazzo might lose his courage at the last minute. But, the baker was needed to carry out the plan. Mattarrazzo froze and did not move forward.

Dan McGann waited in the darkness of the piers on the lower east side. It was late and he was getting tired. There was a game tomorrow and he wanted to look good after going hitless in the last contest. He would wait until midnight and if no one showed he would join the barge workers in the nearby Park Hotel for a pint before heading home. McGann, staying alert, noticed a horse cart pass by. It looked very much like one that had passed earlier. He could hear the water lapping against the wood of the docks. The night was still and cool. There was a full moon suddenly visible which shed its soft light on the dark metropolis. The dim gas lamps left many places in shadow. McGann lit his cigarette and waited in the new light of the moon.

"Forget it," McGann said aloud. He flicked the cigarette into the darkness where even the moonlight did not go, the glow remaining like a distant star in a lonely universe. McGann stepped from his position and moved to his left toward the Park Hotel, he heard someone running and then he spotted a rag picker carrying his bundle of discarded rags.

Petrosino had seen McGann's cigarette and saw Mattarrazzo freeze in his tracks. Suddenly the baker, after seeing McGann head in his direction, ran with the bag across the semi- darkened street, out of the moonlight and into the shadows. Mattarrazzo stayed along the edge of Jeanette Park. He passed an oyster stand and dashed for the darkness of the park on his right. The figure that had lit the cigarette was fast approaching Mattarrazzo, but did not chase him. Instead the figure came toward the disguised Petrosino. The rag picker continued in his course. Petrosino looked at the approaching figure. There in the moonlight was the unmistakable figure of Dan McGann! The detective paused, to consider chasing McGann, when suddenly, Mattarrazzo screamed from somewhere in the blackness.

July 15, 1905

Browne hits a two-run homer in the bottom of the ninth and the Giants win a dramatic game against the Pirates. Pittsburgh clawed its way back after being down 6-0. The potent offense of the Pirates scored two in the sixth and five in the seventh, but it wasn't meant to be for the Pirates this day. McGraw pulled starter McGinnity and substituted Matty, who silenced the Pirates bats. The Pirates couldn't get a hit off Mathewson and Browne came through for the home team with his memorable homer. The Giants led Pittsburgh by 8 games.

14

Tuesday July 18, 1905
*Pittsburgh hands Mathewson his sixth loss, his third to the team
of Honus Wagner and company. This one was 2-1 and featured some
great defensive plays by the Giants.*

"McGraw is nothing but a son of a bitch!"
-Babe Ruth

"There is only one manager and his name is McGraw."
-Connie Mack

"Don't care."
-"Dummy" Taylor, pitcher for the New York Giants

Petrosino dropped his rags and ran towards the sound, his hand
firmly on his gun which was strapped to his waist. He took out his police
whistle and blew hard. He stopped. There was moaning. The trees of the
nearby park hid secrets and prevented the full penetration of moonlight
in the immediate area. Again, the moaning, but the detective saw no sign
of Mattarrazzo. The detective saw the oyster stand and then entered the
park and saw Mattarrazzo slowly squirming on the ground. Hearing the
steady clip clop of horses approaching, Petrosino looked up to see
Muldoon racing down South Street in his carriage appearing and
disappearing in the moonlight, flickering like a Nickelodeon.

"Over here, Muldoon!" shouted Petrosino.

The detective knelt on the pavement momentarily groping in the
darkness. He felt a face with stubble on it, a damp shirt and then warm,
gluey liquid that could only be blood. Muldoon stopped abruptly and
the big man jumped from the carriage. The lamp, still swaying after its
jolting from the carriage, lit up the space and revealed Mattarrazzo's
bleeding chest wound. The lamp, like a pendulum, then swung the other
way and returned all to the darkness.

"Did you see him?" said Petrosino urgently; realizing that
Mattarrazzo would die very soon because his wound was near his heart.
The blood flowed freely.

Muldoon grabbed the lantern and held it closer. Petrosino put his
ear next to the mouth of the dying man.

Mattarrazzo whispered something that could not be understood.

"Again! Say it again!" pleaded the detective.

"Bug," whispered the barber before he died.

The detective stared, trying to understand the incomplete message. "Bug? Bug? Bug!" What did it mean? Was he trying to speak Italian or English? Was it the beginning of a word? Petrosino's mind raced.

Muldoon held the lantern. Clutched in the hand of the dead man was a yellow Tuxedo tobacco tin with the face of Christy Mathewson on it. The detective undid the tight fingers around the tobacco tin and put the tin in his pocket. Petrosino rose.

"Do you see the bag with the money in it, Muldoon?"

Muldoon paced wider and wider arcs from the body.

"Looks like whoever it was that killed yer man here, made off with the money. What did the baker say, sir?"

"Bug."

"Sir?"

"Bug! The dying man said, 'Bug!' Damned if I know what it means! Look a little further Muldoon, maybe we will see something."

Muldoon held the lantern high, to maximize the light. Suddenly, there was a movement in the bushes.

"Over there!" yelled Petrosino.

Muldoon rushed at the shadowy figure trying to get away. For a man his size, Muldoon was fast. He collared the figure and the figure screamed.

"Jesus Mary and Joseph!" cried Muldoon. "It's a woman!"

She struggled and fought but she was no match for the Irishman.

"Calm down lady and tell us why ye were hiding just now."

She was a thin, younger woman. Her face, with accents of makeup, seemed older and at odds with her body, which was still young. Her clothes were not those of a proper woman. They were unclean and had been torn and poorly resewn.

"I didn't do nothing! You can't arrest me!"

"We cannot arrest you for no reason," said Petrosino, "Can you tell us what happened here?"

"Why should I help some Italian fly bull?" she questioned, looking directly at Petrosino.

The Italian Squad started to gather, alerted by the police whistle that Petrosino had blown earlier.

Petrosino immediately took charge, "Men take care of that body. The park was now fairly lit by the lanterns of the additional six men that had appeared. Petrosino turned towards the woman. She was now standing beside Muldoon. The light of the lantern made her look old.

"Can you tell us what you are doing here?"

She was an Irish girl with straight brown hair. The rogue on her face attempted to conceal her paleness.

"I was on my way to meet someone," she looked from Petrosino to Muldoon to Petrosino again.

"There is only one thing ya can be doin as late as this and by yerself no less!" said Muldoon in a tone that was akin to sadness.

"If you are going to arrest me for being out by myself late at night and going to meet someone, I'll never tell you what I saw!"

"It is best to tell us what you saw," said Petrosino.

"Well now, I'll have to think about it," said the young girl with a grin.

"Muldoon, take her to headquarters in the Black Maria we had waiting. Maybe she will stop wasting our time and tell us what she knows when she sees we mean business."

"Yes sir. This way young lady," Muldoon took her by the arm but she threw her arm out to free herself.

"Don't touch me! I can walk by meself. I don't need you to help. I've been in the Black Maria already. Nobody can make me talk. Wild horses can't make me talk! I'll talk only if I want to and nobody can make me," she spit at the feet of Muldoon.

"This way," said Muldoon as he wiped his face with the right sleeve of his shirt.

Petrosino turned to the matter at hand. What was that now familiar Christy Mathewson tin doing in Mattarrazzo's hand and what did he mean when he said, 'Bug.'? Could he have been trying to say something else? Was this the beginning of another word or phrase that Mattarrazzo never completed?

"You!" snapped Petrosino, "What's your name?"

"Corrigan, sir."

"Corrigan. I want to know what this man was stabbed with. When the coroner's report is done, I want it on my desk."

"Yes. Lieutenant Petrosino."

The Polo Grounds on Tuesday July 18, 1905

"What do you think you are doing here?" raged McGraw.

"I came to speak with Mr. Taylor, Mr. Bresnahan, and Mr. McGann."

"You can't just come out here like this!"

"Yes I can and I will," replied Petrosino.

"I have a team to manage and a game to win. Get lost!"

"If I, … 'get lost' you will come with me for obstructing justice and impeding police work." He flashed his badge.

At this, McGraw's face tightened, his jaw became set, his shoulders moved forward, and his hands that were at his hips, went straight to his sides in exasperation. His hands were balled into fists. McGraw took a step forward. Some of the players took notice. A warm breeze blew across the infield. Everything was silent. Eyes were locked. The breeze blew again. All noise and motion stopped for a second.

Petrosino knew that McGraw was a fighter and he said, "Do not think about it. I will get the better of you in a fight. I've beaten bigger men. If you read the papers you will know that. Assaulting a police officer is a charge even you cannot escape. If any of your players try to stop me, I will break some bones. If I am stopped here today, you will never have your championship."

McGraw's lips pressed firmly together. He looked at his players... and stepped aside.

As Petrosino passed the ballplayers, some looked down. Others turned their backs. Taylor was pitching to Bresnahan in the short outfield. As Petrosino passed first base, McGann turned his back to the detective to catch a bullet thrown from third. Just as the speeding ball approached the glove of the first baseman, McGann slightly shifted. The ball got past him and came right toward the detective. Petrosino stopped in his tracks and pulled back at the waist. His derby fell off and the ball whistled by his face. It sailed into the stands and smacked loudly into one of the empty seats. Petrosino was unsure if McGann acted on his own or if McGraw gave a signal. Unperturbed, the detective lifted his derby from the grass and continued.

"Don't go anywhere, McGann. You're next," warned the detective.

As he approached Taylor, Petrosino signaled to the catcher to come forward. Bresnahan immediately got up from his crouched position and came toward Taylor. It was common knowledge that "Dummy" Taylor was deaf and could not speak. He communicated through sign language. McGraw had insisted that all of the players learn sign to not only "speak" with their third starter but to use sign language on the field as a means of communicating tactics which the opposing team could not pick up. Petrosino, as a student of the game of baseball, understood that other teams were imitating the Giants and inventing their own signs for "steal," "fast and inside," "bunt," "hit and run," and anything else the manager wanted to convey to his team. Bresnahan, being the catcher for Taylor, was one of the best at sign language. As the threesome stood in the middle of the outfield of the Polo Grounds, Petrosino spoke first.

"I am here on an important police matter."

"What do you want from us, copper?" questioned Bresnahan as he dropped his glove to the grass and took an aggressive stance.

Petrosino looked at Taylor. Taylor's glove was still on his hands and both hands remained under his armpits. Bresnahan signaled. Taylor spit.

"What do you want?" asked Bresnahan.

"I have a few questions; I won't take up too much of your time."

"Did McGraw OK this?" shot Bresnahan.

"He did. Now, I understand that you both receive Redman Chew tobacco from John McGraw."

"That is true," replied the catcher and he began signaling to his battery mate. Taylor unhooked his hands from their position, threw the glove down, and signaled back.

"What is he saying?" asked the detective.

"He wants to see your badge."

Petrosino flashed the badge on the inside lapel of his suit jacket. The jacket seemed to be an inconvenient formality on such a warm day but it was certainly cooler than the baggy wool uniforms the players were wearing. Taylor flashed hand signs again, this time more quickly.

"Now he is asking why should he talk to you?" said Bresnahan, smiling as he looked straight at the detective.

"A murder has been committed and I am trying to prevent any further deaths," replied the detective, gazing at the downcast Taylor.

Bresnahan kicked his foot towards Taylor's averted gaze and played with the dry dust. This sent up a small cloud around second base, a sign that the pitcher caught. Still avoiding the stare of the detective, Taylor peered at his catcher.

They exchanged hurried signals. The fast hand movement on the part of Taylor seemed to indicate stress or emphasis. Taylor sometimes made slapping noises or smacks when signing. The muscles in his arms were clearly tightened at certain points. Bresnahan's signing was slow and deliberate.

When the movement ceased, the "Duke of Tralee" turned to the detective and said, "Luther says that he knows nothing about murder. All he does is play baseball."

"I want to know about your chewing tobacco. Where do you get the Redman Chew?"

Bresnahan related the information and replied, "We both get it from McGraw."

"Do either of you share it, or get any from anyone else?"

Petrosino watched them sign and felt he was at a slight disadvantage. Deceit on the part of the speaker was sometimes revealed in variation of tone or inflexion. Petrosino could only decipher that Taylor was excited or stressed but this did not necessarily mean deceit. Also, the waving of the hands, sometimes in front of him, partially obscured his face. The detective could not study facial expression as he would like. All eye contact remained with Bresnahan. Subtle shifts in expression or movements of the eyes, twitches, quirks and slight changes in the face were for the most part lost, as the pitcher signed to his catcher and then looked down at the outfield grass. Bresnahan related the information.

"Well, he says he doesn't share it and neither do I. What is this murder all about?"

"Is this your question or his?"

"What difference does that make?" asked the catcher as he looked into the empty seats on the first base side, scanning them with his eyes, waiting for a response from Petrosino.

"Everything in my profession makes a difference. Even the smallest detail can solve a puzzle I am working on. So again, is this question about the murder yours, or Mr. Taylor's?"

"It is his."

"Why is he so concerned?"

By now the pitcher was again looking at Bresnahan. There was movement.

"Dummy is just curious."

"Well, I don't like to discuss my puzzles while they are still under investigation. When I disclose more information, it will be at my... discretion. I can only say that innocent people have been killed."

"How, Dummy wants to know how," pressed Bresnahan.

"Does he have any more to tell me?" questioned the detective, detecting a change in things that may just be a shift in the outfield breeze.

Bresnahan signed. Taylor signed back. The signing suddenly picked up speed and seemed to grow in intensity. Now Bresnahan became more animated.

"What is he saying?"

"I asked him to repeat, he is going too fast. Wait."

The signs continued. "You're wrong!" said the catcher aloud to the face of his pitcher. They continued. Petrosino stared at Taylor. Taylor ended it by bringing his fingers to his nose, closing them, and then pointing them towards the catcher and opening them as if throwing a phantom baseball. He then walked toward the infield, leaving his glove in the grass.

"We both spent too much time talking to a wop. We got nothing to say." said the catcher as he bent down to collect the gloves.

"What was that exchange all about? Why is he wrong?"

"Dummy thinks that all Dagos are nothing, especially ones that are coppers. I told him that there are some good dagos. I think you might be one of them. That's all. I'm sorry."

"We will speak again," was all Petrosino said as he moved back toward the first base side to talk to McGann. He knew that Bresnahan had not revealed everything and yet he sensed that the catcher may have provided an opening for future collaboration.

The first baseman was still taking throws from the infield. Petrosino approached and stood near first base. "Bad" Bill Dahlen kept firing the balls in. The other infielders ran to the outfield for warmups.

"Next time the ball will hit you dago," said McGann.

"You need to answer some questions."

"Blow off," said McGann. He then said to Dahlen, "Bill, aim for the Dago this time."

"McGraw!" yelled Petrosino.

"Dahlen, go run in the outfield. McGann, talk to the man," ordered a yelling and clearly angry McGraw from the bench.

"It's only because he says so," said McGann, as he threw the baseball at the back of Dahlen and hit him with a loud smack.

"I'll get you for that you Irish bastard!" yelled Bad Bill as he kept trotting to the outfield.

Petrosino got right to the point, "Where were you on the night of Friday, July 7?"

"Why do you want to know?"

"It is my job to answer questions and yours to answer them. Where were you on Friday, July 7, around midnight?"

"I don't remember."

"I don't believe you."

"Are you calling me a liar because if you are, I'll fight you."

"On the night of July 7th close to midnight, you were seen by a policeman near Jeannette Park which is located at…"

"I know where it is," hissed McGann, spitting into the infield dirt.

"What were you doing in the vicinity?"

"Walking, smoking, looking for a place to drink."

"Is this your answer?"

"Yeah, that is all I was doing."

"If I get you into Mulberry Street, I will beat it out of you."

"You can't touch me! I play for the New York Giants and I did nothing wrong that night, so blow off greaseball."

"Mr. McGann, when I find out the truth about that night, playing first base for the New York Giants will not help you."

"I said what I said. Stop wasting me time," said McGann under his breath and spitting again while looking away.

"Look McGann, people have been killed. If you have any decency in you, you will tell me what you were doing on the night of July 7 in the vicinity of Jeanette Park."

"I have nothing to say," said McGann, sweating in his wool uniform.

Petrosino looked up to see the manager staring at them. The detective, understanding that he was getting nowhere, left without any parting courtesies being exchanged.

Back at police headquarters, Corrigan made good on his word and left the report on the death of Mattarrazzo on the Lieutenant's desk. The report brought to light some things that had interested the detective. Petrosino decided to meet with the coroner personally. He was fortunate because the coroner, Mr. Zloty, was still working.

"Mr. Zloty?"

"Mr. Petrosino! Good to see you again! How are you?"

"Thank you, Mr. Zloty. And you?"

"Working hard. Everybody around me is dead, so I have to do all the work! It is nice to talk to a living person once in a while." He adjusted his glasses and thrust his small hands into his white lab coat, "You are probably here about the stab wounds I wrote about in last night's report."

"Yes. I did find it. Your report is… tantalizing. You wrote that there seemed to be two wounds."

"Yes. It is very unusual and very interesting. We know he died from loss of blood but there was also a wound on the back of his head."

"What do you think caused it?"

"Well, I don't know. He wasn't directly hit. It seemed that the weapon glanced off his head and when he was on the ground, on his back, he was stabbed. The head wound definitely came first."

"How do you know?"

"From the angle of the wound, if he had fallen and hit his head on the ground, it would have been a very different wound and the position of his body would have been different when he was on the ground. There was a bad scrape on his right hand that showed he tried and succeeded in slowing down his fall. Also, since you say you spoke to him, we know that the blow to the head was not enough to knock him out. He was definitely hit first, he probably staggered a bit, tried to right himself and then fell backwards and then was stabbed landing first on his right hand and perhaps sitting and then lying down. The position of the body on the ground in relation to the head wound tells me that," said Mr. Zloty repeating himself. "If he were stabbed first, the head wound would almost be impossible to inflict and also quite unnecessary."

"What was he stabbed with?"

"A small knife, the wounds were not deep but deep enough to be fatal. It seems that the knife was turned while it was in the body and moved from side to side. Someone very strong had to cause a wound like that. The murderer must have been kneeling close to the body when he inserted the knife into the victim. The killer then wiped the blade on the side of the body, using vertical strokes."

"Is that important?"

"Well, that is for you to decide, but it is unusual. The knife seems to have entered the body only once. The man was not repeatedly stabbed. The one stab left a very large wound created by the movement of the knife when it was in the body. The murderer seemed to have been very strong. When the knife was extracted and wiped, it seems to have been done from a standing position rather than a kneeling position. We can tell this by the angle of the blood smears. There also seems to have been a footprint on the shirt, indication that someone actually stepped on the body."

"Do you have any idea what he was hit in the head with?"

Zloty pushed up his glasses and squinted his eyes. "It was something like a policeman's club or a baseball bat."

July 13, 1905

Michael Mattarrazzo's bakery had been a modest, busy little place tucked behind a cheese shop on Cornelia St. The explosion shook the building and boomed through the alley. Miraculously, nobody was killed, but many were injured.

July 19, 1905

"Mrs. Mattarrazzo! It is me!" said the detective as he walked through the first-floor rubble of Mattarrazzo's former bake shop.

In the small, back room severely damaged by the bomb that destroyed the bakery, sat Mrs. Mattarrazzo. She was dressed in black and wearing a veil which hid her face. She sat eating crackers and drinking water.

"Mrs. Mattarrazzo, I want to find your husband's killers. I need your help."

Speaking in Italian that Petrosino knew was a dialect from Naples, she agreed to help any way she could, but at the same time she wanted to be left by herself.

"Your husband said the word *Bug* to me before he died. Do you know what this might mean?"

"I have no idea. Please, I am sick," she moaned from behind the veil.

"I understand, but this killer may strike again, and I need your help in…administering justice."

"I do not know what this means. I just want to be left alone."

"Please, Mrs. Mattarrazzo I am trying to find a killer. Just a few questions. Has there been anything odd about your husband lately? Was he fearful of anyone?"

"No. Nothing like that. He was generally a happy man, except of course, for the dreaded Black Hand notes."

"Did he have any visitors? Were there strange men at the shop?"

"No, nothing that I know about."

"Is there anything you neglected to tell me?"

"Aside from the Black Hand threats, my husband was quite happy. The only crazy thing he did was harmless really."

"What was that Mrs. Mattarrazzo?"

"Well, he loved the New York Giants and he went to that park up in Harlem whenever he could. He spent too much time up there."

"Did he speak at all about the Giant players to you?"

"All the time. But I didn't listen. My bunny loved to talk to his customers about the Giants. I think they have a good team no? He said even though they were Irish, they were the good Irish."

"May I look into your husband's personal things?" inquired Petrosino softly.

"If it will help to catch those who did this to him, of course, Lieutenant."

Mrs. Mattarrazzo rose slowly from the table and shuffled across the room, never lifting the veil.

"Follow me, please."

They climbed a narrow stairway that led to a simple room with two single beds in it.

"His space is there," she said pointing to the bed still made and untouched from the night of Matarazzo's death.

Petrosino opened the first drawer in the bureau. Black socks, underwear, a black belt, cuff links, a pair of black beaded rosaries, a worn Italian prayer book and an envelope were all that was in the top drawer. Petrosino inspected the envelope. Inside was a photograph of Mattarrazzo at the Polo Grounds. The place was filled and directly in front of Mattarrazzo was John McGraw shaking hands with Christy Mathewson. Mattarrazzo, standing and smiling in the same dark suit he was murdered in, is directly behind the manager and his ace pitcher standing in the fans' seating section. Dan McGann is behind the duo but in front of the fans. McGann is seen standing in front of a vacant seat adjacent to Mattarrazzo's, his arms are crossed, and his eyes are cast downward. McGann is not looking at the camera. He is the closest ballplayer to the deceased baker. The photograph was taken on the first base side of the park. Something small but indistinct can be seen in

Mattarrazzo's hand, which he had been waving at the time of the photograph, causing the object and arm to look blurry.

"What can you tell me about this?"

"Bunny was so proud of that photograph. He wanted to frame it, but never did. It was taken about a week before he died."

"How did he… acquire it?"

"He paid the photographer for it. He paid too much. I know he did. He didn't tell me how much he paid but I know he paid too much. This is what I mean by crazy. He spent money on a photograph that sits in a drawer. He told me he ran after that photographer and pleaded with him to give him a copy of the picture. The Giants were more and more a part of his life. I guess it was because we could not have children. He wanted children so badly. He called those Giants "his boys." I hate to tell you this but I was a little bit jealous of those Giants."

"What is that in his right hand?"

"I don't know."

"Did he mention the name of the photographer?"

"No. I don't even know the newspaper it was from."

"Can I have this? It may be useful."

"Yes, but you must return it."

"Of course." Petrosino put the photograph back into the envelope and slipped it into his vest pocket.

Petrosino then withdrew the pocket tin that was found on the dead man from his inner breast pocket.

"Do you recognize this, Mrs. Mattarrazzo?"

"Yes. My husband has one just like it."

"This is your husband's. He was clutching it tightly the night he died. Did he chew regularly?"

"He never chewed tobacco. That tin was given to him by one of the customers at his shop. Many of the men that bought bread from my husband were Giants fans."

"Mrs. Mattarrazzo, if your husband did not chew tobacco, why was he carrying this tobacco tin around?"

'He took it around to the Polo Grounds because he thought it was a good luck charm. He told me the Giants won whenever he brought it to the ballpark. This is what I mean. He was acting crazy." Her hand went under the veil to wipe away a tear.

"Where then did the tobacco come from?"

"What tobacco?"

"I found tobacco in your husband's tin, a tobacco that was more expensive and much harder to get than the product that was originally in the tin. How do you explain this?"

"Oh that. That tobacco was given to him while he was at the Polo Grounds."

"How do you know?"

"I was upset with him and the chewing tobacco. I asked him how much it cost. He said he didn't buy it. Somebody gave it to him."

"Did he say who?"

"No, probably one of those ballplayers. He told me it is what the players chew."

"Could it have been one of the men in the photograph?"

"Sure, I guess so. He never told me who gave it to him. Come to think of it Lieutenant, the photograph was taken the same day that he came home with the tobacco."

"Can I have this tin as well?" asked the detective.

"That you can keep. That was not him. But the photograph I want back. The only other picture I have of him is the day when we were married. Do you want to see?"

"Yes please," Petrosino was always deeply moved when he witnessed the suffering of those left behind when loved ones were murdered.

Mrs. Mattarrazzo moved brought a picture from atop her chest of drawers. It showed a young Mr. Mattarrazzo with a full head of hair and a slim waistline. She raised her veil to look at the picture more closely.

"It is beautiful," said Petrosino earnestly.

"That day was so full of promise! Such hopes! Now this….," her voice trailed off and she closed her eyes, and after a long wait opened them and asked, "Are you married?"

"No…I am reluctant to get married because I do not want to leave a widow behind. So many people want to kill me and one day they will get me and that day will be a sad one for my wife, if I had one. I do not want to put anyone through that."

"That is no way to think! Look at me! I did not know what would happen when we were married, did I? Now look. Still, I do not regret it. I would do it again! The pain is great now but the love we had was greater. My memories will comfort me for the rest of the life I have left to me."

"I will consider what you have said because there is someone I am in love with. I want to marry her, but I do not want her to get hurt. The Black Hand will not show me mercy because I am a family man."

"Only God knows what will happen! If you love the girl, marry the girl! What is her name?"

"Adelina."

"Adelina!"

"Yes, Adelina."

"Adelina! A nice Italian name! Does she want to marry you?"

"She mentions it every time we meet."

"So what are you waiting for? Life is short. Marry the girl! Create memories for old age. What is she like?"

"Beautiful large eyes, long, thick brown hair."

"No! I mean what is she like? How does she behave? What does she do?"

"She is like an angel, my Adelina! She can sew and she can cook, she is always praying to St. Anthony for me, but…"

"What? You can find something wrong with this angel?"

"No, Mrs. Mattarrazzo, nothing wrong, it is just that she is involved in the suffrage movement."

"Ah! These young girls today. They want to vote. Voting is none of my business, but if she wants it why is it so wrong? Let her be! She will grow out of it!"

"Well, sometimes she marches for the movement and does it illegally!"

"Oh, so she is determined then, a fighter! Good! It will be good if you have a boy. My bunny told me that I would have been soft on boys. I said, How do you know?" She sighed and her sadness came back to her, "None of that matters now. I must get to Our Lady of Pompeii to light a candle for my bunny. I will pray for you and your Adelina, she sounds like a good woman. Marry her! Nobody is getting any younger!" She lowered her veil and once more seemed to retract into her world of grief.

"Mrs. Mattarrazzo, God bless you," the detective then gently held her old, gray head covered in black in his hands and gently kissed her forehead through the fabric of the veil.

The detective searched the rest of the drawers and the room but found nothing.

"I do have one last question."

"Yes?" said Mrs. Mattarrazzo.

"Did your husband ever put his shoes on the bed?"

"Oh no! No! This is bad luck! Don't you know? He knew! He knew it was bad luck. He would never do it. Why do you ask such questions?"

"He really was superstitious."

"Of course he was, I told you so."

"Sometimes people misinterpret the facts and motives of other people, even those that they love dearly. I had to check."

"I want to ask you something, mister detective."

"Yes?"

"The Black Hand has my money. They killed my husband, why do they blow up my home?"

"I think that they wanted to destroy some evidence in this house or kill you to keep you from telling me something. This photograph may hold the clue. Perhaps there is something they do not want me to know. You will have police protection. There is a footman outside now. I will avenge the death of your husband."

"I miss him so much."

"Yes. I know you do. Thank you, and I am sorry for your loss. If there is anything else you can think of please leave a message for me down on Mulberry Street."

Petrosino lightly touched her shoulder and walked on thinking that this man behind the bombings was more dangerous and more intelligent than he had first assumed. His foe had hidden in the darkness of Jeanette Park, knowing that the full moon would reveal everything around and when Mattarrazzo had unexpectedly ran into the park, he had found the killer and they recognized each other. It could not have been McGann in the park because he had seen McGann leaving the area of the park and walking in the opposite direction, before Mattarrazzo cried out. But McGann could have been an accomplice, perhaps a lookout man or the man who would pick up the money. They had searched all around that night under the light of a full moon. How had the killer escaped? One of the keys is held by that prostitute Muldoon found hiding in the bushes. She will talk sooner or later.

July 19, 1905

The policeman who was assigned to watch Don Rizzuto's cheese shop from a hidden spot across the street was awakened by the blast of the bomb. Jumping out into the street he saw rubble and nothing more, then he blew the police whistle. Petrosino wanted to be notified as soon as anything happened at this post. The officer, Jack McNamara, didn't run because he did not know which way to run. He had seen nothing. McNamara waited and dreaded the encounter with the master detective.

In other baseball news: One of the umpires of the July 18, 1905 game between the Giants and Pittsburgh was Bill Klem. It was his rookie year. He would eventually work a record of 18 World Series. "The Old Arbitrator" was an umpire from 1905-1941.

97

15

"Mealtimes at Sagamore Hill were the best education I ever had"
-Teddy Roosevelt, Jr.

Wednesday August 2, 1905 At Exposition Park, Matty defeats Pittsburgh 3-1 and increases his team's lead to 10 ½ games over the Pirates. Perhaps in frustration at falling behind in the standings, Honus Wagner throws a ball at the umpire after he was called out in a close play at first.

Petrosino sat in the Study among some of the more than 6,000 books owned by Theodore Roosevelt. The Study was the hub of the summer White House. The phone, only the second in Oyster Bay (Snouder's Drug Store had the first) and formerly in the pantry, now stood on the desk of the great man. The candlestick phone stood like a soldier waiting for orders to be barked into his ear. Or ready to sound the alarm and then dispatch urgent news. The phone's number was sixty seven. Petrosino wondered if he would ever need to use it. The detective looked at Roosevelt's wall of heroes on which adorned pictures of people admired by the 26th President of the United States. There were pictures of Lincoln, Ulysses S. Grant, Thomas More, and George Washington. The detective thought back to one of his earliest cases in which he had met General Grant. In the place of importance on the wall of heroes was "The best man that I ever knew". The president wrote this about his father, Theodore Roosevelt, Sr.

Like other rooms, animal skins and trophies covered the floors and adorned the walls. Bronze Remington sculptures sat atop tables and fireplace mantles. Petrosino picked up the President's 26th and latest published book, this one published by Scribner & Sons, *Outdoor Pastimes of an American Hunter.* He began to look through it when the President barged into the room slamming the door open, followed by a tall, very energetic and striking young man that had to be James Hazen Hyde.

"Good to see you Guiseppe!" bellowed the President, extending his hand. "Mr. Hyde, this is Lieutenant Joseph Petrosino of the New York City Police Department."

"Lieutenant," Hyde stepped forward and offered his hand.

"I must ask you some questions Mr. Hyde, concerning a line of inquiry I am undertaking regarding a case I am involved in."

"I am at your service, sir."

"Sit down men!" said the President.

Petrosino stepped over the bear head rug and sat on the sofa under the Lincoln picture. Hyde sat in a chair opposite. Roosevelt excused himself and left the room.

"To begin with, what kind of tobacco do you chew?"

"As a rule, I smoke a good pipe. I don't chew tobacco."

"My sources inform me that you do chew tobacco."

"No, I don't chew any tobacco, Lieutenant."

"Do you deny chewing tobacco?"

"Well, occasionally, I do chew tobacco."

"Which variety?"

"Redman."

"How do you acquire this tobacco?"

"I get it from Rossi's Fine Tobacco."

"Do you share it with anybody?"

"Yes."

"Who?"

"My footman."

"His name?"

"Seamus McCarthy."

"How much tobacco do you give to your footman?"

"Almost all of it. As I said, I don't chew much."

"How long has McCarthy been in your service?"

"Since October of 1904."

"How did you acquire him?"

"He came to me by way of a very reputable firm, Corrigan & O'Toole, I remember it correctly."

"I trust his references checked out."

"Yes, well." At this point the most eligible bachelor in New York became clearly uncomfortable. He shifted in his seat. His walking cane was shifted from his right to left hand.

Petrosino leaned forward, sensing that somewhere a door may be opening, a line of thought becoming clear.

"You must know that I am a gambling man. I hired Seamus McCarthy without looking at his references," said Hyde.

"I find this to be... unprecedented from a man in your social circles!" exclaimed the detective.

"Well, he came to me in a desperate way, he sorely needed employment and I liked his attitude. Besides, I trusted Corrigan & O'Toole to do all the research. It is personal qualities that count with me. I liked the man. It doesn't matter what he was like with his former employer. I'm a different man from his other employers and we got along fine during the interview. And Lieutenant, I haven't regretted hiring Seamus for one second."

"May I speak with him?"

"He is my most trusted servant. He is outside, he commandeered the chaise."

"Please bring him in."

"Of course."

Alone, Petrosino again took the liberty of examining the contents of this most interesting room. Animal skins, heads, and other oddities surrounded him. One item in particular captured his curiosity, a gray rhino's foot with oversized nails, severed at the ankle, which now served as an inkwell.

Hyde came into the room, followed by his footman Seamus.

"This is my footman, Seamus McCarthy. Seamus, this is Lieutenant Petrosino. He is going to ask you a few questions."

"This is fine by me, sir."

They took their usual places as McCarthy remained standing, arms straight at his side. He stiffened and maintained a formal stance.

Petrosino began, "Mr. Hyde tells me he gives you his Redman Chew."

"That's right."

"Do you chew it or give it to someone else."

"I chew it, sir."

"Do you have any with you at the moment?"

"I never chew while I'm working, that would be during off hours when I chew the tobacco, so no, I do not have any with me."

"What is your day off?"

"Tuesdays sir."

"What do you do with your time on Tuesdays?"

"I'll go to the Nickelodeon. Maybe down to Coney Island, if the weather is hot enough."

"Have you ever been to the Polo Grounds?"

"Yes."

"Where do you usually sit?"

"I like to sit on the first base side."

"Why?"

"Dan McGann is my half-brother."

Here Hyde, piped up, "You never told me that the first baseman of the New York Giants was your half-brother!"

"It is not something I am proud of, sir."

"Not proud of it! He is part of one of the best baseball clubs ever! How could you not be proud of him!" said an astonished Hyde.

"How are you related?" asked the detective.

"My mother had an affair with Mr. McGann's father. I was born three years before Dan. We share the same father. Dan and I were friends growing up."

"Please tell me more about your relationship with your half-brother," pressed Petrosino.

"My father left when he found out my mother was pregnant with me. My mother would take me to see my half-brother at the park. I don't know if Dan's mother ever knew my real identity. I think she thought my mother was a nice lady who was a widow. My mother told me that this was our secret, but of course, I told Danny. Anyway, one day little Danny told his dad that he played with his brother in the park. He got the beating of his life and was told to never see me again. My father looked for us, my mother and I, probably to threaten us but we hid in the crowds of the lower east side. You see, my mother never married again. I think she wanted me to have family, brothers and sisters, you know sir, playmates.

"She never married anyone after her husband left?" asked the detective.

"Who would want an uneducated woman with a boy? Well, our father was so abusive and threatening to Danny about me that it probably made Danny more determined than ever to see me because I was forbidden to him. For a while we met secretly until my father killed himself. My father never acknowledged me, so I kept my mothers' name."

"You were very quick to tell us about something you are not proud of, I wonder why," said Petrosino, staring fixedly at McCarthy.

"Dan is tied up in some dirty business that I do not want to know about. I thought that if the police are involved, it is best to cooperate rather than be seen as hiding something."

"What business do you mean?"

"I can't say for sure, but he is always in trouble with the manager of the Giants. He stays out late, goes to the Polo Grounds tired, and in general is a worry to me."

"What does he do so late at night?" questioned the detective.

"I couldn't say. I don't speak with him about this."

"Why are you telling me, a representative of the law, all of this?"

"My employer told me that I could trust you. Perhaps, you could help him. I'm hoping you can sir. He needs it."

"Do you share any tobacco with him, or does he with you?"

"Not that I remember, sir."

"What is your..., main cause of concern regarding your half-brother?"

"His drinking, sir. His drinking has become intolerable. It is putting a strain on our relationship. He cannot remember things after he gets sozzled up. I am depressed thinking about it all. He is the only family I have."

"What do you think is the reason for this drinking?"

"It started somewhere in the beginning of May. Danny was drunk when I showed up at Cloke's down on Spring Street."

"Why did you meet with him?"

"If he had an off day that coincided with mine, which was not often, we would meet. Sometimes I would go to the ballgame."

"And so this day in early May, he was drunk, and you were surprised at this?"

"Yes, because he never got drunk."

"Why do you think he was drunk?"

"He told me that a woman had been killed in a blast of dynamite. He had seen it and it upset him. I asked him to tell me what happened, but he would not share any information. All he could tell me was that it was his fault."

At this point the detective focused more intently. His mind instantly recalled the bombing of Iannacone's Meats on May 7 and the death of a young, unidentified woman.

"What else can you say about this? What other details did he give you?"

"Is my brother in any trouble, Lieutenant?"

"It is important that you answer my questions. This is the best way to help your brother. What else did he say about this woman that had been killed?"

Seamus clearly became uncomfortable. "I already told you all I know. I didn't question him. He was so drunk and distraught that I felt he would be better off left alone on the subject. He has a terrible temper."

"Did he ever talk about it at a later date?"

"No."

"Was the dead woman known to him?"

"I really don't know detective. All I know is that he saw her killed in a blast. Why don't you ask him yourself?"

"I think I will. I will need to speak with you again. Mr. Hyde, will you make Seamus available to me at a moment's notice?"

"Anything you say, Lieutenant. Seamus, honestly give the detective all of the information he needs and as much time as he needs. After his visits, you are to report to me that you met with him. Keep me informed of the investigation."

"Thank you, sir."

"Seamus, you will eat with the servants. Petrosino and I are dining with the President."

"Yes, sir."

As McCarthy left the room, Hyde closed the door and looked at Petrosino. "I had no idea. Well, what is your analysis?" said Hyde, feeling he was part of the investigative team.

"Is it possible for him to get out on days other than his day off?"

"Only if I am out of town and that is quite a bit."

"I would like to see your appointment book from the beginning of this year to the present. I want to see when you were not in New York."

"What is all of this in connection with, I am damned curious!"

"Is there anyone else who has access to your tobacco or do you share with anyone?"

"No."

"Are you sure of this?"

"Yes."

Just then there was a knock on the door.

"Come in," said Petrosino.

The President of the United States barged into the room, "I'll have you know Giuseppe, that I hold you in such high regard, that I knock on the door before I enter a room where you are conducting your investigations. As President, I have become accustomed to walking where I please!"

"It is not necessary to knock, sir."

"Just as calling me sir, is not necessary! I have known you for a long time Giuseppe, and we have been through a lot."

"You are the President, sir."

"Loyalty, Hyde, loyalty and respect! It is what makes a man!"

"Indeed," was all that Hyde could say.

"Hyde, I don't know how you are mixed up in all of this, but if you are guilty of anything you should act like a man and admit it now. Giuseppe will catch you sooner or later."

"I have nothing to hide, I assure you. The papers are annoyed by my extravagance, but they cannot find much else because there is nothing else to find."

"I don't like your so-called extravagance either! Extravagance! I call it waste! How can you behave so when men in the mines doing real work are paid in one day, what you spend in a minute?"

"It is not against the law to spend our money any way we want."

"Responsibility man, where is your responsibility?"

"The people that are entertained by my parties are important financial connections."

"BAH! There is no talking to you! If Giuseppe finds you guilty of anything, I will flatten you like a pancake. My presidency will not be undermined by my friendship with you! I have too many important things to accomplish! Enough gentleman! Let's enjoy what is left of this beautiful summer day!"

The threesome walked the grounds and talked of hunting, horse racing, and history. At the four o'clock hour, Roosevelt excused himself and played with his children. This was his daily routine and it consisted of general roughhousing, football, some baseball, hide and seek and much laughing.

Afterward, Roosevelt joined his companions for dinner.

The table was set for eight. The dinner consisted of all the president's favorites, venison, oysters, and asparagus. The end of the meal featured some Hu Kwa Tea and cookies.

As they began their meal, one seat was noticeably vacant. Suddenly, Alice ran into the room. Roosevelt sniffed the air in an exaggerated way.

"Alice, you have been smoking on the roof again! You see Giuseppe, I can identify tobacco in various circumstances. HA!"

"Mr. Hyde, do you like baseball?" asked Petrosino.

"Well, I gambled on it in the past, but it does not interest me much."

"Have you been following the Giants?" asked the detective.

"I guess most people in New York have been following them. Do you think they will be champions?" asked Hyde.

"Yes, if their catcher, what is his name, Donlin! If Donlin keeps hitting like he does, they should win. He is one of the best catchers in all of baseball," replied Petrosino.

"I've heard that McGraw is a good manager," said Hyde.

Roosevelt interrupted, "Giuseppe, I thought Donlin played outfield."

"No, Donlin is the catcher."

"Are you sure of it?"

"Quite sure, Donlin is the catcher."

The rest of the meal was spent in questioning the young Roosevelts about their studies and recounting Roosevelt's adventures with Petrosino in Newport, Rhode Island. Teddy also entertained with stories about being with the Rough Riders in Montauk.

After dinner, the men retired to the study. They drank port wine in privacy.

"Mr. Hyde, I will reveal to you what this current mystery is about because I am convinced that it is connected to baseball in some way and because you did not correct my obvious mistake about Mike Donlin. It seems along with other information I have, that you are not involved," said Petrosino.

"I knew Donlin wasn't the catcher! A clever little trick!" smiled Roosevelt.

"A true crank would have told me that Donlin played outfield as the President pointed out. There is a pattern I have detected that makes me almost positive that the man behind these bombings is a fan of the New York Giants."

"Tell me Lieutenant, what this is all about? My curiosity is getting the better of me!" smiled Hyde, enjoying the conversation.

After Petrosino had detailed the case from the discovery of the tobacco tin back in January to the present time, he began asking questions.

"Your man Seamus, do you think he is capable of any aspect of this terrible business?"

"I don't think so Lieutenant, but one never knows. He is a very private man."

"Do you ever notice any changes in his behavior?"

"I must admit," said Hyde as he sipped his port, "that I do not know him as well as I should. I have noticed that he becomes very depressed at times. He seems preoccupied. He withdraws deeper into himself and well, Dang it! I respect the man's privacy. I don't pry Lieutenant, if you know what I mean."

"I do, but now, to save lives you may try to discreetly get information from him."

"What sort of information?"

"What he does when you are away. Any information you can get about his half-brother Dan McGann would help. I have two conditions for you."

"What are they, Lieutenant?"

"One. You do not reveal this conversation to him. Pretend you are in the dark about everything. Mislead him into thinking that you don't trust me, and you would rather I be gone."

"I do like the man, Lieutenant, but I will do as you say because it will probably be for the best. I want to help him and go along with your investigation in any way I can."

"Smart move, Hyde! Giuseppe will set things right!" roared the President.

"What is the second condition, Lieutenant?"

"I want you to stop giving him tobacco and take him with you when you travel. Get to know the man. Let's see if he opens up to you."

"What about his day off?"

"Find an excuse to keep him with you. Offer to compensate him with some extra money. I don't want him to meet with his brother."

"Why, Lieutenant?"

"I have detected a pattern developing with these bombings. If the bombing occurs again, on the day I predict, and you can prove that Seamus was with you, and I can find out where his half-brother was on that day, then I can close some doors in my mind and open others."

"Everything will be done as you say Lieutenant, with utmost alacrity!"

"You are a good man, Hyde."

Roosevelt, who had been listening intently said, "Hmff! You would be a better man if you watched your extravagance!"

Hyde looked down at his glass of port. Petrosino studied Hyde and Roosevelt looked up at the portrait of his father. The discussion meandered a bit from there but shortly after the first glass of port disappeared, the three parted company.

Seamus brought the hansom around. Hyde offered Petrosino a ride, which the detective accepted. To keep up their ruse, remarks to one another remained perfunctory all the way to Manhattan.

The next day, Petrosino visited the hospital where Bresnahan was recuperating from a hit in the head by Dummy Taylor while he was catching. The detective was first rebuffed when he wanted to see the Giant catcher, but after he identified himself, he was led to the half-slumbering Giant. Bresnahan sat up and started looking at the day's paper when the detective walked in.

"How are you today, Roger?" asked the detective. From their first encounter, Petrosino had sensed the Giant catcher to be indifferent, even antagonistic towards him. Was this in Bresnahan's nature or was he trying to hide something?

"You again! I have better things to talk about than chewing tobacco! And what right do ye have in calling me Roger? If I speak to a Dago, he has to call me Mr. Bresnahan!"

"That was a nasty hit you took."

"It's all part of the game," replied the catcher, as he placed the newspaper aside. "What do ye want, ye grease ball?"

Unfazed, Petrosino pressed onward. "Your team is winning without you," grinned the detective as he sat in the wooden chair close to the bed.

"This is why I must get better soon. Someone may realize that they don't need me."

"I'm sure your position on the team is secure."

"Nothing is secure in this game," said the catcher, slightly touching his head.

"Well, two years ago you batted .350, which I believe was fourth in the league," said the detective.

"Wow! I didn't know you were a crank!"

"Crank?" questioned Petrosino, feigning ignorance of the word as he leaned forward.

"Sure. It means fan. Baseball has its own lingo. We have alternate words for many things. It just happens, I guess."

"I'm not really a crank, as you would say, but I have been studying and researching the game to understand..." Petrosino trailed off.

"Understand what?"

"I want to understand the game, and the people behind the game. I want to understand the ways in which this great game can be connected to life."

"What does murder have to do with baseball?"

"In this instance, perhaps everything."

Bresnahan, sitting erect, folded his hands on his lap and looked intently at the detective, "Did you come here to talk about baseball or murder?"

"Who threw the ball that made you unconscious?" "It's all over the papers. You should know. It was Dummy."

"What happened?"

"What does that have to do with anything? Is this part of your investigation?"

"Please, Mr. Bresnahan, I will ask the questions. Again. What happened?"

Since Bresnahan considered it some form of manliness to get hit with a fast ball and live to tell the tale, he was happy to oblige the great detective on this point. "I called for Dummy to throw it low and outside. He came up and in. I haven't spoken to him about it yet, but we probably got our signs crossed or the ball just got away from him."

"What do you think is most likely?"

"The kid has pretty good control. It was probably a mix up in signs."

"Why do you say that?"

"Well, that is all I can remember. Once that ball hit me, I can't remember anything."

"McGraw told me that you are working on protective gear. Tell me about that."

"I've been working with a football helmet. The batter can wear it when he is at the plate."

"I think the shin guards are truly innovative," said Petrosino.

"I didn't know McGraw had such a mouth!" Bresnahan paused. "Yeah. Some players wear protective gear under their pants but me, I am thinking about borrowing what they use in cricket and ice hockey and maybe modifying them a bit for baseball. Wear them leg pads on the outside."

"I think that is an excellent idea. I have been to a few games at the Polo Grounds and I have seen catchers injured by your teammates because of high spikes on a close play at home plate."

"I am also inventing something else, but nobody sees it."

"What would that be?" questioned Petrosino.

"When the ball hits the catcher in the face mask, it still hurts. Especially when Matty or McGinnity throws it. So now, I am wrapping little pieces of leather around the wire of the mask and it sort of absorbs the blow, makes it less painful. I get beat up more than anybody else out there, and don't get paid any more for it."

All of this talk about innovation in protective gear for catchers was the detective's way of gaining the confidence of Bresnahan. For many years now, Petrosino had practiced getting people to talk to him that were at first reluctant. He questioned them about something that interested them. This appealed to that pride found in every man. By degrees, the conversation imperceptibly turned to subjects that Petrosino wanted information about.

"McGraw appreciates innovation, how did you begin your acquaintance?" asked the detective.

"You mean how did we get to know each other?"

"Yes, that is what I mean."

"We were on the old Baltimore team together. I started as a pitcher and then worked outfield. When I was pitching, the previous catcher couldn't handle my stuff. He dropped everything. I complained to McGraw. I still remember what he said. 'If you're so smart, get in there and catch yourself.' I did. Now, I am the catcher for the best pitchers in baseball and the best team in baseball."

"You are very close to McGraw."

"He is my best friend in the game."

"I heard Dan McGann was your best friend on the team."

At this, the catcher became irritated. He shifted under the sheets. "I'll never talk about another Irishman to a wop. What are you here for anyway?"

"I only meant to inquire about his health. He looks tired at the ballpark."

"You go ask him about his health. I don't know nuthin' about Dan McGann. Are you done? I need to rest."

"Either you answer my questions here or I bring you down to police headquarters and you can answer them there."

"You devil!"

"What does Dan McGann do all night to make him tired for Giants games?"

"I don't know. I've only gone drinking with him once or twice down at Cloke's."

"What's so special about Cloke's?"

"Many of the guys like to go down there for a pint. It's away from the press and the men that work the docks will never bother you. They are there to drink. A lot of the Giants go to Cloke's. They like the atmosphere."

"During this time, has McGann ever mentioned something to you about what he does at night or if he was involved in something that he wanted to get away from?"

"I'm tellin' ya man! I don't know! Jesus Mary and Joseph, can ya leave me be?"

"Mr. Bresnahan, I am trying to do my work. My work is to help others."

"It's a sick man yer talking to. Go and leave me alone!" Bresnahan moved his head to the left, away from the detective, seated near the bed.

Petrosino rose. "If you can think of anything, you can find me at Mulberry Street."

When Bresnahan was released from the hospital the next day, he reported to the Polo Grounds for work. He was greeted by John McGraw.

"How's the head?" asked the manager.

"Dummy threw it at the wrong head. The signal I gave was ta throw it at the head of the batter!" They laughed as Bresnahan taped his catcher's mask with some new leather.

"I heard the grease ball visited you," said McGraw.

"He did. I don' like him. He had me talking away before I caught myself."

"What did he want?"

"I don't really know. He was asking about Danny."

McGraw's face muscles tightened, "Don't say anything to that wop!"

"I didn't"

"What did he ask?"

"He's asking about Danny and what he does when he's not playing."

"We're a team. We'll stick together as a team. I don't know what he is after," growled the manager.

Bresnahan continued to tape his mask. Without looking up, he said, "Do you think he wants you?"

McGraw growled, "Damn it!" He spit into the dirt, "He'll never get me. I mean too much to this town! What I do on the side is my business. I don't mean to hurt anybody! Don't you mention this to anybody, Roger, and tell McGann to watch his back!"

"Mr. McGraw, we had a fight, Danny and I, and we're not talking. Can't somebody else tell him?"

McGraw grew red in the face, rather quickly, "Grow up and go tell him yourself! I don't want any part of this! I don't want you to talk to this about anyone unless I talk to you first. Understood?" roared McGraw.

"Yes," said Bresnahan, as he stood up to adjust the mask.

"Good," McGraw patted him on the backside, "get a few hits today and keep your eye on the ball, not your head, you thick Irishman!"

Bresnahan went to the back of home plate and crouched, ready to take some pitches from Matty. Various players gathered in the field doing exercises. Dan McGann had not arrived yet. It was still early. The loud POP! of the ball in his catcher's glove told him that Matty would be strong today. Through the slits in his masks, he saw Seamus, Dan's half-brother. They had spoken together in better times, over a Guinness at Cloke's. The catcher signaled his pitcher to stop throwing by holding up both arms. Matty held on to the ball and kicked the dirt around the pitcher's mound. Bresnahan approached Seamus, who seemed to be in an agitated state. The catcher began the conversation.

"Yer brother, he ain't here yet."

"Yes, it seems so," said Seamus not looking at the catcher.

"There's a copper interested in Danny."

"Do you mean, Lieutenant Petrosino?" asked Seamus, turning to look at Bresnahan.

"The same."

"Do you know what it is all about?"

"No, and I don't want to know. Just tell your brother to keep his mouth shut. Those are orders from McGraw."

Seamus sat down in one of the fan seats. "This must be serious."

Matty yelled something from the mound. Bresnahan punched his glove and adjusted his mask.

"If Danny can't keep his mouth shut, we are all in trouble," warned the catcher as he turned and trotted back toward home plate.

Seamus kept his head in his hands, fearing the worst. He sat slumped in his seat. His torment was broken half an hour later by his half-brother.

"What are you crying about?" asked Dan McGann, first baseman for the New York Giants.

"I came here as soon as I could get a day off. I had to lie to Hyde. I told him I was going to the doctor. The police are looking for you."

McGann became visibly angry, "What are you saying? What do ya mean?"

"Lieutenant Petrosino was asking about you and now your teammates are telling me that you should keep your mouth shut. What have you done?"

"Nothing they can prove. Which teammates are talking to you like that?"

"Please, I don't want any fights."

"Tell me Seamus."

"I'm trying to help you Danny. You're the only family I got. I'm worried about you."

"I can take care of myself. Let the coppers talk to me! I'll set em straight!" said McGann, as he punched his glove.

McGraw yelled, "Get to work Dan, I want you to take some throws at first!"

"Danny, tell me what happened. I may be able to help."

"Seamus, I might be in some trouble. An innocent woman died because of me. I didn't mean to kill her but the coppers may try to hang me anyway."

"You told me this Danny. How are you responsible for that?"

"It is a long story. I'm ashamed at what I've become. Somehow they got me for the night of July 7. They must be following me. I don't know what tipped them off."

"What do you mean? What happened on the night of July 7?"

"Nothing! I can't talk now. I'm ashamed of meself. We'll talk again Seamus."

McGraw yelled again, "Slackers get pay cuts, Danny!" McGraw tossed the ball lightly into the air and hit it directly at Dan and Seamus. Dan turned at the sound of the bat and with quick reflexes snagged it.

"We'll talk Seamus. I'll try to explain. Although nothing will bring that girl back." Dan trotted with the ball towards first, fired the ball towards McGraw and said, "Is that the best you can do old man?"

He then turned back to his half-brother, "Hey Seamus!"

"Yes Danny."

"Say the beads for me."

Seamus, deeply troubled, left the ballpark.

16

Saturday August 5, 1905
The score was tied at 5-5 in the bottom of the ninth at Exposition Park in Pittsburgh. Claude Ritchey led the inning off with a double. George Gibson followed with a bouncer back to the mound. Matty threw to Devlin at third to get the lead runner but Ritchey was called safe. McGraw raced onto the field to argue the call. The umpire told him to get off the field and resume play. McGraw and the Giants refused to play. After timing the delay the umpires Bausewine and Esmile forfeited the game to Pittsburgh 9-0. The Pirates took the last three games of this series and got to within 7 ½ games of the Giants. Under the 1905 rules, Matty was given the loss, his seventh overall for the season and his fourth against Pittsburgh.

"I must confess it was with a heavy heart that I turned my face towards that antique and shabby palace, that sepulcher of reputations, that tomb of character, that morgue of political ambition, that cavern of intrigue and dissimulation-the Police Headquarters at Mulberry Street."
From Guarding a Great City by William McAdoo, Police Commissioner, New York City, 1904-1906.

August 6
Nicky Vivona had been threatened by the Black Hand for months. He started to carry a Baby Hammerless Revolver that sold for $1.80 in the Sears catalogue. If anyone came close to him, he would kill them. He closed his shoe repair shop as usual on the night of the 6th. He looked around and saw no one. He walked home, ate a bowl of macaroni, some wine and then went to bed sweating from the heat and the thought that his shop might be visited by the Black Hand.

After midnight, a cab slowly moved past Vivona's shop. The driver stopped and after waiting, looking, and listening, he dismounted. The door on the side of the cab was opened. A body was pulled out, dragged across the sidewalk and laid to rest near Vivona's shoe repair shop. The driver then mounted the wagon, looked up and down the deserted streets, and lit a double stick of dynamite, which he tossed nonchalantly in the direction of the limp body. He whipped the horse and they started off in a trot. The tremendous blast shattered windows.

The unfortunate body was blown to many bits. An ankle with a white shoe landed across the street.

Not more than ten minutes later, Petrosino was awakened by his telephone. Immediately alert, he feared the worst.

"Yes," answered the detective, never giving his name before he knew the identity of the caller and could recognize the voice.

When he heard a crackly voice say, "Sir, there has been an explosion and a death on Varick. 180 Varick Street."

"I'll be there immediately." The telephone, still a rarity and distraction or annoyance for some, was another tool Petrosino used to combat crime. He then lit his candle and dressed for his walk to the crime scene at Varick Street. He had wanted to be informed of any blast and he was somewhat satisfied that someone was doing their job.

Shortly, he arrived at the crime scene where he encountered a few police and fewer bystanders, due to the late hour and remote location.

"Has the owner been notified?" started the detective.

"We haven't been able to locate him yet, sir." Most everyone on the force knew Petrosino and this young recruit was no exception. To work alongside the master, if even only for a few minutes, was considered a privilege, thus was Petrosino's reputation. Petrosino's twenty-two years on the New York City Police Force effectively made a myth out of the man. The new recruit carefully watched the detective, hoping to learn something. Already, the young policeman began to imagine how he would tell some of his mates about his encounter with the great detective.

"What have the men found?"

"We didn't touch anything, sir," said the young man with a quick, salute and awkward smile.

Petrosino neared the shop. Police followed him with lanterns. There were body parts in various places. He noticed the blue pinstriped suit on what was left of the torso. This could be the man whom he had seen at Rossi's and he had suspected of being *Angelo*. Turning, he stepped from the street. A policeman in front of him cursed.

"Damn horse dung! There is too much of it in the city streets. You! Hold the lamp here so I can get this off my shoe."

Petrosino knelt closer to the source of agitation.

"Shine the lamp here," said Petrosino, as he knelt to look at the shit.

The waste was soft and recent and there was a lot of it. The policeman stepped in just one part of many. How did it happen that the *Angelo* was killed by his own bomb? Petrosino noticed the grooves of carriage wheels that went through the horse manure, almost dividing one plop into two at one point. Who was in the carriage pulled by the horse

113

that had left this clue? He walked further and saw something in the street. He bent to look at it. It was an ankle and a foot inside of a white shoe. He examined the white shoe and noticed horse dung on the back of the sock, dung tucked into the shoe and smeared along the back. The front of the shoe was free of any horse plop. This seemed to imply that the wearer of the shoe was dragged. This confirmed his suspicions. *Angelo* the bomber, one of his major leads, was knocked unconscious or killed prior to the bomb going off and was laid at the storefront to make it look like an accidental death. Who killed him? Was it Dan McGann? Had the mastermind behind all of this made his first mistake? Surely there were people connected to the man with the blue pinstriped suit. He would be missed. People would look for him. Petrosino didn't have much to go on. The deceased seemed to be a baseball fan and someone was supplying him with Redman Chew. The great detective thought about the time when he actually saw the man while he was in disguise and decided not to follow him. This was probably a mistake, but at the time he did not think so. He had wanted to preserve his identity and in most cases this is the prudent thing to do. Petrosino's work, like that of McGraw's, was a mix of using statistics, hunches or impulses, and creativity. The detective believed an important part of his work was identifying his mistakes and learning from them. What could he learn from preserving his disguise and allowing *Angelo* to get away? Petrosino took from his pocket the sketch of *Angelo* that had been drawn for him by a police artist at headquarters. He compared the drawing to the bloodied head on the corpse before him. The moustache, size of the head and ears, and general shape and contour were all in agreement. He thought the best course of action was to confront the suspects with this drawing. He would have to detect shifts in emotion when he presented the drawing of the deceased. Very few people were good at hiding their emotions when confronted with a surprise of this sort. Is the person who killed *Angelo* the same as the person who killed Mattarrazzo the baker?

The following day, Petrosino's plans were interrupted by an early morning phone call he received from Sargent Muldoon. The ringing of the phone seldom brought good news.

"Hello."

"Sir, Seamus McCarthy, Dan McGann's half-brother, is dead!"

114

17

"How long will the National League stand for the hoodlum tactics of this New York team both on and off the field? During a game McGraw and his men are fighting umpires all the time, questioning every decision against them and resorting to all the dirty tactics known to baseball in order to win. McGraw and his crowd are intolerable during a game to all decent, self-respecting people in the stands."
-A Philadelphia newspaperman

"Sportsmanship and easygoing methods are all right, but it is the prospect of a hot fight that brings out the crowds."
-John McGraw

"Where are you?" barked Petrosino.

The voice of Muldoon could be heard faintly, "At the residence of James Hazen Hyde."

"Hold everything Muldoon! I'm on my way!" Petrosino hung up and made his way to the street. The new subway was usually quicker but at this early hour, horse and carriage may be better. He went to his friend the grocer who lived nearby and always had a second horse and cart available for Petrosino.

Mr. Eckert was stacking oranges when the detective entered.

"I need the horse and wagon!" yelled Petrosino.

"Son, do whatever he tells you," said the father, "And son, give him the most rested horse, we'll get by with the other one."

Every time Petrosino asked for the horses, young Master Eckert was always curious about how his father was in such debt to this Italian policeman. His father once told him, "I know this may not make sense to you, but you must never question the detective. When you are ready, I will tell you everything." The boy hopped up on the cart and Petrosino jumped up next to him. Halfway up Fifth Avenue, they encountered a standing traffic officer holding the STOP sign. Petrosino blew his police whistle, they were recognized and were waved on. They arrived at the residence of James Hazen Hyde. It was an imposing mansion on Fifth Avenue, the scene of many elaborate parties for the most eligible bachelor in New York City.

"I will settle with your father, you may go," said the detective as he jumped down from the wagon.

Muldoon had been waiting on the sidewalk and was there to greet his superior.

"This way sir," said Muldoon as he led him through the doorway, and into the cavernous interior of the grand house. Petrosino instantly noticed the absence of house staff.

Muldoon led the detective past rooms filled with early American furniture, oriental rugs, and Chinese vases on small tables. They ran up the marble stairs and into a room near the top of the stairs. It was a study filled with books. The window looked out onto Fifth Avenue and was open. Slouched behind the desk was Seamus McCarthy, gun in hand and bullet in his head.

"Nothing has been touched," said Muldoon, although he didn't have to make this announcement.

Petrosino looked at the body.

"Look here Muldoon. The bullet entered the head from behind. See the blood splattered over the front of the desk? Do you think it is strange that the gun is still in his hands? Further, do you think it is odd that he should shoot himself from behind rather than through the mouth as most people do when doing this… act of self-annihilation?"

Muldoon considered this. "Well I guess that if he held the gun tightly enough and died instantly from the bullet, he might still be clutching it."

"Was there any suicide or farewell note?" asked the detective.

"Nothing has been found yet, sir."

"Who was in the house at the time of the tragedy?"

"Just Mr. Hyde sir."

"What? Where were all of the other servants?"

"They were let go for the day, sir."

"Where is Mr. Hyde now?"

"Downstairs in the drawing room."

"Then that is where I shall go. Lead me Muldoon!" Petrosino and Muldoon retraced their steps to the bottom of the magnificent marble stairway. They made a sharp left into the drawing room and found James Hazen Hyde sitting on a yellow sofa, pouring and quickly swallowing a small dose of whiskey. When he saw Petrosino, he brightened, laid the shot glass on the nearby table, and rose from the sofa, extending his hand to the detective.

"Lieutenant Petrosino! I am glad to see you!"

"Give me the details," said the detective, not acknowledging the greeting.

Hyde allowed his arm to flop to his side and awkwardly asked, "Do you want some coffee or tea? One of your men has a pot going."

"No thanks. Tell me what happened."

"Well, as I said to your men, I heard the shot from down here and raced up to find Seamus dead."

Petrosino turned to the officers gathered and asked, "Who wrote down Mr. Hyde's testimony?"

"I did sir," said a bald officer with a big handlebar moustache that Petrosino recognized as Officer Cadbury.

"Good, well, I will ask you again Mr. Hyde, so I may hear with my own ears."

"Yes. Of course."

"I understand from Muldoon that all of the servants were given the day off this morning."

"Yes Lieutenant. That is correct. I was going to be traveling today and only Seamus would accompany me."

"Where were you going?"

"To Philadelphia to race my horses."

"Why did you give the rest of the servants the day off?"

"Why not? I didn't need them. I can afford to be generous."

"Did you disturb anything, touch anything or take anything in that room?"

"No."

"So, there was no note left behind from the deceased?"

"No. I didn't see anything like that."

"Where were you when you heard the shot?"

"I was in the dining room reading the morning paper and finishing some breakfast, anticipating our journey."

"Please describe your last conversation with the deceased."

"Well, he seemed agitated by something. Usually, he is a bit more talkative and focused. I had the horses readied and breakfast was served. I then released all of my staff. I instructed Seamus to finish the last minute preparations for our journey and check to see if all of the servants were gone. He reported to me they were released and I told him to write a note to the cook, reminding her about the dinner party next week in Newport. The Astors needed to be added to the list as well as a final count of wine cases and champagne cases. The desk where he shot himself is used by the staff. It is the place where all of the staff receive their correspondence."

"Are you sure all the other servants were gone?"

"If Seamus said they were, then they were."

"Could anyone else have been in the house?"

"What are you getting at Lieutenant? Are you thinking that Seamus might have been killed?"

"I must entertain every possibility, no matter how... outlandish it may seem!"

The room Seamus was found in is closed to everyone except myself and house staff. It is locked at all times and there are only two keys, one which hangs in the kitchen. When one of the servants reports to work, they first get the key and then go to the room and check for their daily messages. It is also a room in my house in which the servants can rest. I never use it for personal reasons except to socialize with my servants."

"This seems a rather elaborate system," noted the detective.

"Not at all. The servants actually like it. Everything is in one place and they can mingle a bit and relax there. I provide newspaper, broadsheets, and books for them to read."

"Well, what if someone needs the key and it is not in its place?"

"The key will only be in that room with another person. Servants are strictly forbidden to walk around with the key. When the last person leaves the room, they should lock the door and go directly to the kitchen and replace the key. The key has never been lost."

"Where is the duplicate key kept?"

"Seamus carries it."

"Who does the gun that killed Seamus belong to?"

"It is my gun. It is the gun that Seamus had access to if he ever needed it. We carry it on trips for protection. He was probably cleaning and loading it for our trip when he decided to kill himself."

"What makes you so sure, he killed himself? Couldn't someone have hid, shot him, put the gun in his hands and hid until you appeared and then run away?"

"But why, Lieutenant? Why would anyone do that? What could the motive possibly be?"

"Why do you think Seamus would kill himself?"

"I really don't know Lieutenant. Don' you have a clue? This is your line, not mine."

"Have you seen, or has he spoken about Dan McGann recently?"

"No. Seamus is, that is, I mean *was* very private. He never spoke to me of personal matters. When you interviewed him at Oyster Bay, it was the first time that I knew he was Dan McGann's brother."

"Half-brother. Well, that will be all for now. I will have Muldoon contact you if I need anything."

"Lieutenant, I feel terrible about this. If there is anything I could do, I mean if he has any family that I may help, please let me know... He was a good man. I don't understand it."

"Muldoon. Notify his brother, Dan McGann."

"Yes sir."

Thursday August 10, 1905

Matty improves his record to 19-7 by outpitching Chicago's Ed Reulbach. New York scored all they needed on an unearned run in the sixth. Strang was safe on an error, stole second, and scored on McGann's single.

Thursday August 17, 1905
Matty blanks Chicago 3-0 for his twentieth win of the season.

Monday August 21, 1905
Petrosino walked into headquarters and went over to the Rogues Gallery to study it. Men, women, old and young of all nationalities were displayed on the gallery. Petrosino memorized faces and profiles. He saw the picture of the man that had thrown the knife at him while he was on the scaffold in the Hippodrome and removed it. The empty space the picture had left behind would soon be occupied by another picture.

"Sir!" said a familiar voice behind him.

"Good Morning, Muldoon," he replied, without turning around.

"Good morning, sir. There is something I want you to hear. Please follow me."

Muldoon led the way down a hall and to his own office on the right. Inside was a young policeman.

"Sir, this is Officer LaSalle. Tell the Lieutenant what ye just told me."

"Well sir," began LaSalle, with an officious tone, "I was walking on my beat which is the Lower East Side. I was looking carefully, at faces, like you told us to do during our training. Anyway, I follow the New York Giants. I know all the players. I'm always at the Polo Grounds. I saw Mr. Luther Taylor. He is a pitcher for the Giants. I know it was Taylor because, well, I have his baseball card and I like him because he is a deaf mute as my own brother is and well, he was with another gentleman that seemed familiar to me. At first I thought he must be another baseball player. I looked at my cards when I got home but I didn't see him on any of those cards. Then I remembered sir where I saw the man that was with Taylor. It was here at the station. It was the man you are looking for sir. The thin man with the thin moustache. His drawing is in the Rogues Gallery."

"Are you sure about this?" asked Petrosino.

"Very sure sir, I like to paint sir and I am one to notice details."

"Did you notice anything else? Did you see where they went?"

"Nothing out of the ordinary, sir. They were just walking along together. They looked like they were friendly with each other. Dummy was smiling. When they parted, they shook hands. If I knew then that the man was in the Rogue's Gallery, I would have followed him. I'm sorry if I let you down, sir."

"LaSalle, I will keep my eye on you. Continue work like this and you will get a promotion. Are the Giants at the Polo Grounds today?" asked Petrosino.

"They are. They should be getting ready for this afternoon's game," answered LaSalle.

"Muldoon, let's visit Mr. Taylor. Officer LaSalle, you come with us. We'll take the subway."

Fourteen thousand fans watched New York defeat Pittsburgh at the Polo Grounds 10-2. Matty is in command throughout, and the Giants steal five bases, including Devlin's steal of home.

Just before this game finished, Petrosino, Muldoon, and LaSalle made their way down to the field to talk to the players. Both policemen wore plain clothes. Only LaSalle was in uniform. McGraw saw them right away.

As they approached the bench, the manager yelled, "You're on my territory now. I don't talk to anybody during game time, especially some short New York copper who thinks he is a big man!"

Most of the players on the bench averted their gaze. As Matty continued to dominate in the top of the ninth inning, Petrosino spoke.

"Mr. McGraw, the score is 10-2. This is no longer a contest. I would like to address your players on an individual basis out in right field and then..."

"What? We don't have time for that. Say what you have to say to us as a group. We live and die together. There should be no secrets on this club."

As Pittsburgh made the last out, the Giants came in to the benches. Dan McGann, being closest, was one of the first to come in.

Petrosino wanted to express his sympathies and began simply with "Mr. McGann..."

The first baseman came close to the detective and he threw a lightning punch, a left hook that caught the detective in the midsection.

Seeing Muldoon step forward, Petrosino barked, "Stay out of it, Muldoon!"

Some of the ballplayers crowded in front of LaSalle.

The other players came running in and those on the bench stood to watch. McGann assumed a boxing stance. McGraw remained silent. Petrosino also assumed the boxing stance. For some men, watching a good fight is a pleasure. Many of New York's National League team saw it every day; fighting was part of their job. However, scrapping with a policeman on a baseball field, was something special. The adversaries eyed each other up. They danced around first base and their feet kicked up some dirt that made small dust clouds. McGann threw another punch a left to the midsection, but Petrosino surprised him using his knowledge of martial arts that he had learned during the Tong Wars. Petrosino released all emotion and tried to remain fluid. He grabbed the left arm of McGann and bent his clenched fist downwards to attempt to touch the knuckles to the wrist. As a boxer, this was the last thing McGann expected, and he tried to resist the pain. The detective used his weight and leverage, to gain the best angle to place himself to exert the most pressure. It worked. In an instant McGann was on the ground, dust flying everywhere.

"Alright! Alright! Enough!" was all McGann could utter.

The rest of the team was, to varying degrees, impressed, shocked, and angry.

McGann rubbed his wrist and stood up. "Damn you. My brother is dead because of you! I ought to kill you, you greaseball dago!"

"I am sorry for your loss. I would have prevented it if I could have. My job, my life's work is to save lives, not take them. I regret your loss and I am sorry that it happened. Your brother was a good and trusted servant to an important man in our city."

Red Ames, the pitcher stepped forward, "Nice little speech but I still say get out of our ballpark." He spit a large wad of chewing tobacco on the black shoes of the detective.

Turkey Mike Donlin, one of the offensive leaders on the club spoke next, "He saved my life. I think we should listen to what he has to say."

Bresnahan piped up, "Luther wants to know how the copper saved your life."

"We were at the Hippodrome, high up on one of those scaffolds. Some guy tried to jump on our scaffold and we almost fell about forty feet. This detective almost lost his own life until that crazy man fell into the water himself."

Bresnahan signed to Taylor.

McGinnity spoke up, "I say we ask McGraw. What do you say, Mr. McGraw?"

McGraw hesitated. The team trained to rely on his judgment waited for orders. If he told his men to assault the detective, they would have.

"Let's hear him out!" shouted Little Napoleon.

So Petrosino stood atop first base and had Muldoon organize the players to stand in a group and face him. It would be more difficult to assess personal reactions in this way, but he had to take what he could get. When he revealed the drawing of the man with the white shoes, he knew who he would be focusing on.

"I have been trying to catch a criminal who has killed at least three people, maybe more up until today. Here I have a rendering of the latest victim. I hold this man's killer responsible for the death of Mr. McGann's half-brother. I want to bring this killer to justice, but I need your help. I have reason to believe that someone on this team may know the killer or his latest victim. The victim was a Giants fan. He enjoyed your baseball. He might have come to the park. You might have given him an autograph. You may have shared your tobacco with him. Please look at the drawing carefully."

"Stop wasting our time!" yelled Red.

"How do you know what you know?" asked McGinnity

"I cannot tell you much because the investigation is still in progress."

"Who is it that you're talkin' about?" questioned the Iron Man.

"I have a drawing of a man, the Giants fan killed by the man I am looking for. I am going to pass it around and I want to know if any of you know him."

Nobody moved except for Bresnahan signing to Taylor. Petrosino took the picture of *Angelo* with the white shoes from his pocket, showed the team, and focused intently on faces. Some shook their heads, a few walked away, downturned lips, slanted heads with no real sign of recognition. McGraw looked.

"He looks familiar in some way, but I don't know him. He could be a fan I see in the stands every home game. How am I supposed to know?" yelled McGraw.

Bresnahan examined it next and paused. Petrosino noticed the catchers jaw firm, his lips together. The catcher handed it to Dummy Taylor. The deaf pitcher looked at it quickly, passed it along, and stared at the detective. Petrosino felt that he had something. Donlin got it, made a clucking noise, shook his head, and passed it on. When McGann got the picture, he studied it. He held it longer than anyone else. He passed it on. He looked down at the infield grass. Muldoon took it after the last player looked at it.

Petrosino yelled from his first base perch, "If anyone recognizes him. Please let me know. Information you have may lead me to the killer."

"Muldoon, I've discovered a hole in my front pocket. I hope I didn't lose anything," said Petrosino.

This was a code word used by the detective in the company of others. Depending on where the "hole" was, Muldoon would stand. The Irishman stood directly in front of the detective allowing his supervisor to watch Bresnahan and Taylor sign back and forth without the appearance of staring.

The men dispersed.

McGraw approached. "The game's over. We won. Stay as long as you like. I hope you catch the bastard."

The pitcher and his catcher were still signing. Muldoon and Petrosino were alone in the first base area. Most of the players were gone now, no longer interested. The Giants did not chatter and gossip, nor did they need to know who knew what. McGraw's only concern was to win ballgames and as long as that kept happening, everything else was nobody's business. The New York Giants just had to be prepared to come to the field and play their best.

Finally, the opportunity that comes from hard work and perseverance came to Joseph Petrosino.

Bresnahan started, "Dummy thinks he knows this man. It looks very much like a man named Luigi Francella. Dummy wants to know how the man died."

"He was hit over the head with a blunt instrument and then a bundle of dynamite was left on his body to make it look like he died in a botched attempt to blow up a shop. My man LaSalle positively identified this man with Taylor. They were seen on the Lower East Side together about a month ago," replied the detective.

"Dummy says there is a mistake because Luigi would never blow up a shop."

"When did he last see this man, Luigi?"

"He says not since the end of July."

"Does he ever give this man his chewing tobacco?"

"He says he does."

"Why didn't he tell me this before, when I first asked?"

Signs flew in all directions.

"He didn't want cops bothering his friends; now that he is dead it doesn't matter."

"How does Luther Taylor know this man?"

They exchanged silent signs. Taylor looked sad and slow.

"He says that he is a Kansas boy and that when he came here to play with the Giants, well, New York was a little bit too much for a deaf country boy. He was crossing Fifth Avenue in Manhattan and a trolley was clanging its bell to warn him, but he never heard the bell. The trolley tried to stop. Everyone else heard the warning bell, including Luigi Francella. Luigi pushed Taylor to the ground and saved his life. Luigi knew sign because he had a deaf brother who he lived with. As a sign of thanks for saving his life, Taylor gave Luigi some tickets. Luigi loved the game. Taylor became friends with Luigi and his brother Rocco. Dummy knew that the Francella brothers did not have a lot of money. When McGraw handed out tobacco, Taylor took some anyway, although he didn't really chew. He gave what he had to Luigi who grew to like the chew. Sometimes, he gave the Francella brothers some food and even money, but they never wanted to take much."

"What do you know about where he worked?"

Bresnahan was signing and saying, "Dummy now says that Francella recently told him that he did work for someone, but he wanted out. He was looking for another job. Luigi said that his boss was violent but that was all that he said. They didn't talk much about work."

"Can you take me to his brother?"

"Will it help to catch his brother's killer?"

"Yes, it might."

"Then of course."

Bresnahan, Taylor, Petrosino, and Muldoon looked at each other as Lasalle, not believing that he was on the field at the Polo Grounds, stood by. The empty park was very quiet. LaSalle looked for the seats where he usually sat. One well-dressed fan was far out in right field, sitting and watching them.

"Well, let's arrange a meeting," announced Petrosino.

Thursday August 24, 1905

New York wins their twelfth straight from Cincinnati behind the pitching of Mathewson. His 8-0 win brings his record to 22-7. McGraw gets ejected for the third straight day.

August 25, 1905

The Lower East Side of Manhattan in 1905 teems with humanity. People from around the world come together to struggle, strive, suffer and starve, all participating in the same determined tentation. Some sell homemade soap, other sell rags. The immigrants combat their new environment with its many languages and mixed traditions, its newness and modernity. They know there is a rich city beyond these rat infested, crime ridden slums. The stench; the lack of fresh air, clean water and basic food, the filth and absence of privacy all combine to make life on the Lower East Side a hell. People sometimes cooperate, but mostly struggle with each other for jobs, opportunities, space and food. The immigrants also combat their innermost selves. They battle their fears. Fears of newness and fear of a world so different from the one they left behind. This fear makes it sometimes impossible to see this new world as promising and inviting. Many newcomers battle the urge to give up, or become depressed. The air of the Lower East Side is foul with sewage and dead horses. Some in this new world, especially fellow countrymen, are dishonest and scheming. Conditions are cramped and living spaces lack sunlight. Rats live everywhere. Alcohol, homemade and potentially lethal, is readily available. Some succumb to its numbing, deceptive balm. This is the dirty, crowded, hopeful world that Luigi and Rocco Francella lived in and tried to escape from. Petrosino, Luther Taylor, Muldoon, Officer LaSalle, and Officer Fitzpatrick, who knew sign language quite well, approached the Lower East Side tenement house at 97 Orchard Street where Luigi Francella had lived with his brother Rocco. The squalid interior had a mixture of smells that changed as one walked along the darkened hallways. Grease, garlic, human waste, rotting meat, vomit, tar, stale beer, and then a smell so awful that was a repulsive mixture of all of them. Buckets of dirty water lined the hallway. A ripped brassiere filthy and forgotten was underfoot, in a building where most went without the luxury of such a garment.

Taylor led them down the hall past the ragged, disheveled and bewildered occupants. One intoxicated boy unconscious on the floor, had to be stepped over. Suddenly, a man walking through the dim hall towards them with his head down, looked up saw the representatives of the law. He ran in the opposite direction and disappeared down a back exit.

Taylor paused before a door smeared with stain and grease and slowly pushed it open. The police remained hidden from view on either side of the door, motionless in the hallway. Taylor observed a man asleep on stacks of bundled newspapers. A mouse scurried to a hiding place among the papers. A scent of urine filled the air.

Taylor approached and shook Rocco Francella awake. Startled at first, Rocco relaxed when he saw his friend Taylor. They began signing, Taylor standing. Rocco, dressed in crumpled clothes, remained sitting on the old newspapers.

"I have some bad news, my friend," signed Taylor.

"Tell me." Instinctively, Rocco knew it was about his brother. What else could it be about? There was nothing else in his miserable life. His brother had not been home since August 6. Food was running low. Now it seemed his worst fears had been correct. Something had happened to Luigi.

"It is about your brother."

Rocco seemed to sink into the couch of papers. Although expected, the news still had the power to shock and disturb.

"There is no easy way to say this. Your brother is dead."

Rocco let out a primal scream. It sounded like a horse panicking. He shook and crawled up into a ball, pulling his legs up into his chest, his bare feet dangling over the dirty copies of newspapers. Taylor sat beside him and ignoring the stench and dirtiness, embraced his friend.

Minutes passed. In those minutes worlds collapsed, a part of life for Rocco was closed. His eyes shut tight, and he swayed back and forth. Only years later, upon reflection of this day and its mixture of sad and happy events, would Rocco realize a small seed of acceptance was planted when Taylor attempted to console him with a gentle embrace. Silent tears streaming down his face, Rocco broke the hold of his only friend Luther.

"How?" was all he could sign, after many minutes of personal agony.

Taylor began, "He was killed in a blast of dynamite. The police are trying to find the killer so justice can be done. They need your help to find this man. Can you help them?"

"Yes."

"They are here. They want to talk to you. They want to help. Can they come in?"

All Rocco could do was nod in the affirmative. Taylor went to the hall and summoned the waiting party. Petrosino came in with Muldoon and Fitzpatrick. LaSalle, nightstick in hand, went out to have a look around the building.

Rocco kept his sad, tortured face on Luther Taylor.

They signed, and the watchful Fitzpatrick said, "you can ask questions now, sir. He is ready."

"Do you know who would want to kill your brother?"

Fitzpatrick signaled to Rocco as Taylor and Petrosino looked on. Rocco returned the signals in a halfhearted way, insipid and slow. After a while, Fitzpatrick spoke.

"He tells me his brother worked as a ditch digger and that he was working hard for little pay when Mr. Rossi approached him with a better job offer. He took it because he saw how nice Rossi was dressed."

The signals went back and forth. Petrosino asked many questions and Rocco Francella answered them with honesty. His sadness could not express itself in the silent voice that was quiet since birth. Rocco's story was basically as follows:

When the Francella brothers came through Ellis Island, one of the agents, an Italian, took all their money when he found out that Rocco could not speak. Still, they had an opportunity now in America. They lived in the street until Luigi got a job digging ditches. As the only Italian on the work site digging a tunnel for the subway, Luigi took a lot of abuse from the Irish and German workers. When Rossi came along with the prospect of a better job and the same pay with extra tips for delivery and with no Irishmen involved, Luigi took it. He was overjoyed at the extra money because Rocco could not acquire any employment. Luigi worked for the both of them. They were saving for a move out of the East Side. Luigi was determined to succeed in their adopted country and he was serious about maintaining his honesty. He was ashamed that so many of his countrymen were criminals. It went fine for a few weeks until Luigi was asked to deliver notes. Neither of the brothers could read or write in Italian or English. Luigi, however, was quick to learn how to speak English. Luigi was told to copy the notes in his own hand, something he thought strange, but Rossi told him that he should learn to write. He saw the number on the notes and believed what he was told, that they were tobacco bills. One day Rossi told Luigi the real nature of those letters. They were letters asking for money and signed by the Black Hand. Luigi was now trapped. There were many witnesses who would remember Luigi and identify him as a Black Hand mobster. If Rossi was ever suspected or if Luigi ever went to the police, Rossi would say that he too had been a victim of the Black Hand and that Francella was delivering notes to him as well. Rossi convinced Francella that nobody would believe him should he go to the police and that Rossi, due to his successful business and many years in this country without incident, would not be suspected of any wrongdoing. In this way, Luigi was blackmailed into setting off dynamite at a barbershop in January and in that blast, someone was killed. Now, he was a murderer and firmly bound in the clutches of Rossi. The dynamite they used was acquired from someone that Luigi worked with while as a ditch digger. Rossi never revealed himself to anyone. Luigi Francella was the only face that victims saw. Francella worked in the back of the tobacco shop and was never allowed to come into the main entrance. Now he, Luigi Francella, and not Rossi, had killed someone. Luigi became desperate. One day, Luigi decided to confront Rossi. He walked into the shop from the front entrance. He argued with Rossi and said that he had had enough.

Luigi threatened to go to the police, but never did. He was too afraid. Rossi was a big baseball fan as was Luigi himself. When Mathewson had lost a close game earlier in the season, something tipped inside of Rossi and the bombings became sort of a vent or a release of frustration for Rossi. It became a game. When another innocent person died in an explosion that Luigi had set, Luigi decided that he would use less dynamite to do less damage. Once someone had paid up, but Luigi was still instructed to bomb the shop anyway and it was at this point that Luigi and his brother plotted on how they would kill Rossi. They didn't want to intentionally kill anyone, but they felt trapped and they knew that Rossi was not reasonable. Rossi was a dangerous man. They convinced themselves that if he were dead, the bombings would stop and people would not die. Also, they were afraid of Rossi because he seemed less sure of Luigi since Luigi had threatened Rossi about wanting to quit. The last time Rocco saw his brother was in early August. Luigi was going to talk to Rossi about leaving, promising to never say anything to anybody. If Rossi did not agree to let him go, then Luigi would kill Rossi. He never saw his brother again. All of this was done through sign language as Petrosino and Muldoon stood by politely, not asking questions, until Rocco had seemed tired and unwilling to go on.

Petrosino remembered watching Rossi and Francella through the window. He imitated the motion that Luigi made towards Rossi. He brought his fingers together, close to his own nose, flicked his wrists and mimicked a claw, pointing towards Fitzpatrick.

"Enough sir? Enough of what?"

"I saw Luigi do this to Rossi, but at the time I did not understand that it was sign language. Luigi used sign so much that he sometimes used it to express himself in verbal speech." Turning to Rocco he asked, "Tell me, why haven't you earned enough money to afford a better place than this?" Fitzpatrick signed.

Rocco responded, and Fitzpatrick related, "After Rossi told Luigi that he was sending Black Hand notes, he stopped paying him. He did not stop giving him some chewing tobacco, but that was all he got. It made us more reliant on Rossi than ever. At the end my brother wished that he had never left the ditch digging. Even the Irishman would never have done what this dago, er Italian, sorry sir, had done."

"This tobacco that you are talking about, the stuff that is given to him by Rossi, is there any around the house?"

"Yes, we keep it here."

Rocco produced a bag of tobacco and handed it to Petrosino. Immediately he identified the Redman Chew.

"Can we have some of this?"

"You can have as much as you like."

"Muldoon take this, we may use it for evidence."

"Mr. Taylor, ask Rocco what he will do now."

"He has no idea, sir," replied Fitzpatrick.

"Fitzpatrick," said Petrosino, reaching into one of his inner pockets, "here is twenty dollars. I want you to clean Rocco up, buy him some new clothes and take him to see James Hazen Hyde. Tell Hyde that Petrosino sends him. I'm sure Hyde will have a job for this man. There is plenty of work that a silent man can do. Also, arrange for housing. He will not stay in this squalor another night! Also, Fitzpatrick, if I hear the word Dago again from you, you will be put behind a desk and no one will be able to get you out from under it. Is that understood?"

"Clearly, sir."

When Petrosino's plan was revealed through the signing of Fitzpatrick, Rocco seemed stunned. Here was something he had always wished for, yet his brother was not here to share his happiness. Such mercy amidst such pain! It was too much to comprehend. Rocco cried, out of sadness or deep gratitude.

"Mr. Taylor, we must go. Please take care of Rocco. Maybe he can stay with you tonight? When he is ready, you know where to find Muldoon," said Petrosino through Fitzpatrick.

Automatically, Dummy Taylor signed, "Yes, sir."

The policeman left the two friends alone, one sobbing in his hands, the other a deaf pitcher for the New York Giants signing, instead of shouting after Petrosino, "Thank you, sir!"

Saturday August 26, 1905

After winning the first game of a doubleheader against Cincinnati by 2-0, the Giants play a close one in the second game. The bases are loaded for the Cincinnati club in the bottom of the ninth. The Giants have a 6-4 lead. McGraw pulls McGinnity and puts Matty on the mound who shuts the Cincinnati nine down.

Monday August 28, 1905

Matty wins his fifth straight and his twenty third overall against St. Louis 8-1. The Giants are now 8 ½ games ahead of the Pirates.

Friday September 1, 1905

Matty strikes out nine in a three-hitter against Philadelphia to up his season record to 24-7.

Monday September 4, 1905

Matty wins his 25th game despite giving up five runs to Philadelphia in the second. The game is called in the eighth inning on account of darkness, but the Giants bats hammered the Philadelphia pitchers and the Giants come away with a 11-6 victory for Matty.

Thursday September 7, 1905

Matty pitches a three hit gem and wins the second game of a twin bill at the Polo Grounds against Boston 3-0.

18

In New York City, a woman is arrested for smoking a cigarette in an automobile.

"You can't do that on Fifth Avenue!" the arresting officer says.
New York Times 1905.

The bell tinkled above the door to Rossi's shop as Petrosino entered the place for the third time. He slammed the door behind him and the glass in the door shook with violence and warning. Petrosino was prepared to arrest Rossi.

Rossi, finely dressed as usual looked up from behind the back counter and smiled, the left hand disappeared into his dark, finely tailored coat pocket and his right hand holding his distinctive walking stick.

"Ah, Mr. Petrosino, I was just on my way out."

Petrosino stood in front of the same counter when he had waited in disguise for Rossi to bring him the Redman chewing tobacco. Petrosino began, "You are under arrest Mr. Rossi for the murders of Luigi Francella and Mr. Michael Mattarrazzo. You are also under arrest as an accomplice to the murder of Richie Venuto, and a Ms. Palmer who died at Iannocone's meats."

"You are not as smart as you think, Guiseppe!" Rossi pulled a Leather Billy from his pocket, a nine-inch, nine-ounce revolver that was small and quiet, but effective. "You are a fool to come here alone! I was checking my pocket for this handy little pistol when I saw you come in."

"Why did you kill Francella?"

"The Great detective does not know? I will tell you. He laughed and sneered with all the assurance of a cat that has a mouse trapped. I saw you in the dugout at the Giants game. I saw you communicate with Dummy Taylor. I knew that Taylor was friends with Francella. That idiot Francella bragged about it all the time. After I killed Mattarrazzo, yes it was me hiding in the park that night who had killed Mattarrazzo, and saw you as the rag picker reveal himself to be the Great Petrosino! After Mattarrazzo, Francella became increasingly uneasy and reluctant about doing business. Francella wanted to leave me and I couldn't allow that to happen. To finish this business, I will now kill you. You were that Spanish gentleman that requested Redman, were you not? He paused and glared at Petrosino. Your silence betrays you, fool! At first, you did have me deceived, but when I saw you as the rag picker, I realized that the coincidence was too much. Nobody knows I have access to Redman tobacco except for the men on the list I gave you and none of them knew any Spanish gentleman. All of us, McGraw, Hyde, Thompson, would meet occasionally to gamble on horses. I have been looking forward to killing you for quite some time."

"You kill with… such nonchalance!" said Petrosino.

"I was planning to accuse Francella of fabricating the whole story about me. I would say that he was blackmailing me and threatened me with death if I should tell the police. This would explain his presence here and my being seen with him. Who would believe that scum? Why should I, the owner of such a fine shop, bother with crime? I don't need the money. He always had the dynamite, I never touched it, except to kill him. Besides, I am from the north of Italy. I am not one of his kind!" Here, Rossi paused as if wondering whether to go on. "But you are relentless, and you may have found me out sooner or later, so I decided to blow up my own shop to avoid suspicion." When this shop is blown up, I will produce Black Hand letters and contradict everything Luigi said. It would in the end be my word against his. Yes, he is dead, but I had a story for this as well, I could convince the investigators that Francella bungled the use of the dynamite, but he has an accomplice, which I have never seen but was told about and he must have bombed my shop! You see, I had it all planned."

"But did you know that he had a brother who told me everything?"

"Bah! I would still contend that the story had been made up! I would say he created a clever ruse to hide his own guilt!"

"Did you really believe that the Black Hand ruse would work?" asked the detective, thinking about possible outcomes to this unfortunate situation.

"You yourself asked me if the Black Hand had bothered me. This led me to believe that for the time being I was above suspicion. It also led me to believe that you did not suspect our high stakes gambling club. Dundy, Hyde, and McGraw were all high stakes gamblers. We gambled on everything. They sent someone to me with a sealed envelope which held the wager. I never communicated by note. They sent wagers to me and I sent Redman to them as a sign that I got the bet. Even their winnings were sent in sealed tobacco tins. They were all so busy and we did not want to be seen together. We thought we had a good system and we did until Dundy panicked when you questioned him. He thought you were after us for our high stakes gambling."

"You will… never get away with this!"

"You are mistaken once again. There is dynamite in the front of my shop. It is at the end of a very long fuse. There is enough dynamite to blow this building to nothing! You will die in the blast. People will think you died from the Black Hand. Do you know why I did it? Why I got that Francella to bomb for me?" questioned Rossi, almost proud of his cunning and novelty.

"You love the New York Giants and especially Christy Mathewson. Whenever he lost a game you would… vent your anger by ordering Luigi to blow up a shop, even one that had paid you. You are.., a sore loser. You are sick."

Rossi smiled, lips pressed together he slowed his speech by becoming thoughtful. "At first, I wanted to see if I could control Francella, bend him to my will. I did it for the control I could have, the power I could have over another human being. Then it became boring. But, one day I became so upset from thinking how McGraw refused to play in the World Series last year and all the money I could have won that I decided to blow up a shop. Francella set the dynamite for me. It did relieve the tension I was feeling."

"Now I understand," said Petrosino. "Fassett had told me that Francella had said, 'he should have played.' I didn't know what he meant but now I know he was referring to McGraw refusing to play the 1904 series!"

The conversation took a turn and it almost seemed as if two friends were talking about ordinary things.

"After that temporary relief, I realized that venting my frustration in this way did help. Soon I became angry again. I felt distraught over Christy Mathewson's losses. Francella walked into the shop and I was so angry about that loss, that I told him to go immediately and bomb Iannacone's Meats. I was angry because the Giants should have won. Also, that damned Iannacone kept his finger on the scale when he was weighing my meat! Mathewson loses a game 2-1 at the Polo Grounds, against Boston! Against Irv Young who is, at best, a mediocre pitcher. I think your mind Petrosino can appreciate the irony of that first loss and the fact that games like that are unacceptable!"

"Unacceptable? When innocent people die as a result of your madness, that is what is truly unacceptable." Petrosino spoke with a grim tone, his mind racing, thinking of alternatives, wondering how a shot from a thirty five cent Leather Billy would feel.

"Well, Iannacone and the rest of them should have paid. Iannacone should have been honest. This became a game for me and they lost the game."

"A game?"

"Yes, a game like baseball. Baseball is an infinitely interesting game. I am sure a mind like yours would appreciate all the subtleties.

However, when the Giants lose, when Mathewson loses I am very upset." Here he paused, "but I never hit women, I order someone's place of business to be bombed. I could never hit a woman."

"Why Mathewson? Why not the Iron Man?"

"Mathewson elevates the game. He is after all, the Christian Gentleman just as the newspapers refer to him. He is well read, a scholar and a fine athlete. He compensates for some of the Irish trash in the game. He paused again, "enough of this," said Rossi, fingering the pistol.

Petrosino wanted to keep him talking.

"Mattarrazzo whispered 'Bug' before he died. I didn't know what it meant at first, but I learned from an interview I had with Donlin that bug is another word for fan. You were the fan he was talking about. You gave Mattarrazzo the Redman Chew the day you met him at the Polo Grounds. You sat next to him but you left early. Mattarrazzo has a photo of that day. The empty seat next to him was yours. You are the bug he referred to when he died in my arms. He recognized you that night in Jeanette Park as you recognized him."

"You are clever, but not clever enough. I am after all, holding the gun," Rossi smirked, unable to conceal his triumph.

Petrosino calculated outcomes, and tried a semi bluff, "When they find me here with a bullet in my chest, they will become suspicious. Justice will have the final word. For such a man as myself, there will be an autopsy. They will find a bullet and all suspicion will focus on you. You cannot escape justice."

Suddenly, Rossi swung the cane like a baseball bat. For a small, stout man the detective was nimble. As he ducked, Rossi adjusted his swing halfway and connected with Petrosino's head. The detective, who had been holding on to his derby, became dizzy and tried to maintain his balance. Rossi leaned over the counter and swung again. This was a direct hit and the detective slumped to the floor, feigning unconsciousness. Had he not been wearing his protective padding underneath the derby, the damage would have been severe.

Rossi moved around the counter and began to arrange the dynamite in the front of the shop. He lit the fuse. The bell jingled above the door as Rossi exited by slamming the door shut. Petrosino, on the floor, reached for his flask of Sambuca which he carried at all times to revive himself and others. He unscrewed the top and gulped down twice. The detective dropped the flask and steadied himself on the counter, blood, trickling down his face. He knew the dynamite would go any minute. He had no time to try to stop the detonation. Everything was spinning. He felt his hands shake. His knees were weak. He vomited. He moved along the shop using the counter as a hand rail. He was unsteady and tried to keep moving. When he reached the front door, he vomited again. He opened the door, the bell tinkled he saw Rossi at the end of the street, hopping into a horse drawn cab. Petrosino became dizzy.

The backup police officer, who had been flirting across the street and had missed Rossi coming out, rushed to the wounded detective.

"Keep everyone away. There will be an explosion. Stay across the street, far from the building. Keep people safe." was all Petrosino could say. Feeling the fresh air, he felt a little better. He approached a hay transport standing nearby. He looked up at the driver, his face bloodied, his voice struggling to be audible.

"Police. I want you to discreetly follow that cab, you will be rewarded handsomely."

"Which cab?" asked the confused but delighted cabbie to have such an interesting encounter, a good story for the supper time, and the promise of extra money for an extra pint.

The dark one closest to the White Wings, just pulling out."

The detective climbed onto the flat wooden platform and lay among strands of hay. "When he stops, you stop at a distance. Tell me what he does. He must not see me," said the detective, laying at the flat of his back and talking to the sky. As they slowly moved from the curb to join the stream of light traffic, a terrific boom occurred with shattering glass. People began shouting. Petrosino hoped that the policeman had done his job correctly this time. Later he would find out that the flirting policeman had lost his life in the blast. But, at the moment, all he could think was that Muldoon would never have allowed Rossi to escape. These were his thoughts as he fought off unconsciousness.

"Keep driving," ordered the detective.

"When I put me life in danger, sure it will cost a wee bit more than what ye may be thinkin'," replied the driver, apparently enjoying the excitement.

"Come to the police precinct on Mulberry Street and mention the explosion on Pearl Street. There will be an envelope for you with money in it. The amount depends on how pleased I am about the outcome of this little chase," said the exhausted detective, forcing the words in a voice barely above a hoarse whisper.

"Then I'll hav to make sur yer well pleased."

"Your horse is very calm, sir," said the detective, feeling sick again.

"She's deaf, so nothing spooks her."

Meanwhile Rossi, admiring his cane, heard the blast and despite losing his shop, he smiled at the thought of having outwitted the master detective.

Petrosino started to feel sleepy again. He fought to stay awake. He

134

knew he must not sleep, must not let Rossi get away.

"Follow him at all costs," he whispered and rolled over so that his shoulder touched the platform. The blood formed lines down the side of his face and stained his collar. Some pedestrians stopped and stared at the strange sight. He became dizzy and vomited again. Then, everything went black.

The next morning, Petrosino woke up in a hospital on West 59th Street and the corner of Amsterdam Ave. A doctor looked down at him.

"Rest, Lieutenant. I spoke with Police Officer Muldoon, so the Commissioner knows you are here in Sloane Maternity. I am to call them as soon as you are able to have visitors. You are our only male patient over one month old." The doctor chuckled at his own joke and smiled at his patient.

"Where is the cab driver?" What day and time is it?" questioned the master detective.

"It is September 11 and just about 5:30 am. I liked your derby Lieutenant, that extra padding saved your life. You have been out for awhile but you will be alright. Nothing very serious, but you need rest. The cabby's been here all along. He is a fine fellow. He brought you here, and considering your condition, we had to take you in even though this is a maternity ward.

"I must speak with the cabby," said Petrosino, as he lifted himself up a bit to adjust his posture to a sitting position.

The doctor studied him, "How important is this?"

"Lives are in danger!"

"I'll send him in, but not too long, you need rest."

Petrosino noticed that he was still wearing his clothing and his hat and shoes were nearby. The room was small, clean, and private.

The cabby walked into the room. A sincere Irishman with jet black hair and happy green eyes, he dressed in dark clothes and black shoes that were well worn and in sharp contrast to the white backdrop of the walls and floor. His hands were those of a laborer and his ruddy complexion hinted that he had spent many days working outdoors. He was very deferential in his approach towards Petrosino.

"I've been saying the beads for ye ever since ye passed out on me wagon. You look much better."

"Thank you," said Petrosino. "What happened to the man you were following?"

"Well, when I first noticed that you were passed out, I decided to follow him, feeling that he had something to do with that awful explosion on Pearl Street. I followed 'im all the way to 59th Street. He got out of his cab and walked into St. Paul the Apostle Church. It's a magnificent church. I was there last Easter and I will never forget the music. They had trumpet players there! Anyway, after he went into the church, I started to think about what to do with you. This hospital was the closest one and I felt that they would not turn you away. I don't know where the man we were following went after he entered the church."

"Help me with my clothes. I must go to Saint Paul the Apostle." The cabby did not argue but immediately began to assist Petrosino with his shoes.

"I don't see any socks, who took your socks?" was all the cabby could say.

Petrosino steadied himself as the cabby helped him with his jacket.

The polite cabby helped Petrosino to the door.

"Wait a minute!" shouted the doctor as soon as they appeared. "You can't go anywhere."

"This is police business."

"I just spoke to Muldoon, he is on his way."

"Tell him I am at St. Paul the Apostle Church on 60th Street."

"But you are not ready for this, you need rest."

"I am going to St. Paul the Apostle Church."

"Where are his socks?" persisted the cabby.

"Forget the socks. I already have my shoes on," replied Petrosino.

The doctor, having read about Lieutenant Petrosino in the papers, was a secret admirer of the great detective. "It is against my better judgment." He stepped aside and let him pass.

"Is your horse ready?" asked Petrosino, turning to the cabby, who was now fully involved in the adventure.

"He's chompin' at the bit."

"Good, take me to St. Paul's."

19

"Accidents there have been on railroads far removed from centers of population, so gruesome and terrible that the printed descriptions of them have failed to convey to the human mind the real horrors. This one, occurring in the very center of the greatest city in America, contains elements that the human mind can scarcely realize."
The New York World, September 12, 1905

"As the car struck the sidewalk a big hole was torn in its roof, now hanging over the street, and through this dropped the bodies of several men mangled beyond recognition."
New York Times, September 12, 1905

At close to 6:40 on the morning of Monday September 11, 1905, Lieutenant Petrosino rolled off the wooden flat bed of the hay cart and stood in front of St. Paul the Apostle Church. Petrosino looked up at the statue of Saul knocked off his horse and in a perpetual state of being blinded by the angel. Petrosino wondered if he been blind to anything in this case.

"You wait here," he told the hay dealer/laborer turned cabby. "If you see Rossi, try to stop him, but be careful."

Petrosino entered one of the largest churches in Manhattan. Why would a murderer like Rossi come here? Petrosino crossed himself, his head was still hurting. He felt weak but he tried not to think about it. He splashed holy water on his face. He put some more around his neck, praying as he did so. He needed to revive himself. He felt dizzy. He felt as if he would collapse. Petrosino sat in one of the pews to collect himself. He sat near the Altar of the Annunciation. Carved by Nicolo Antenucci in Chieti, Italy, it depicts the pregnant Mary, arms outstretched. Petrosino knew this statue well.

School children from the nearby Catholic School were lighting candles in front of the church as a nun looked on. Petrosino prayed for help.

A man who had been cleaning the floor approached.

"Are you alright? You look sick." The man stood, arms akimbo, and stared at the detective.

Petrosino, wearing his crumpled, blood-stained clothes held his head and sort of waved the man off and mumbled, "I am looking for a man named Rossi."

The cleaner straightened up. "I can take you to him."

Petrosino got up and said, "No, Rossi!"

"Yes, this way."

With the excitement of this news, adrenaline filled his body and renewed his strength. The cleaner directed the metal pail filled with gray, pine smelling water towards a side altar with his left foot. It made a loud noise in the early morning church as it scraped along the stone floor. He then led the detective past the school children toward the front of the church. Rossi was a very dangerous man. An encounter with Rossi now would not be in the detective's favor, but Petrosino must not allow the terrorist to strike again.

The cleaner led him to the sacristy. A priest was there alone.

The cleaning man spoke first. "Fr. Rossi, there is someone here to see you."

Fr. Rossi turned to look at the detective.

The smile of Fr. Rossi disappeared as his eyes met Petrosino's. The priest was a large man. In appearance, he was not at all like the Rossi that Petrosino knew. This man was bulky under his white alb, and his overall appearance was not as polished as the Rossi who owned the tobacco shop.

"Father, I am with the police. I am here about Anthony Rossi."

The priest replied, "I am preparing for the 7AM mass, so I do not have much time. My brother is coming here soon. Do what you have to do, but please do it outside of the church. You can wait for him at the main entrance. Go quickly so as to avoid a scuffle in the House of God."

"Thank you, Father Rossi."

"What is your name?"

"Petrosino."

"Yes, I knew that," Rossi kissed the stole before wrapping it around his neck. "I will offer up the mass for you and my brother. I am sorry. My brother is a mystery to me."

Without a word, the detective turned and walked quickly down the cavernous interior of the church to get to the front door.

Petrosino opened the door and saw Rossi bounding up the church steps. Rossi saw him, froze for a moment with mouth wide open in astonishment, and turned and fled. The cabby that was watching and waiting for the tobacconist, approached Rossi and awkwardly put his arms out, but was not quick enough to avoid the heavy cane. Rossi expertly swung the stick like a baseball bat and hit the cabby in the face without slowing his stride. Churchgoers entering St. Paul the Apostle for the morning mass, cried out when they saw the commotion. They froze, not understanding the bizarre and unexpected behavior on the church steps. The cabby staggered, holding to his face his hands unable to hold back the flowing blood. Petrosino followed Rossi, feeling dizzy again. Rossi ran down the crowded sidewalk and mounted the steps to the elevated southbound Ninth Avenue train.

Petrosino slowed due to his head injuries and he feared that the elusive Rossi would escape yet again. The cabby regained his composure and followed Petrosino by about ten yards, at a slow pace.

On the platform, unsuspecting morning commuters waited for the downtown train. Rossi made his way to the platform just as the train was pulling in to the 59th Street Station. The train screeched to a halt, and then lurched forward a bit, before finally stopping. Rossi paused and waited to spot his pursuer. Petrosino, holding the railing, arrived on the top step just as the doors opened. People rushed onto the platform and into the train. Rossi entered the train with the crowd. The detective went around the turnstile and into the nearest door in the car behind Rossi. The cabby, now feeling better, ran around Petrosino and entered the same car as Rossi just as the doors closed. The train pulled out of the station. Petrosino steadied himself on the shoulder of a woman with a baby in her arms before he began to move through the crowds to the front of the car. Passengers looked at Petrosino and some moved aside to let the unshaven, disheveled man by. The train quickly picked up speed. Faster and faster it went. The detective made it halfway through the car when there was a terrific crash. Suddenly, panic erupted and fear gripped everyone, causing some to shout. The subway car lunged forward. Brakes screeched. Glass shattered. Bodies slid and fell to the front of the car. Another thunderous crash occured, more powerful and louder than the first. With both hands, the detective held onto the floor pole. People screamed. The lady was separated from her baby. People pulled at each other. Another loud crash added to the confusion and terror. Petrosino tried to focus. The train had stopped, but it was at a strange angle. Petrosino looked to the next car, but it was not there. Instead, there was an empty space and people were falling into it and disappearing. Blood was everywhere, smeared on the train floor. Petrosino did not know if it was his own blood. Somehow, glass was in his hand. He thought of the crinkling glass at Fassett's barbershop and remembered how the chill of that night. He became cold. He shivered. He saw someone else fall through the void, the hole where the train should have been. He wondered if going through that hole would be better than this hell. Someone had jumped out of their bench seat and had fallen through the void. Petrosino now crawled on top of the seat, afraid to face the gaping hole. Crying, moaning, cursing, pleading, praying and groaning came together to form a chorus that had never before been heard in New York City. This mangled moaning is what Petrosino heard when he lost consciousness.

A policeman, who had been standing in the street, was killed when the first car of the train ran off the tracks separating itself from the second car. It then hit a building and landed in the street. Eyewitnesses noted bodies as they splattered on the street below. Heads looked like exploding tomatoes when they hit the pavement. There was some silence between the terrible sounds of destruction and chaos and the ensuing sounds of frantic rescue. It was this in-between silence that was truly remarkable. The sounds of metal, glass, screaming and some new sounds that could never really be described were so incongruous with the usual way of life that people that witnessed it thought they were witnessing the end of the world. It was the silence however, that followed this hellish growl and preceded the panicked response and recovery that was most memorable. The intense noise made the silence that much more surreal. It seemed as if someone had turned off the volume of the world. There was no bird sounds, no traffic noise, no voices, no footsteps, no breeze, no breathing. It was as if the city had received a terrific blow to the head, and was at the point of unconsciousness. The city held its breath and paused, and almost stopped, but New York held on and righted itself. Although groggy and disoriented, it held on and slowly sounds came back, tentative at first, unsure but then determined and with purpose.

Father Rossi was saying mass when he heard the sounds of hell.

"*Et clamor meus ad te veniat*," said the priest.

Someone ran into the church and screamed, "There's been a train wreck! The train left the tracks!"

Some of the congregation departed the church running, but Fr. Rossi continued. After the last communicant received the Eucharist, Father Rossi ended the mass, remained in his vestments, and mumbled his prayers. He fingered his rosary beads while making quick strides to the scene unfolding a few blocks south.

Muldoon received the message sent by Petrosinio and was approaching the church, when the elevated train suddenly left the tracks, then hit the building nearby and landed in the street. Screeching brakes and screeching humans mingled with the sounds of crunching metal and the incredible bang of subway cars on pavement. Muldoon froze and looked. Bodies spilled from the second car, falling in freefall and becoming squashed on impact with the sidewalk. Instantly body parts appeared everywhere.

Muldoon, for the first time in his career, paused in his duties toward his superior. The site held him transfixed. He overcame his initial shock and sprang into action. With great discipline, he ran towards the church and asked the first priest he saw, who was running out of the church about Petrosino.

"He left before mass started," said Fr. Rossi.

Muldoon ran down the steps and towards the incomprehensible. When he arrived, the second car hung over the tracks and seemed as if it still might fall. The dead were everywhere. Soon the area was filled with people. Stunned onlookers and helpful citizens were joined by police officers, firefighters, priests and eventually medics and newspapermen. Muldoon felt that the people of the second car, if they were still alive, would need the most assistance but would be the most difficult to reach. With priests delivering last rites to those that had fallen or were in the first car and ambulance personnel covering the dead, Muldoon climbed the stairs and went out onto the elevated track. People formed a slow but steady column along the tracks going the opposite way as Muldoon, like a fish swimming against the current, boldly approached the train. He entered and attempted to reach the second car overhanging the street. The closer he came to the second car, the more injuries and more shock and traumas he saw. He was descending into a horizontal hell of increasing madness and pain. In the third car he saw, hunched between seats, was the unmistakable form of Lieutenant Petrosino.

"Jesus Mary and Joseph!" was all he could say as he rushed to his fallen friend.

Petrosino was unconscious, but still alive. Muldoon boomed, "We need a doctor here now! We have a policeman down!" But there was no doctor. No one paid any attention. Everyone crouched in their own safe haven between the seats. Some were crying and shaking, others were unconscious or dead. Muldoon carefully lifted his friend and carried him. It was a superhuman effort to carry the detective back up the slant of the train. He carried him through the train car, momentarily rested in the next car, and then continued across the tracks, down the stairs and finally, gently laid him in the street amidst the noise and confusion. Other people were being placed in the street on gray Civil War blankets that someone had spread on the ground. Muldoon knelt and was transfixed on the unconscious form of his friend. He pulled away and yelled, "We have a policeman down! We need a medic now!"

Hours later, a medic pronounced that he would live and bandaged the head and hand of the detective. Petrosino woke to see Fr. Rossi staring at him. Behind the priest loomed Muldoon.

"Your brother..," began the detective, when he saw the priest.

"He was killed in the wreck. He was in the first car, the car that fell to the sidewalk and he is among the dead," said Fr. Rossi.

"What about the cabby who helped me?"

"We haven't identified him yet, sir," offered Muldoon.

Petrosino was attended to again, his wounds examined and rewrapped, with his vital signs checked and found stable. It was agreed that he could go home. However, Petrosino wanted to go to the West Forty Seventh Street Station to identify the dead. Muldoon and Petrosino said goodbye to Fr. Rossi and slowly walked down to the station.

"Sir, I have bad news," said Muldoon as they walked down Ninth Avenue.

"Yes," said Petrosino, his head bandaged and his right arm in a sling.

"We lost two men in the wreck. An officer Aiken, who was hit with the train as it fell to the ground, and a Joseph Bach of the Arsenal Station in Central Park. Bach died when he got to the hospital."

"What other information do you have?" asked Petrosino grimly.

"It was the southbound train sir. It went through the light and was going too fast around the curve. We are looking right now for motorman Kelly. He has disappeared. Kelly is from St. Louis, so we have all outbound trains being watched as well as all ferries."

They reached the station where the bodies were kept to be identified. There was crying and screaming that could be heard from quite a distance and as they approached, it became louder and more real.

When the coroner in charge saw the policemen, he went right over to them.

"Gentleman, we have ten dead and more I suspect. I've never seen anything like it. I must warn you. Some of the bodies were mangled beyond recognition. Whom did you come to identify?"

Petrosino remained silent. He surveyed the scene with the eye of a detective.

"This is Lieutenant Petrosino. We are here to look at the bodies. The lieutenant was in the wreck himself and he is looking for two males," volunteered Muldoon.

"Yes. Well, the males are here. Feel free to look."

Petrosino could see the expensive shoes worn by Rossi protruding from the blanket. He thought of Richie Venuto's body under the barber towel at Sam Fassett's. To make sure, he picked up the blanket and looked at the deceased. Rossi's face and body were severely battered. Petrosino's positive identification of Rossi came from the fine clothing, once impeccable, now tattered and bloodied. He let the blanket drop. In death, they were all the same, lifeless. The contents of the pockets, the quality of the clothes, what did it matter now? Petrosino looked for the tired shoes of the good cabby. They were behind him. He lifted the blanket and saw the surprisingly fresh face of the cabby.

The coroner approached. "He is the only one I've managed to clean at this point. He was the cleanest to begin with and well, my resources here are quite limited, as you can imagine."

"Has the family been here yet?" asked Petrosino.

"No."

"If anyone arrives, I want you to send them to me at Police Headquarters at Mulberry Street. Can you remember it?"

"Yes. Of course. I'll leave a note on the body for the next coroner."

"Let's go, Muldoon. I've seen what I was looking for."

October 4: In other baseball news, Honus Wagner of the Pirates and Cy Semour of the Reds are one point apart in season batting average. Their teams play each other in a double header on the last day. Wagner goes 2 for 7 and ends the season batting .363. Seymour is 4 for 7 and wins the National League batting title with a .373 average.

20

"When we clinch the National League pennant, we'll be champions of the only real major league."
-John McGraw, when asked why his club refused to play the 1904 World Series

The Giants are... "one collection of peerless ball tossers."
The New York Times October 15, 1905

October 9, 1905
Philadelphia owner Ben Shibe won the coin toss. The first World Series game to be played in two years would be in Philadelphia. Eighteen thousand bugs were in attendance. The Giants created a stir with their new uniforms, which were a bit intimidating. The new, all black jerseys had a large NY in white covering the chest and were complimented with white caps and white belts. They were in sharp contrast to the tired gray wool uniforms that had seen a year of play and now hung like old rags worn by the Athletics. Christy Mathewson would take the mound for the NL Champions and the lefthander Eddie Plank would represent the AL team. Plank was 25-12 on the season with a 2.26 ERA, not quite Matty's 31-9 and league leading 1.27 ERA, but pretty formidable anyway. The pitchers dominated until the Giants half of the fifth. Mathewson opened with a single. Bresnahan forced Matty and stole second. After Browne popped to the shortstop, Donlin singled to left scoring Bresnahan from second. The throw home wasn't close and it enabled Donlin to take second. McGann walked and Mertes then doubled scoring Donlin. Dahlen flied to left to end the inning. The Giants got an insurance run in the ninth to make it 3-0, but didn't need it. Matty pitched a four-hit shutout while striking out six to get his first Series win.

October 10, 1905
Charles "Chief" Bender, a member of the Ojibwa tribe, evened the score at the Polo Grounds against the Iron Man. The twenty-one year old Chief was 18-11 on the year with a 2.83 ERA. The thirty-four year old McGinnity was 21-15 with a 2.87 ERA. The Chief, who was later credited with inventing the slider, threw a four hitter, with Turkey Mike Donlin getting two of them. For the "white elephants," Topsy Hartsel and Ossee Shreckengost were the catalysts behind the 3-0

144

Philadelphia win.

October 12, 1905

Back in Philadelphia, Dummy Taylor missed a start on October 11 due to wet grounds. Some said the small turnout of 4,000 fans was the real reason for the postponement. This gave Matty a chance to pitch on two day's rest. This turned out to be the most lopsided score of the Series. McGann led the way for the Giants by driving in four runs on three hits. The final was 9-0 with Matty pitching a four-hit shutout, now 2-0 in the Series. Andy Coakley was on the losing end for Philadelphia. New York went ahead in games 2-1.

October 13, 1905

McGinnity faced Plank in the fourth game of the World Series. The two combined for a classic pitching duel. Each team had only five hits and the Giants lone run came in the fourth was unearned. In the Giants fourth, Mertes reached first on an error and after Dahlen flied out, Mertes advanced to second on the groundout by Devlin. Gilbert then singled to left and Mertes scored. In their half of the eighth the A's had Hartsel on third with two out but McGinnity got Seybold to strike out, preserving the 1-0 score. The Giants left for New York leading the series 3 games to 1.

October 14, 1905

Men hung on fences and sat on the grandstand roof. Fans perched atop distant poles and houses with black spy glasses in hand to view their beloved Giants from afar. Boys of all ages risked punishment for spending all day at the Polo Grounds. They squeezed between legs and ducked under the view of taller men. Being agile and small, boys found watching points not accessible to their fathers, big brothers, and uncles. When McGraw appeared, some in the crowd yelled, "Clinch it today Mac!" He tipped his hat in recognition. Behind home plate, the boxer and team friend, Gentleman Jim Corbett posed with Bresnahan and the Irish flag. Corbett, a Giants fan and the former world heavyweight champion at six feet one inch, proved an imposing figure. A carnival-like, almost giddy atmosphere pervaded the park. Fans expected their team to clinch the championship at home. There was singing, hugging, laughing, and yelling. The Giants exuded confidence.

There was one major obstacle to the plans of the thousands who packed the stadium on this cold day. Charles "Chief" Bender, the twenty-one-year-old was an fine hurler and winner of game two who proved that he could handle the Giants. In his private life, Bender was a kind gentleman. In the pitcher's box, Bender was an intelligent, aggressive competitor. The Chief would need some run support from the Philadelphia team. In their three previous losses, they had been blanked all three times. Not one player wearing the big A had crossed the plate.

Hartsel opened the game with a single to left but the A's could do no more damage. In their half of the first, the home team went down in order with three ground outs.

The Athletics got two hits in the second but the leadoff man died after Murphy hit into a double play. Cross followed the double kill with a single of his own and was caught trying to steal second on a fine throw by Bresnahan. The Giants got a single in their second and another single in the third. The fourth inning was also silent and the suspense and excitement of the pitching duel between Matty and Bender became the focus of the game.

Mertes walked to lead off the Giants half of the fifth. Dahlen walked sending Mertes to second. Devlin advanced the runners to second and third with a bunt. Gilbert hit the ball off of the end of the bat for a sacrifice fly. At the same time Dahlen was caught at third and the inning ended, but not before the Giants got that all-important run. The fans delighted in the way Mathewson was pitching. The A's responded in their half of the fifth with a single and no more. In the sixth, Mertes struck out with two on. Things were quiet until the bottom of the eighth. Gilbert lined out to center for the first out. Then Matty walked. With their star pitcher at first, Bresnahan came to the plate. The catcher was 4 for 13 at this point in the Series. "Swat it off the earth!" someone yelled.

Bresnahan loaded up on dirt and looked carefully at the fat end of the bat. He extended the drama. "Put it in a balloon Roger and send it away for good!" yelled some bug. Bresnahan doubled, sending Matty to third. The way Bender was pitching, most fans felt that Matty had to score for an insurance run. Browne was up next, and he smacked it back to Bender, who tried to grab it with his bare hand. It deflected off his hand and the infielder got Browne at first, but Matty scored from third for the second run of the game. Turkey Mike ended the inning by striking out. In the bottom of the ninth, Matty induced three ground outs and the World Series of 1905 was history.

The crowd celebrated, clapped, sang, and ran all over the field. Petrosino ended the season ·as he had begun it, next to the Commissioner, field glasses in hand.

"Great game! Great team!" bellowed McAdoo.

Petrosino handed the glasses back to McAdoo without looking at him. The great detective took everything in.

"I saw the report you filed on the bomber case, good job. Thank God you weren't killed on September 11.

Petrosino looked at his commander. "What are you going to do about McGraw?'

"What do you mean?" asked McAdoo, knowing what Petrosino meant.

"It's in the report. McGraw throws games, and bets illegally."

"Look, the police of Gotham have a hard job. We need public opinion behind us. To go after McGraw for those things would hurt our reputation. The press would be all over us. The public would who knows what. Besides, McGraw can get the best lawyers money can buy and they would find a way to get him off."

Petrosino looked at him, "But no one is above the law."

McAdoo said, "Yes, true, but if we go after McGraw it would hurt us in other areas."

"If it were my choice, I would arrest him. If it weren't for your order, I would arrest him."

"Yes, and I am repeating that order now, hands off McGraw! Look, I wish more of my men were like you. I do admire your integrity, but I can see the whole picture. Your focus is more narrow. Please don't bring this up again." The Commissioner made no attempt to show that he was upset that Petrosino was working against the festive mood.

Petrosino looked hard at McAdoo, "The game of baseball is very instructive."

McAdoo, welcoming the change in topic said, "I'm glad to hear you say that. I've loved the game since the days of King Kelly!"

As the crowd moved about, refusing to leave, Petrosino's serious face was in stark contrast to all around him. "As you know Rossi had nothing to do with the Black Hand. It seems I will have to work harder to shut them down."

"Whatever I can do to help," said McAdoo.

Petrosino lightly doffed his derby and left the Polo Grounds not saying what was on his mind.

In the three World Series games in which he appeared, Christy Mathewson threw three shutouts, in six days, allowing only fourteen hits. He struck out 18 and walked just one in the 27 innings of play. No player on Philadelphia ever reached third base. Each Giant player received $1,141.41 in World Series money.

The Eclaircissement

"Mathewson was the greatest pitcher who ever lived. He had knowledge, judgment, perfect control and form. It was wonderful to watch him pitch when he wasn't pitching against you."
- Connie Mack manager of the 1905 American League Champion Philadelphia A's

"The very symbol, the outward and visible expression of the drive, and push and rush and struggle of the raging, tearing, booming nineteenth century."
-Mark Twain on baseball at Delmonico's in New York April 8, 1889.

November 30, 1905. The orchestra of forty began playing a march and Samuel Clemens, with Mrs. Freeman on his arm and Andrew Carnegie right behind him, led the party of 170 into the Red Room at Delmonico's to celebrate the 70th birthday of the great American writer Mark Twain.

It was prearranged that Petrosino would have a small table in a corner where he could meet John McGraw and settle a few scores. Twain and Roosevelt perhaps thought Petrosino was attending the celebration for enjoyment. President Roosevelt had arranged the meeting in a correspondence with Twain. "Teddy" could not attend and asked if "his good friend Giuseppe Petrosino" could show in his stead. Petrosino asked for a guest list and saw that John McGraw was invited because Mark Twain was a "bug" and wanted to meet the champion manager. Petrosino then requested that he sit with John McGraw. Twain thought it was a capital idea because in a room filled with writers, statesmen, and businessmen from around the country, the guest of honor feared that a baseball genius and master detective might feel somewhat out of place.

Petrosino anticipated McGraw would be punctual, but he was slightly surprised when he entered the Red Room following all the other guests, trying to be inconspicuous. Petrosino saw McGraw already sitting at the table, beer in hand, cigar clenched in his teeth, grinning.

McGraw stood up to greet the detective. The Yellow Monkey, *El Mono Amarillo*, was a moniker given to the baseball genius because of the brightly colored clothes and fancy shoes he purchased in Cuba. McGraw came dressed in a deep lemon-yellow shirt covered over the shoulders by a white linen jacket. Despite the late November chill, he was dressed lightly. McGraw stood in contrast to the detective who never wanted to draw attention to himself and thus wore only subdued clothing in the most ordinary grays, blues, or blacks of the day.

"I hope there are no hard feelings. Dummy related the whole story to me." said McGraw, before Petrosino could sit.

They vigorously shook hands and sat down. A waiter instantly appeared.

"Red wine, please," said the detective, without looking up.

"Good to see you, Joe. I'm glad the season's over and I can't wait until the next! It feels good to be a champion," said John.

Petrosino learned that in private John McGraw could be a very respectful and kind man. His gruff, public persona was mostly for fans and publicity.

"Tell me how you solved the crime. Was I really a suspect?" questioned the manager.

"You were. But do not take this personally, I suspect everyone and follow every lead. When I discovered the pocket case of Tuxedo chewing tobacco left behind by the bomber, I knew that my chances of solving this problem increased. A master criminal would never leave anything behind except to deceive me, that is, want to make me think something else. To put it more accurately, the purpose of a skillful deception is to send me in a direction away from where I should be going. I felt that in this instance this was not the purpose of the forgotten tobacco tin. The barber shop murder was not intended. This was originally for money and not to kill someone. So I surmised that the tin was left by an amateur. Christy Mathewson's face was on the tin left behind by the bomber and I decided to buy a similar tin."

"I didn't know you chewed," said the champion manager.

"I don't but I wanted to see how easy it was to buy, where I could get it, how much it costs and so forth. So I went to Pearl Street where there is a high concentration of tobacconists. I purchased a pocket tin of the Tuxedo tobacco with Mr. Mathewson's face on it, an exact replica of the one left behind by the bomber. When I arrived back in my rooms, I opened the tin and immediately discovered that what I had purchased was very different in color with the tobacco found in the pocket tin left behind by the, I will say, terrorist. Not only that, the Tuxedo tobacco was twist tobacco and the tobacco I found was not. I purchased three more tins of this type and none matched what I had picked up in the barber shop. There was even a taste difference. I discovered that a very high grade, very expensive tobacco was being carried around in a pocket tin that is meant for a cheaper, more readily available tobacco. Why is this?"

Little Napoleon attempted an answer, "The criminal...."

The wine was served. McGraw then ordered beer.

"Thank you," nodded the detective.

"The criminal purchased the better tobacco in a container too large to fit into his breast pocket," said McGraw.

"Good," started the detective, "but why would he buy a cheaper tobacco to begin with?"

"Well," thought McGraw, dusting his Cuban cigar in the tray. He then moved his eyes up to look at the detective.

Petrosino started, "I immediately thought that either this better tobacco was a gift from someone else or quite possibly the criminal was a fan of the New York Giants, or at least Christy Mathewson. After all, advertising does work with some people and if the criminal is a fan he may purchase the tin for the identification with your team and dump the tobacco altogether."

"You understand the human mind. I could use you in the clubhouse," said the manager, his eyes squinting into two thin slits.

"I was directed to a certain establishment on Pearl Street that sells this quality tobacco. Solving a mystery like this requires luck. The fact that the tobacco was so rare in New York, it was only sold by one proprietor in this city, was again in my favor. When I came into the shop as a representative of the New York City Police Department, I did not suspect the proprietor of the shop to be the mastermind behind this dirty work, which in the final analysis is my mistake. Mr. Anthony Rossi gave me the short list of customers and you Mr. McGraw, were on the list. I visited a few others on that selective list but what intrigued me about you was that you seemed to be the only one who regularly shared his tobacco with quite a few others. Luther Taylor, your pitcher, did not chew tobacco. Instead, he gave what you gave him away to the bomber Luigi Francella, the man who did the dirty work for Rossi."

"Dummy Taylor is a good kid. It's too bad his World Series start got rained out." Little Napoleon paused. "Still, that gave Mathewson the chance to shine. How did Taylor get mixed up with this Luigi fellow?" asked McGraw.

"When Mr. Taylor started playing for the New York Giants, he was walking to the Polo Grounds and was nearly hit by a trolley. He was born in Kansas and you can imagine that he was somewhat, shall we say, overwhelmed by the size and busyness of New York. Although everything is up to date in Kansas City, I don't know if he ever saw a trolley in Kansas. People shouted to him, but of course, being deaf he heard none of the warnings, the trolley clanged its' bell but couldn't slow down fast enough. Who do you think saved him from serious injury or even death?"

"Luigi!" said McGraw, leaning back and enjoying his cigar.

"Exactly! They became friends and Luigi became a Giants fan. Luigi had a deaf brother, so he understood sign. As another instance of luck, when I was in the shop of Anthony Rossi, Luigi came in and they started an argument that I could not hear. Luigi became upset and made peculiar motions with his hands that I remembered because they were so unusual. When Luigi became very angry he would sign. Some people get angry and speak in Italian. Luigi gets angry and uses sign."

"So the pocket tin you found was because Luigi was a Giants fan?"

"A Giants fan that used baseball terms like double kill and dying quail, in his speech. This is also what focused me on you. Any peculiarity in speech or word choice can be a clue to identity or association. Once I was focused on the Giants baseball team I noticed another pattern developing. The bombings occurred after Christy Mathewson would lose a game. I look for patterns. Some patterns are easier to identify than others. Since the Big Six, as you say, only lost nine games, this was fairly easy to see. The baseball language used by the bomber, the Christy Mathewson tin, the bombings occurring after a loss by that great pitcher, and you as a customer of the Redman tobacco, taken together, had me almost convinced that my mystery would be solved in connection with your team. What was very interesting was the bombings occurring after a loss by Mathewson."

"Those losses would be," McGraw leaned back and was clearly enjoying himself, "May 6, that hurt, that was 1-0 against the Beaneaters, May 18 against Pittsburgh, he only lost one in June that was also against the damn Pirates on the 9th, July 4, that was also a close one 2-0 against Philadelphia, July 12, the eighteenth , August 5 again against Pittsburgh but this time we forfeited, September 23 a 1-0 game and October 5! He paused. But couldn't that be a coincidence?" questioned the manager as he stamped out the stub of his cigar.

"Is it a coincidence when a batter strikes a ball and it moves like a missile through the infield and the shortstop doesn't have to move left or right but remain exactly where he is to perfectly field the ball? I must assume there is no coincidence and in this instance, there was not. However, I must… keep the idea that there may be another answer. The pursuit of one lead cannot blind me to other possibilities. Detective work is very much like chess, or even like baseball, there are countless moves one could make but as the game progresses the choices remain numerous, but the wise moves are narrowed. The more I discover about a theory I have on a crime the better able I am to determine… *it's worth.* However, I must always be prepared for the unexpected that is outside of my theory. Anyway, all of this led me to believe that the bomber was, if not you, then perhaps a player on your team, but the description given to me by those threatened, fit no one on your team. All of your men are husky and big, the man I was looking for was slender, almost like a skeleton. Also, some bombings occurred while the team was away. So. if not someone on the team, then maybe a friend of someone on the team or someone associated with the ,team who never leaves New York. The grounds crew for instance. When I discovered that you gave your tobacco to the players, I was sure that the bomber was getting it from one of them."

"How were you so sure?"

"At first, I did not think that the bomber, that is Luigi Francella, was getting his tobacco from Rossi. I thought Rossi was a possible victim. This was my initial mistake. In the end, I was partly correct because Taylor was passing to Francella what little you gave him. Dundy did not share his tobacco and Hyde shared only with McGann's half-brother Seamus McCarthy."

"What about coincidence in all of this?" persisted McGraw.

"Again, I must assume there are no coincidences, if there was a connection between a Mathewson loss and a bombing then the motive may be something other than money. You motivate people every day McGraw. You understand that when people are very upset or angry they can get drunk, or beat their wives, or feed an addiction. Other, more rationale people will read a book, go to the opera, take a walk in the Central Park or pray. Some people will even shop at Wannamaker's to relieve stress! There is a wide range of possibilities within the rational and irrational. Human behavior is nearly limitless in its reaction to events. Reactions that are not... normal can be criminal. One of the possibilities is that when the Mathewson loses a game then, let us say, an overzealous fan can decide to blow up a shop."

" How did you catch him?" asked McGraw.

A Mr. Mattarrazzo, a man who had been threatened by Rossi, had seen Dan McGann, your first baseman at the drop-off site, panicked and ran into Rossi, hiding in the darkness. I know now that McGann was waiting for a prostitute. A prostitute had also been killed in one of the bombings and by coincidence she was on her way to a tryst with McGann. McGann knew the prostitute and saw her die from the explosion and he felt he was to blame because she was on her way to meeting him. Again, when your first baseman was close to the drop-off site for the money that night, it was purely coincidence. But I of course, did not know this at the time. I assumed he was involved. We picked up a prostitute the night Mattarrazzo died and she later told us that she had a boyfriend on the Giants which I knew was McGann. She also said that she saw Mattarrazzo killed by a man with a baseball bat although we now know that it was the walking stick of Rossi that first hit poor Mattarrazzo. When he was still groggy, Rossi released the knife hidden in the tip of the cane, plunged it into the chest of the barber and held it there until Mattarrazzo hit the ground. He then screwed the knife into the body, put his foot on the barber, and extracted the knife. He wiped it on the body and then retracted the weapon back into the walking stick. The prostitute closed her eyes when Rossi swung, so she did not see him hide in the nearby bushes.

"McGann does too much of that meeting with prostitutes. He is always with a floozie. I told him to knock it off or at least do it a little earlier!"

McGraw drank his pint and listened intently, his blue eyes focused on the detective.

"Anyway," Petrosino continued, "Rossi had met Mattarrazzo at a Giants game and they sat together. Mattarrazzo carried around an empty Tuxedo tin as a good luck charm. His wife told me so. She also told me that the day he had come home with the tobacco, this picture had been taken."

He handed the photograph to McGraw.

"I've posed for so many of these. Which one is Mattarrazzo?"

"This one," said Petrosino, pointing to a happy, waving, living Mattarrazzo.

"The last word Mattarrazzo whispered to me was 'Bug' as he grasped the tin."

"Does he mean fan? Bug is a popular word for fan you know."

"Yes! I later found this out. When Mattarrazzo ran into Rossi they recognized each other despite the darkness. Mattarrazzo said 'bug' to give me the clue that a fan had killed him. Mattarrazzo probably remembered the photograph that had been taken the day he met Rossi but had forgotten that Rossi left before it was taken. Mattarrazzo probably knew I would find the photograph and hoped I would make the connection. He clutched the Tuxedo tin with the tobacco that had been given to him on the day the photograph that you are holding was taken."

"Rossi was in this photo?"

"Rossi was in the seat that is now empty. He left early that day. Had he remained I would have had my man and perhaps prevented the death of Francella."

"Go on," said McGraw, gulping his beer and clearly enjoying the story.

"All of this gave me the thought that the man behind this is very intelligent. More intelligent than I first assumed. Also, a shop was bombed of someone who had paid. This made me think Why is this? Why is he bombed if he paid? This could mean and it did mean that it was not about the money. Most police work is boring. I waited five days in a barber chair, disguised in lather, waiting for the bomber to come back to a certain barber Rossi had been harassing to collect money. I had compared handwriting, in style and sophistication. I also compared paper. Luigi was writing the notes himself. He was copying what Mr. Rossi had written. Mr. Rossi wanted to protect himself by not having to write the notes. They could not be tracked in any way back to him but this also... backfired on him. Luigi did not take the precautions in writing the notes that Mr. Rossi would have taken. Luigi always wrote on a certain very commonplace, thin paper, in an unfinished hand with a black ink that always seemed slightly smudged because he was left handed and his left hand would move across the paper before the ink fully dried. Anyway, Francella never showed up at that barber where I sat because he was killed by Rossi."

McGraw finished his beer and signaled for another.

"What if Mathewson wins?" asked the manager, fully interested.

"If Mathewson wins there is no bombing. It is, after all, not about the money. It is about venting a frustration. Even when shopkeepers did not pay and Mathewson won, they were given more time. The only consistency between the number of letters, the time allowed before the bombing took place and the actual event was if Mathewson lost or not.

"Dummy received only a small amount of tobacco from me. Just enough for a few chews. Just enough for a very small tin," said the manager, understanding the process by which Petrosino had put everything together.

"Right. Francella was carrying around more than anybody could have given him, which showed that he was getting Redman Chew from Rossi. I found a bag of it at his apartment that he shared with his brother."

"Well look, if this is such a big case, why didn't I read about any of this in the papers?"

"Most of what I do is not known by the press. Freedom in the United States is a good thing but it doesn't help me catch criminals. We have our methods. In the end, justice prevailed."

"Who killed Danny's brother?"

"It was a suicide. Bresnahan had warned Seamus to keep his mouth shut to me about McGann. This made it appear to Seamus that his brother was in more trouble, doing worse things than he actually was. McGann told his half-brother he was in trouble but did not give details. Seamus couldn't take the pressure. He feared the worst of his half-brother. Dan couldn't tell Seamus that he was meeting a prostitute that was killed in a midnight blast. He was too ashamed. Meeting a prostitute is something you Irish... worry about more than Italians. When Dan said he was responsible, he meant that he had asked her to be there at that time, if he hadn't she would have lived. We captured the other prostitute in Jeanette Park who, and this is a coincidence, was on her way to meet Dan McGann. McGann got tired of waiting for her and he came directly into our path. The prostitute heard all of the commotion and hid in the park on her way to meet McGann. She actually saw Mr. Mattarrazzo being killed but she saw no details as I said she had her eyes closed. She was friends with the prostitute that was killed, Dan's original floozie and she told us that McGann was bad luck. McGann thought we were after him for being with prostitutes. When Dan did not tell his half-brother the truth, Seamus probably thought the worst. Seamus couldn't take all of the pressure that he was building up inside of his mind. He killed himself. This is..., ancillary to the case of course, but I was not sure of this at the time. Dan McGann was the only family that Seamus had. He would become severely depressed sometimes and when he thought about... the prospect of his brother going to jail or worse he couldn't deal with the pressure he had created in his mind. His release was death."

"I'm glad everything turned out fine for the both of us," McGraw said.

"By the way, forgive my oversight. Congratulations on being baseball champions!" said Petrosino.

"Thanks," started McGraw, "By the way, did you notice that when we won it was the first time that baseball was reported on the front page of the *New York Times*?"

"There is something you must know, McGraw," but before the detective could continue, Petrosino saw coming across the room toward them, the man of the day himself. Dressed all in white, with his shaggy, lion-like white mane that so distinguished him, a cigar in one hand, a chair being dragged over with the other and a smile on his face.

Petrosino stood as he always did to greet someone.

"Hello Mr. Clemens," said Petrosino, straightening his vest by pulling down on it from the bottom as he did so.

"Stay seated John," directed Clemens with a pat to McGraw's back and placing his chair between the two men, sat down.

"Congratulations on being the manager of the world champion New York Giants!" Clemens said, turning towards John, "Congratulations to you Lieutenant Petrosino on solving the Barrel Murder case. I know it was a few years ago but when you are 70, it is as if yesterday. I followed that case in the *World*, and your powers of observation are almost as good as mine!"

The waiter approached the table.

Bowing at the waist, "Can I get anything for you sir?"

155

Clemens took the initiative, "Another lager for John, another, red is it, for this gentleman, and I will smoke this cigar."

"Yes, sir." and the waiter receded.

"Try this McGraw. It's better than what you're smoking. The master writer pulled a Havana cigar out of his pocket and put it on the table for McGraw to pick up. "Do you follow that wonderful sport known as baseball, Lieutenant?"

"I have recently acquired an interest in the game," replied Petrosino.

"You and tens of thousands of others," remarked Clemens and continuing, "Perhaps my most interesting story about baseball is the following: It was in May of 1875 and I was attending a contest between the Hartford Dark Blues and the visiting Boston Red Stockings. The visitors scored twice as many in a 10-5 win but that wasn't the worst thing to happen that day. I had brought with me an English-made, brown silk umbrella and when I was focused on the skill of the players, a boy with very different skills made off with my irreplaceable umbrella. The Hartford team could use such a boy. He could steal bases all day and not get caught! Anyway, I put an ad in the Hartford Courant offering a five-dollar reward in return for the undamaged article. I never saw it again. That was thirty years ago, and I am still waiting for it, although I may have to put in a new ad, raise the reward to ten dollars, and hope that the boy who is now a man hasn't given the stolen property to his son. Maybe I should put you on the case Petrosino."

McGraw laughed heartily. "Try this Twain, it is better than what you are smoking!" He pulled a cigar from his breast pocket and gave it to the writer.

Clemens sniffed at the cigar, looked at it and pronounced, "For my birthday I would like as much of these as you can get. I forgot how often you have been to Cuba and how much extra cash you can throw around on such foolish things!"

Petrosino added, "McGraw, it seems that every time I talk with you, you are giving tobacco to someone."

"Joe just solved a case involving tobacco and baseball. He is a genius, Twain."

"Everybody in this room is a genius, except for this waiter, where is he?"

"I was a suspect in the case," informed McGraw with a grin.

At this point Twain became interested. "This is the beginning of a good story," said Twain.

"As I was about to tell Mr. McGraw, when I went to arrest Rossi he hit me over the head with his cane and I nearly lost my life. He had planted dynamite just before I entered. He was going to blow up his own shop to repel any suspicions I may have had about him. When Luigi Francella was killed, I had no evidence against Rossi. Rossi left me in the shop for dead and I followed, leaving the shop just before the explosion destroyed the building. The tip of his cane was weighted with solid metal and if I hadn't wisely taken my precautions, the blow would have killed me."

"What precautions are they?" asked Twain.

"I have special derbies that are filled with a protective padding of my own design that protects me from blows to the head."

"He thinks of everything," marveled McGraw.

The drinks came. The waiter receded.

"Thanks to a gentleman who looked after me, I was able to leave a hospital and find Rossi at St. Paul the Apostle Church, where his brother is a priest. I chased him to the 9th Avenue line. It was September 11. He was in the car that flew off the elevated rail. He was one of the many killed as was the gentleman who had helped me."

McGraw raised his beer, "A toast!"

The three drank for a moment in silence. The photographer who had been photographing every table for posterity came to this little group.

"Please, no photographs!" Petrosino said as he held up his hand to shield his face. Twain, with a jerk of his head, signaled the photographer to move along.

"I try to avoid public appearances and newspaper photographs. I do not want certain individuals to know where I am and what I am doing. If I can keep my enemy guessing, then it gives me a slight advantage. Although most criminals on the Lower East side would recognize me, it is better to let them think they saw me, even if they did not."

Twain said, "I sit with two very rare men. Joseph, even when you are not working, you are working. Always thinking. Always anticipating. You notice detail and yet you have an excellent grasp of how things are related. It is the same with you John. Your baseball men are talented. I mean it helped that Donlin batted .356 for the year but how the players think and how they execute as a team, that all comes from you."

"Donlin was my offensive powerhouse. Don't forget with seven home runs he was only two behind the leader Fred Odwell," said McGraw.

"The Cincinnati player, isn't it?" asked Twain.

"Yes."

"Cincinnati also had the best hitter in Cy Semour, his average was ahh..." Twain leaned back in his chair, mouth open as if he were in the dentist chair.

".377!" smiled John, appreciating Twain's knowledge of the game.

"Yet, Cincinnati finished fifth which proves my point about managing," theorized Twain.

"Well, good pitching wins ball games. Our pitchers were the best. Mathewson had an incredible year," said John, deflecting some of the praise to his players.

"Pitching three shutouts in the World Series is something that will be talked about for a long time." said Twain.

"Do you think the World Series will continue?" asked Petrosino slowly sipping his wine.

"Owners can see how much money they can make, and I think that 1904 was a fluke. I'm sure the Series is here to stay. The fans want it."

With this, Col. Harvey came over to the table. He was the Master of Ceremonies and he wanted Twain's attention

"Sam, I am going to read a letter from President Roosevelt. You may want to reply," and the Colonel departed.

"How is the former Police Commissioner?" asked Twain, looking directly at Petrosino.

Petrosino sensed a change to coldness in Twain's voice.

"He is fine. I have not seen him for some time. I am happy that he arranged this meeting," Petrosino answered.

"So am I." Twain seemed to relax.

The colonel now had the attention of those in the Red Room.

"A letter from President Roosevelt!" the Colonel exclaimed as he adjusted his monacle.

My Dear Col. Harvey: I wish it were in my power to be at the dinner held to celebrate the seventieth birthday of Mark Twain - it is difficult to write of him by his real name instead of by that name which has become a household word wherever the English language is spoken. He is one of the citizens whom all Americans should delight to honor, for he has rendered a great and peculiar service to America, and his writings, though such as no one but an American could have written, yet emphatically come within that small list which are written for no particular country, but for all countries, and which are not merely written for the time being, but have an abiding and permanent value. May he live long, and year by year may he add to the sum of admirable work that he has done. Sincerely yours, THEODORE ROOSEVELT.

Without saying goodbye, Twain stood up and approached the head table. The smoke swirled in the room. Twain spoke with good humor about his age and the feat to make it so far in life. When he finished he went to another table.

Petrosino turned to McGraw and said," There is something else I must tell you. In fact, it is the main reason I am here today."

"Yes," said McGraw studying, staring at Petrosino through the cloud of cigar smoke he had just created.

"I know about your high stakes gambling club. Dundy, Hyde, you and Rossi were all a part of it. When I visited Dundy at the Hippodrome, he thought that I was after this. I knew that Dundy knew something, that he was holding something back. All of you met Rossi through James Hazen Hyde. Each one of you started gambling on Hyde then it became gambling with Hyde. The four of you had this little high stakes gambling club. It seems that all of you are addicted to gambling."

"How do you know this? Did that greaseball Rossi confess?"

"James Hazen Hyde, out of respect and admiration for Theodore Roosevelt, told me everything. He didn't want to keep anything secret."

"That ended months ago!"

"I know but you continued to gamble sending various people to Rossi's under the guise of buying tobacco. All of your messengers thought it was a tobacco transaction. Instead it was an elaborate system of payoffs and bet making. Rossi controlled the gambling and delivered payoffs. Rossi was "the house" he made money from this. This is why he never charged for it and he was so defensive when I came into his tobacco shop disguised and asked for Redman! Why should he be apparently annoyed or upset when a customer asks for something that he is supposed to be selling? Why didn't he have any Redman Chew on his shelves? He instantly figured that my disguised self knew one of you. When I visited him as myself, an agent of the law he quickly put everything together and decided to cooperate with me. He also initially thought it was about the high stakes gambling because only the high stakes gambling club received Redman Chew. Rossi's mistake was to give the Redman to Francella. When he gave the Redman Chew to Francella because Francella was an avid fan and wanted what the Giants chewed it was what finally led me to Rossi. Now, I know you gamble illegally and it is rumored that you...fix games. You also leave Giants games early to go to the track. It is not in my jurisdiction, and I haven't had enough time, being so busy with another more important matter, to collect enough evidence, and, well, the Commissioner thinks that I should focus my attention elsewhere."

Here, McGraw's smile vanished. He leaned forward and quickly became red in the face, "You son of a bitch! It'll never stick." said McGraw in a measured, deliberate way.

"Mr. McGraw, I have been also gathering evidence about Rube Waddell, the star pitcher for the Philadelphia team."

"What about him?"

"I have strong reason to believe that he was paid a good sum of money to feign an injury during the World Series that your team just won."

"You are crazy! He was hurt roughhousing on the train with some of his teammates."

"Yes, he was, but I believe that has healed. If I had a bit more evidence and if I could speak with Mr. Waddell, I might be able to pin this on you. I think you are behind Rube's refusal, but I cannot prove it yet. No one is above the law, not even the manager of a championship team. If I were the assigned officer to this case, you would be made to pay for your wrongdoings. I also know you have paid police officers in the past, sometimes enough money will cause policemen to forget everything. I, however am immune to the... power of money."

"You can't prove I paid police officers! I have access to good lawyers," said McGraw.

"I wanted to arrest you myself, but Commissioner McAdoo told me to stay away from the case."

"You wop! Do you know what I had to get through to come where I am today? Diphtheria killed me mother and me sisters! I was eleven! I was twelve years old when I put a baseball through a window pane and my father had trouble coming up with the fifteen cents it costs for a new one. He beat me and threw me around the room. I packed my things and never lived with him again. Don't mess with me greaseball!"

McGraw then started to fidget with his shirt collar and unbuttoned his shirt in order to pull out a gold medallion on a chain. "Ya see this greaseball? This was given to me by Cardinal Gibbons! It means something!" He clutched the medallion and shoved it under his shirt without giving Petrosino a proper look at it.

The waiter came to the table, a young man that didn't recognize McGraw. "Would you like another stein sir?"

"I'm done for today," he said in measured tones, staring at the detective. He rose and dramatically waved the jacket off his shoulders with a flourish akin to a matador swinging a cape over the shoulders of a bull. McGraw then pulled out a wad of bills from his breast pocket. He shifted his eyes to the waiter and handed the young man a twenty-dollar bill.

"Thank you, sir!" said the astonished waiter, shocked into immobilization.

"I'm feeling generous today," and without looking at Petrosino or saying goodbye, he left the room.

The waiter was so stunned that he forgot about the detective. He walked away, staring at the bill.

Petrosino sat and peered into the crowd. McGraw was forgotten about, his superior told him hands off, so he obeyed because it was his duty to obey. He had to focus on the Black Hand. They were still out there. He stood and took the white bust of Mark Twain, given to all in attendance as a gift from the man himself. He didn't say goodbye to Twain. He left Delmonico's unnoticed, which was how he liked it.

The Final Chapter

"That was all he knew- all he could hope to unravel from the story."

    -Edith Wharton from The House of Mirth

Petrosino sat in his now usual place at Lanza's. The year 1905 was ending as it had begun, with snow. He was reading the latest book from Edith Wharton, *The House of Mirth*. It was wrapped in an Italian newspaper to hide it. There were advantages to pretending that one could not read English.

Petrosino's recent trip to Frederick Bourne on Dark Island put him in a group of elite society. In crime, all people seemed alike. Greed, power, jealousy, cowardice, betrayal, misplaced love; these were some of the basic elements that contributed to criminal character and motives. How crimes were committed varied from one economic class to the next. Petrosino studied the book to educate himself on human weakness, hubris and every other frailty. Petrosino knew that studying human nature helped him solve crimes. Petrosino felt that Wharton was an excellent observer of the human condition. He had read all of her work and called them to mind now, briefly gazing out at the snow. *The Touchstone, The Valley of Decision, Sanctuary*, her short stories, *The Descent of Men* and the *Great Inclination*. One of his favorites was her nonfiction work entitled *Italian Villas and Their Gardens*.

However, there was one line from her newest book, *The House of Mirth* that haunted the detective. An unexpected line that unknowingly taunted Petrosino. This sentence arrested the thoughts of the great detective. He wrapped the book in the folded newspaper and slipped it easily into an extra-large inner breast pocket that his tailor had especially sewn into all of his suit jackets. He sipped his cappuccino. He looked out onto First Avenue. He stretched his right leg out from under the table to relieve the stiffness caused by an old thigh wound, a souvenir from the Tong Wars.

As the detective sought to relieve the stiffness in his leg, a beautiful woman walked into the restaurant. She had thick brown hair, a full figure, large brown eyes, smooth olive skin with a color that could be considered dark for winter. It was Adelina, the woman who wanted to marry him. She saw her beau and smiled instantly. She quickened her step and approached the table. Petrosino stood to greet her.

"Joe," she said, giving him a kiss on the cheek.

"Adelina," was his whisper-like response as if her appearance had arrested his breath.

They looked at each other for a few seconds until Petrosino offered her a seat at the table.

The waiter came over and Petrosino ordered her a cappuccino, without asking her.

"It is good to see you, Joe. How was your trip upstate?"

"Believe it or not, there was a murder."

"What? How terrible. Trouble seems to follow you. What happened?"

"You know Adelina, I cannot really speak of my cases. I can tell you about the house. It was a huge house, a mansion on its own island. There were secret rooms and secret passageways. Someone was killed. There were less than a dozen guests and I had to find the killer. The killer did not know who I was at first but then…"

"Then what?" she asked, as her cappuccino came to the table.

Although it might pain her, Petrosino had decided to tell her realistically about the dangers he faced. He looked at her eyes, felt her hand lightly touch his. He loved her more and more, but he did not want her to be a widow someday. He resisted marriage to her because of the dangers inherent in his job as a Lieutenant for the New York City Police Department. He felt that if he related some of the more dangerous situations that he would make his argument for not marrying more convincing. Although in truth, it is not an argument he wanted to win.

"Well, there was a speed boat chase, I nearly died."

"How? How did this happen?"

"Let's leave it at this. I don't want to discuss cases that are closed. I must concentrate on those that are still winnable. What happened on Dark Island is finished and done. I can't waste time thinking about it. My energies must be expended on the next cases."

"What are your next cases?"

"The Black Hand bombings are continuing. This madness is far from over. Rossi and Francella are both dead but others continue to terrorize the public. There are many layers involved in the Black Hand. This case with the New York Giants led me to a dead end. Rossi was one of the many Black Hand impersonators, imposters who profited from the names and habits of the authentic terror group. I had hoped to catch the major puppeteer behind all of this, the man who pulled the strings. I am sure that it was my nemesis, Ignazio Lupo."

"Please don't mention that name. I will spit on him when I see him."

"Dear Adelina, if you spit on him, what do you think he will do to you?" Petrosino knew she was brave and very capable of taking care of herself.

"Well, didn't you say 'the wolf' has been eluding you since 1902, the year of the Barrel Murder Case and he is still evading justice?"

"Yes," said Petrosino. He looked down at his coffee, somewhat embarrassed by his inability to nail Lupo once and for all.

"Ever since you gave Lupo that public beating and stuffed him in a trash can, he has carried a picture of you in his pocket and brags to everyone, 'Someday I will kill this man!' Isn't that true, Joe? I read it in the papers."

"Yes, it is only a matter of time before Lupo and I have a showdown. There will be only one victor. Even if justice prevails and Lupo is put in jail for life, the Black Hand will continue because men like Lupo, how shall I say it? Animal-like men that crave power above life, are ready to take the place of Lupo. Dons like Lupo are more likely to be killed by someone within the organization than to be arrested by the police. So Adelina, you are right. Ignazio may never get the opportunity of killing me but he will take the opportunity if it comes. The outcome of our battle is far from certain. There are so many variables. The Black Hand is a vast, secretive, and an increasingly ruthless organization.

Frustrated, Adelina asked, "Why don't the victims of the Black Hand speak out?"

"Victims are afraid to testify against them! People in high places protect them. They have protectors everywhere!" The thoughts of the detective swirled like the snow piling up on First Avenue and he kept his suspicions from Adelina. He looked down at the solitary, white porcelain cup on the red and white checkered tablecloth. He idly played with the small spoon.

"Look at me, Joe," said the woman across from the small table, who was now holding one of his hands in both of hers.

Petrosino looked up.

"I love you."

"I love you too, Adelina, but this is not the problem. If we were married, you could become a widow any day."

"I am willing to live that life. I understand."

"What about the pain and grief it would cause you?"

"If you were killed tomorrow, I would still feel much pain and grief. You know that."

"I can't think about it right now. The Black Hand has been threatening Enrico Caruso and I have been ordered to be his personal bodyguard. I must follow him around in disguise."

She smiled, "Well, you do love the opera."

"Yes, but I love nothing on this earth more than you." He felt awkward after he said it even though it was true.

"How much longer will you put me off?"

"I must study. I am going to have a small part in Carmen and we will be traveling to San Francisco as part of the 1906 opera season if the Black Hand case with Caruso is not solved by then."

"Can't you do all of this and be married at the same time?"

"If the Black Hand knows I am married to you, and they surely will, they may come after you."

"Maybe there is a place where we can be safe, far from everyone, like Staten Island or Queens."

"That is too far. I need to be close to Manhattan for my job."

"Could you ever give this job up?"

"I have a duty. I feel I have a responsibility towards my countrymen who now live here and well, justice. Justice must be done."

"When two people love each other like we do, is it unjust to keep them apart?"

"What about Mr. Roosevelt. He made my career."

"You made your own career! He just recognized your talent. He didn't give you anything you didn't deserve."

"But..."

"No but!" Adelina let his hands go and she became, as was her way, emotional.

"Please..."

"You risk your life for others, you made Mr. Teddy Roosevelt look good while he was police commissioner, and if they had listened to you, President McKinley would still be alive! You should be more than a Lieutenant for all you have done!"

"Don't forget. I am an Italian Lieutenant!"

"Is all of this more important than being my husband?"

"Let me tell you something, Adelina. Do you remember when we were at this restaurant and that strange, bald man came in and sat at that table?"

"How could I forget that vulture face?"

"Well, a few months ago I killed him at Pete's Tavern. He found me there while I was with Muldoon and he wanted to kill me."

At this Adelina looked down. She remained quiet. She listened.

Petrosino continued, "This man was with the Black Hand," he pulled a letter out of his inner breast pocket and unfolded it. "This letter was sent to me at Mulberry Street. The Black Hand is so bold that now they send me letters! They threaten me! I keep it as a reminder to remain... vigilant! I want to read it to you. 'You killed our man at the tavern. You miserable dog. Now we will kill one of your policemen. Someday we will kill you. There will be a note on the dead policeman to show you that we mean business. You cannot escape the Black Hand.'"

He folded the paper and put it back.

She looked at him with tears in her eyes.

"Three days later I got this note that had been pinned to a policeman with a knife. The policeman was with us for three years. A young boy, really. He was from Ireland. He came here for a better life. He had three children. The note said: "For Petrosino, this is for Pete's Tavern.""

"This is what I am up against. I don't want you exposed to them. They are animals."

"Love never counts the costs," Adelina said through her tears.

Petrosino took her hands into his. He combated the most intelligent criminals in all circles and he usually won but he never could seem to win an argument from Adelina. Maybe it was because he only half-believed his side of the argument. Maybe Adelina was right. He remained silent, a sign of his defeat.

His silence only enraged her.

"We could get married in secret! The Black Hand would not have to know. I know how you feel about your work and I won't ask you to choose between it and me. There must be a middle ground."

"If there is, I do not see it," said the detective.

"I am continuing to work with the women's movement. It is important work but I want more in my life. The love I have for you is stronger than my feelings about the injustice of our society. I'd like you to join me in this crusade."

"What?" Petrosino pushed the coffee cup away from him.

"I think I can get a job for you working for our cause."

"I am made for police work and nothing else."

"Do you love your police work more than me?"

"Adelina, if you loved me, you would not want me to give up my police work."

"You work for justice! You told me this yourself! Isn't working for the women's vote a matter of justice?"

"Adelina, I am not a politician. It is the thrill of the chase, the problem that needs to be solved that tugs at me."

"Can you give this up for me?"

"If you loved me, you wouldn't ask me this."

"Enjoy San Francisco!" At this point she stood, looking intently at him for signs of acquiescence. When she did not get this, she abruptly pivoted around, twirling her long brown skirt, which mimicked the movement of her long brown hair. She left the restaurant.

The detective knew that she was sad and that he could relieve that sadness. He knew that he should marry her, but he did not because he loved her so. Petrosino looked forward to working so closely with

Enrico Caruso, yet he knew that he would miss Adelina. He was trying to decide what to do about his sometimes feisty, but very loving Adelina when the line from Edith Wharton's new book *The House of Mirth* again unexpectedly visited him. Petrosino hoped that it did not foretell anything about his attempt to catch the leaders of the Black Hand. He wanted the upcoming Caruso case to be the beginning of the end for the Black Hand. But still, it echoed in his mind.

"That was all he knew- all he could hope to unravel from the story."

He looked out the window onto First Avenue. White flakes gently fell from the sky.

"We talked, lived and dreamed baseball." -John McGraw

About the Author

James Carmody a former Peace Corps volunteer, met his wife Olga while serving in Ukraine. Today they have three wonderful children. James lives in Stratford, Connecticut and teaches in New York City.

www.ingramcontent.com/pod-product-compliance
Lightning Source LLC
Chambersburg PA
CBHW011523240626
47154CB00009B/2945